IF I KISS YOU

"Jagger," she said, her voice husky with what he hoped was desire. His name had never sounded so sweet to his ears. He wished she would say it again. He wanted her to moan his name as he possessed her body, as he possessed her soul.

He wanted her to love him. If he kissed those lips, would she swoon or slap his face?

BOOK YOUR PLACE ON OUR WEBSITE AND MAKE THE READING CONNECTION!

We've created a customized website just for our very special readers, where you can get the inside scoop on everything that's going on with Zebra, Pinnacle and Kensington books.

When you come online, you'll have the exciting opportunity to:

- View covers of upcoming books
- Read sample chapters
- Learn about our future publishing schedule (listed by publication month *and author*)
- Find out when your favorite authors will be visiting a city near you
- Search for and order backlist books from our online catalog
- Check out author bios and background information
- Send e-mail to your favorite authors
- Meet the Kensington staff online
- Join us in weekly chats with authors, readers and other guests
- Get writing guidelines
- AND MUCH MORE!

Visit our website at
http://www.kensingtonbooks.com

FOREVER YOURS

Janmarie Anello

ZEBRA BOOKS
Kensington Publishing Corp.
www.kensingtonbooks.com

ZEBRA BOOKS are published by

Kensington Publishing Corp.
850 Third Avenue
New York, NY 10022

All Kensington titles, imprints, and distributed lines are available at special quantity discounts for bulk purchases for sales
promotion, premiums, fund-raising, educational, or institu-
tional use.

Special book excerpts or customized printings can also be created to fit specific needs. For details, write or phone the office
of the Kensington Special Sales Manager: Attn. Special Sales
Department. Kensington Publishing Corp., 850 Third Avenue,
New York, NY 10022. Phone: 1-800-221-2647.

Zebra and the Z logo Reg. U.S. Pat. & TM Off.

ISBN-13: 978-1-4201-0000-6
ISBN-10: 1-4201-0000-9

First Printing: April 2007
10 9 8 7 6 5 4 3 2 1

Printed in the United States of America

For Carol,
my mother, my hero, my best friend

For Ala and Matt,
for sharing your dreams with me

And for Michael, with all my love

Chapter One

Calcutta, 1816

The bamboo shutters, pulled tight against the monsoon winds, trapped the stench of cigars and unwashed bodies in the crowded tavern. Orange lamplight flickered through the silvery haze, casting shadows over the room.

Jagger Remington eyed the man seated across from him at the table. He wished the man would go away. Conversation was not on his list of things to do tonight. He wanted nothing more than to get drunk and bed a willing wench or two, preferably in that order. Still, he owed this man more than he could ever repay. He had to listen to what the man had to say, even if it did concern the odious subject of matrimony.

He downed his brandy, then called for another.

The tavern maid sauntered over and refilled his glass. She slowly circled her tongue around her full, sensuous lips. "Need anything else?"

Her blatant invitation teased a reluctant smile out of Jagger, despite his foul mood. For reasons he did not understand, women seemed to find his black hair and blue eyes wildly attractive, so much so that they rarely seemed to notice the hideous scar that marred the left half of his face. He fingered the jagged flesh beneath his eye, a grim reminder of the past he had left behind, the promises he had yet to keep.

The tavern maid crossed her arms on the knife-scarred tabletop. Flashing him a saucy smile, she leaned toward Jagger until the scooped neckline of her smock gaped open, giving him a tantalizing view of her big breasts bulging out of her stays. Honey-blond hair curled around her face. Sea-green eyes opened and closed seductively.

He was about to suggest they head to his room when the tavern keep, who was as big as a bear and looked just as mean, growled her name in a tone that clearly bespoke ownership.

Jagger grinned. "Just leave the bottle."

She shrugged her shoulders and strolled away, her hips swaying flirtatiously as she walked toward her man.

The slurred voices of drunken soldiers and sailors mingled with sultry laughter as a kaleidoscope of painted whores circled the room, plying their trade. All the while, the man sitting with Jagger droned on and on about the benefits Jagger would gain in a match with the man's sister.

"How on earth did you ever find me?" Jagger asked when the man finally paused for breath.

Stephen Treneham, the fourth Earl of Hallowell, crushed his handkerchief in his fist, then mopped the sweat from his brow. He glared at Jagger. "What difference does it make? I have followed you through the backwaters and malarial swamps of this godforsaken region for nigh unto a year now."

The earl's voice trembled with anger, but Jagger refused to rise to the bait. He would explain himself to no one, not even to Stephen, whom he had once loved like a father.

The space between them filled with a charged silence, broken only by the incessant chatter of voices in the taproom and the drumming of Stephen's fingertips on the table.

Murky lamplight played over the earl's bony hand.

Jagger was amazed at how much the man had aged since the last time he had seen him. Gone was the full head of blond hair, replaced by thin, silver strands combed from ear to ear. Harsh lines cut into the flesh around his mouth, as if he never smiled, and his sagging cheeks were flushed from the heat.

His eyes were the same as Jagger remembered, though—vibrant blue and burning with determination as he pointed at the legal documents spread out on the table. "With no entail attached to that estate, once you sign the papers, it's as good as yours. Granted, I have made no recent improvements, but you know as well as I what that property is worth. Why, there is a fortune just in timber on that estate!"

Jagger couldn't mask the momentary interest that no doubt flashed across his face. The fact that Stephen noticed, as evidenced by his satisfied smile, goaded him into irrational anger. "I am not for sale."

Stephen shrugged. "Nor am I buying. I am merely making a settlement upon my sister."

"She is agreeable to this?"

"She signed the papers, did she not?"

Jagger picked up the documents. Her signature was at the bottom of each page, a graceful, flowing sweep across the paper. It was the most bewildering aspect of this ludicrous scheme. Why would she agree to wed a man she had never met?

"I didn't even know you had a sister."

Stephen snorted. "Why would you? You have been gone from England for what, fifteen years now without a word?" His voice had grown louder with each word he had spoken until he finally bellowed, "Did you never think to let me know you were alive?"

The accusation rang through the room. Conversations stopped as the drunkards around them turned to stare.

Jagger clenched his fist but said nothing. He could never explain the anguish he had suffered over his exile from England. Nor did he want to. He would return when he was ready. When the time was right. Then he would have his revenge.

"Did not my mother mention my letters?" Jagger asked, pinching the bridge of his nose. He had written to her as often as he could and had provided for her maintenance, but he'd never invited her to join him. Given her delicate health and the drastically reduced life span of a European in India, he had not thought she would survive.

"I've not spoken with her," Stephen said in a voice so low, Jagger had to strain to hear him. "Not since the arrangements were finalized and she retired to the country."

Stephen cleared his throat, waved his hand. "Never mind. It does not matter. Sophie is my stepsister. From my father's third marriage. There is no blood between us, but I would see her safely settled before I die. In truth, I should have seen to it long ago. So, what do you say?"

Jagger laughed. "You honestly expect me to do this thing?"

"Why not? I admit it's a bit out of the ordinary way."

"That's a mile short of nowhere," Jagger drawled.

"But I see nothing wrong with it," Stephen continued as if Jagger hadn't spoken. "That is, of course, unless you are already engaged?"

Jagger shook his head. He tossed back his brandy, relishing the warmth as the smooth liqueur slid down his throat.

Stephen smiled. "Then I see no reason not to proceed. What say you?"

"I say you have gone daft, man. I have no need of a wife."

"Why not? Every man needs a wife. If for no other reason than to care for him in his old age."

"Nonsense." Jagger poured himself another bumper of brandy. "You cannot be more than fifty. I am certain there are any number of nubile, young maidens eager to wed a man of your station, regardless of your years."

"No." Stephen stared into his drink. A hint of despair crept into his voice. "I loved a woman once . . ."

Wretchedly uncomfortable at the mournful expression on the man's face, Jagger shifted on his seat. Romantic drivel, he thought harshly. He had never met a woman who inspired anything more in him than momentary lust, and that was easily assuaged by a night spent in carnal bliss.

Stephen drew a shuddering breath. "But she was lost to me, so I did my duty and married another."

He leveled his piercing gaze on Jagger. "When everything is said and done, duty is all we have. Unfortunately, my wife died in childbirth along with the babe. Now the title will go to my brother, but *I* need to see to Sophie's future. *I* need to know she is safe."

"Why me?" Jagger asked bluntly. "There must be a dozen or more eager young bucks vying for your sister's hand. Choose one of them."

Stephen shook his head.

Jagger narrowed his eyes. He stroked his thumb and forefinger over his stubbled chin as he studied the earl. The man was definitely hiding something.

"What's wrong with her?" he said.

"There is nothing wrong with her!"

"Oh, cut line, Hallowell. Why else would you be fishing in *India* for a man to marry the chit?"

The earl slammed his fist on the table. "There is nothing wrong with her. Watch what you say!"

Jagger merely lifted a brow.

Stephen sighed. "I admit, she is a bit headstrong and set in her ways. But given the right man to guide her, she will make an exemplary wife. And I assure you, she is fair of face and form. You will not find her displeasing."

"I tire of this game," Jagger said. "I ask you again—why me? And this time, give me the truth."

"Why not you?" Stephen snapped. "You are my godson, after all. Jagger! I am offering you more than wealth. I am handing you a treasure beyond compare if you would only have the sense to reach out and grasp it."

Jagger swirled the brandy in his glass. The steady buzz of voices around him faded away as he contemplated the offer.

He had to admit that he was tempted.

The land they were discussing was deep in the heart of Norfolk. Rich, arable land with less than a third of it being properly used. With the new agricultural methods available, Jagger knew he could double, perhaps even triple, the corn harvest in the first year alone. The fact that its northernmost border marched along with his father's principal seat sweetened the prize indeed.

Why not? Why the hell not?

It wasn't as cold-blooded as it sounded. Most marriages amongst the *ton* were arranged entirely for financial reasons or for matters of estate. And God knew he was heartily sick of the life he was leading. He was tired of the heat. Tired of the disease. Tired of roaming from place to place, searching for something—he didn't know what—that would ease the ache inside of him. The wealth he had amassed over the years meant nothing to him. Oh, yes, he wanted the land, if for no other reason than to drive his father mad.

There was only one problem. He did *not* want a wife.

But it wasn't as if it would be a real marriage. It would be a business arrangement. Nothing more. Nothing less. With no pretense of love involved, no foolish emotions would complicate the issue.

Unless the lady in question wanted children.

Jagger most definitely did not want children.

He shook his head. What the hell was he thinking? To contemplate marriage to a woman he had never met was completely insane.

Stephen leaned forward as if he were about to impart

a state secret. "Your father tells all and sundry that you are dead. Though he has yet to seek a formal declaration, I am certain it is only a matter of time."

Jagger grinned. "So, like our Savior before me, you want me to rise from my grave? No doubt my father would suffer fits, not to mention my dear uncle Anthony, who has, I am sure, grown quite accustomed to my absence." Jagger could well imagine the outrage that would distort his father's face when his long-lost son returned to hearth and home.

He tightened his grip on his glass until his arm ached from the tension. "He knows I'm alive. He just wishes I were dead."

He drained his glass, then pushed it away. "I will return to England when *I* am ready. Do not ask me again."

Stephen rubbed his hands over his face. He started to speak, then stopped. Finally, he whispered hoarsely, "There is no longer any reason for you to stay away."

A piercing pain gripped Jagger's chest. He sucked in a deep breath. "What do you mean?"

"I did not want to tell you like this. Not here."

"Tell me what?" Jagger said, though a sickening suspicion twisted in his gut.

Stephen slowly shook his head. He rubbed the fingertips of his left hand along a gouge in the tabletop. When he looked back at Jagger, his face had gone ashen. His eyes glistened. "Your mother is dead."

Jagger's vision went dark at the edges. The room swirled around him. He was perilously close to fainting, he realized with chagrin, and that made him furious.

Grown men didn't faint. That was for vaporish young women and shriveled-up old maids. Then why did his limbs feel so weak, as if he would topple over should anyone so much as cast a heavy breath upon him?

"When?" The single word was all he could manage to push past the knot in his throat.

"Shortly before I sailed from England."

Jagger closed his eyes. Fifteen years he had stayed away. Fifteen long years to protect his mother's life. Now she was dead. He hadn't expected it to hurt so much. Until this moment, he hadn't even known if he loved her or if he hated her.

Now he knew, and it was too late.

He didn't know whether to laugh at the irony or cry for her passing. Instead, a cold fury settled over him, seeping through his pores to the very marrow of his bones. Oh, yes, it was time he went home. It was time he made his father pay.

It would take him six months to reach England. He had no time to waste. He pushed to his feet and headed for the door.

Stephen grabbed the documents from the table, then shoved them into his pocket as he rushed after Jagger. "Wait."

"This discussion is over," Jagger snarled. He did not need to marry this girl to gain his revenge—even if she was the sister of his father's worst enemy.

His thoughts turned to more pressing matters. He had no idea how long he would be away. He had contracts to sign, shipments to arrange. His man of affairs would have to—

Stephen grabbed his arm. "Someone is trying to kill me."

That snapped Jagger's attention back to the present. "Good God, man. You tell me this now? Who?"

"I do not know." Stephen rubbed the back of his neck. "Ever since I left London, there has been one attempt after another. At first, I thought it was a series of random accidents. Then two nights ago . . ."

He pushed up his coat and shirtsleeves. A long, ugly gash rent his skin from wrist to elbow. "I was attacked by a man with a knife. He jumped out of an alley as I walked by. I did not recognize him, but it was no accident. He meant to kill me." He lifted his gaze to Jagger's.

"Had he succeeded, I shudder to think what would have happened to Sophie."

Jagger groaned as he felt the shackles of matrimony clamp around his legs. He searched for an excuse, for any honorable means of escape from the trap the earl had skillfully woven around him.

"What you need is a bodyguard," he growled.

Stephen sliced his hand through the air. "No. I need a man I can trust. A man who will fight to protect what is his, who will guard my sister with his life. There is no one else I trust in this, but you.

"Besides," he added, ramming his words home with deadly precision, "you owe me."

Chapter Two

"I do not understand why you persist in doing the servants' work," a stinging voice said from behind her.

Sophie Treneham gave the mahogany banister one last swipe with the dust cloth before she turned to face her companion, a distant cousin from her stepbrother's side of the family.

Lynthea Washburn stared at her through narrowed gray eyes. Her red hair, artfully arranged about her face in a flurry of delicate curls, did nothing to soften the tightness of her lips or the sharp angle of her chin lifted in haughty disdain.

Sophie curled her mouth into what she hoped would pass for a smile. She silently cursed her brother for forcing Thea's company upon her. He'd said he wanted her to have a companion close to her own age, but Sophie rather thought she would have preferred it if he had bought her a dog. Then she felt mean and petty. She knew Thea had nowhere else to go. For if she did, she certainly would not remain here in exile with Sophie.

She wanted to warn Thea to smile or her face would freeze like that, but she bit her tongue.

"I like to keep busy," she said instead. Or rather, she needed to keep busy. The alternative was to sit and think, and thinking was the last thing she wanted to do.

Thea plunked her hands on her hips. "Can you not at least do something more befitting of a lady? Despite your, er, unfortunate circumstances, you are still the sister of an earl."

"Stepsister," Sophie said, turning back to the gleaming banister. The fresh scent of beeswax filled the air as she rubbed her dust cloth over the intricate pattern of flowers and leaves she had just finished polishing.

Unfortunate circumstances, indeed. "And what would you have me do? Unlike you, I do not enjoy watercolors or stitchery. Nor do I have the time."

"You could practice on the pianoforte. Or study your French. Honestly, I do not understand it. Lord Hallowell has let you run wild. I mean to give him a piece of my mind when he comes home."

If he comes home, Sophie thought. So much time had passed, she was beginning to doubt he would ever return. Maybe the rumors were true. Maybe he had fled the country for good. Or maybe he was dead—no, she would not believe that!

Then why hadn't he written to say he was safe? It was so unlike him to go off without a word. And for so long.

Determined not to let her worries prey upon her mind, Sophie turned her attention to the foyer floor. Made of white stone with black insets, it could stand to be washed.

She added it to her mental list of tasks she wanted to complete before noon, along with sweeping the Turkish carpet that ran the length of the hall. The walls would have to wait for another day, she decided with a sigh as she walked through the arched entryway. She did not have the energy to attack the elaborate stuccowork today.

She moved to a satinwood table along the wall, rubbed her dust cloth over the wood in circular motions until her arm went numb. She could hear Thea pacing the floor behind her.

Sophie prayed she would go away.

She did not. "I vow I shall run mad if I do not get out of this house. It is a beautiful day, Sophie. Let us walk to the village."

"No," Sophie said swiftly. "I have too much to do."

"But—"

"I cannot, I said. I want to dust the drawing room. It has been at least a week—"

"But I cannot go without you," Thea shrieked. "You are so selfish. I tell you, I am bored."

"You could have accompanied Betsy and—"

"The nursemaid? Are you out of your senses?"

A sharp rap on the door saved her from having to reply.

Sophie shoved her dust cloth into her pocket as she headed for the door.

"Whatever are you thinking?" Thea shouted, chasing after her. "You're not going to answer that! Let the butler get it."

Sophie did not bother to remind Thea that the butler was long gone and the only manservant who remained had accompanied Betsy and Cecelie on their errands.

Before she opened the door, she paused.

What if it were another bill collector?

No, it couldn't be. She could not possibly owe anyone any more money. Could she?

Another sharp rap on the door set her heart to racing.

Maybe she shouldn't answer it after all.

What was she thinking? She wasn't a coward.

She yanked open the door. Her spirits went from bad to worse as Sir John Shays, parish magistrate and notorious rake, stepped into the hall.

Sophie forced herself to smile at her unwanted guest as she dipped in the obligatory curtsy. "Sir John."

His hat in his hand, the handsome roué bowed a

formal greeting. Not a single strand of his perfectly cropped blond hair moved. He wore an elegant rust riding coat over tan breeches tucked into perfectly polished black boots. Anyone looking at this gentleman would never guess that beneath the veneer lurked the heart of a perfect scoundrel.

As he straightened, Sophie watched his blue-eyed gaze scan her up and down, taking in her gown, which was as brown as mud and spotted with grime, the shapeless white apron she had borrowed from Betsy, the oversized cap into which she had tucked her mahogany hair.

His lips thinned in obvious distaste.

Sophie lifted her chin. She needed approval from no man, least of all him. "What a pleasant surprise," she lied. "Won't you come in?"

"Oh, yes," Thea echoed. "Do, please come in. Would you care for tea?"

"I'm afraid I haven't time for tea," Sir John said. His gaze skipped about the entryway, then finally settled on Sophie. Or rather, on Sophie's chest, what little of it was visible above the square neckline of her shapeless shift. "Rumor has it you are interested in selling your mare. I thought to purchase it for my sister."

Thea pouted. "But, Sir John, can you not stay for even a few minutes? We have not seen you since Sunday service and we would so enjoy a nice chat. Wouldn't we?"

Thea glared at Sophie, silently demanding that she agree.

Before she had a chance to say anything, Sir John shook his head. "I am sorry. I am expecting guests this afternoon. I must return to the manor straightaway. If this is an inconvenient time, I could return on the morrow?"

"No," Sophie said, eager for the chance to sell that mare and earn some much-needed cash—even if it meant having to spend time in close proximity with Sir John.

But to venture into the stables? The mere thought

quickened her breath and set her heart to pounding in her chest. If she wanted to sell the horse, she had no choice. Timmons was with Betsy and Cecelie and wouldn't return for hours yet.

Sophie stiffened her spine. She would do what she had to do to survive. "Miss Washburn, would you accompany us?"

Thea wrinkled her nose. She looked about to refuse, then she smiled at Sir John and said, "Why, of course."

She linked her arm through his. "Shall we?"

Thea's obvious flirtations as they walked to the stables brought some relief to Sophie's growing apprehension. The morning fog had burned off. Bright sunshine and endless blue sky stretched across the horizon. The pleasantly mild breeze was a hopeful sign that spring would soon give way to summer.

With each step she took, Sophie found it harder to block the thoughts and memories trying to invade her consciousness. She forced herself to focus on the chattering birds darting in and out of the trees rather than the pressure growing in her throat, trying to choke off her ability to breathe.

She did not pause outside the stable doors. She was afraid she'd never get her feet moving again if she did.

A small window at the back of each stall provided a meager amount of light. The air felt cool against her heated cheeks.

The mixed aromas of leather and horse and hay triggered a sudden onslaught of forbidden memories that nearly brought her to her knees. She held up her hands as if she could physically push them away and forced her mind to the moment at hand.

A soft nickering called to her from the first stall.

Sophie kept her head carefully averted until she reached the only other horse in her possession, Lady May, a bay mare with a golden mane and the sweetest disposition.

She could hear Sir John's boots pounding on the stone floor as he stepped up behind her. He was standing close.

Too close. She could feel his hot breath against her neck, smell his cologne and the sweat on his skin.

Sophie shivered. She took a deep breath, forced herself to relax. She would not give him the satisfaction of knowing his proximity disturbed her. She turned around, searched for Thea who was nowhere to be seen. Then she caught a glimpse of her standing outside the door, backlit by the sun. No doubt Thea thought it beneath her dignity to step foot in the stables, but to let a man accompany Sophie alone was beyond all bounds.

Especially when that man was Sir John.

She lifted her chin. "It is much too dark in here for you to judge. If you would wait with Miss Washburn, I shall lead the mare outside."

"Please, allow me," he breathed against her cheek.

"As you wish," Sophie said, eager to get away from him.

She took a step back but before she could make her escape, he grabbed her arms.

She clawed at his fingers. "Sir John, what are you doing?"

He tightened his grip.

"Release me at once," she said through her teeth.

She had known he was a scoundrel. She had known he had dishonorable designs upon her person, but she had never thought him capable of accosting her in such a way as this, especially considering he was the keeper of the peace.

She should kick him in the shin but she doubted her well-worn shoe would do much damage against his knee-high Hessians. Besides, she truly did not want Thea to catch her in a scandalous embrace with this man. Her reputation might be in tatters, but Sophie took pride in her knowledge of the truth and the fact that she had always behaved with perfect propriety, regardless of what anyone else might think.

She was not about to let him take advantage of her. She would give him one chance to redeem himself.

"Unhand me at once!"

"Sophie," he said in a low, urgent voice. "You need a man to take care of you. I want to take care of you."

"I can take care of myself."

His gaze raked her from head to toe, then settled on her chest, indistinctly outlined by her thin cotton apron. "And a right poor job you're doing of it. You dress like a maid, and you work like one, too. You deserve satin and jewels—"

"What I wear has nothing to do with you. Now, release me."

He leaned into her, pressed her against the cold stone wall. "I know you are not frightened. You know what it means to love a man. I want you, Sophie. Let me love you."

Sophie grimaced. She was now convinced he had no intention of releasing her. Still, she doubted Sir John would want anyone else to see him like this. She drew a deep breath and opened her mouth to call for Thea's attention.

His lips came down hard upon hers.

The shock of his mouth against hers stunned Sophie into immobility. His lips were wet and slimy, as if he were drooling against her mouth. Her stomach clenched. She tasted bile in her throat. Every muscle in her body constricted. She was incapable of thought as panic raced through her. She dragged air in through her nose. A scream built in her throat.

When he pushed his tongue against her teeth, her paralysis snapped. She struggled against him, but he clutched her arms in his fists, his fingers pinching her skin. He gripped her tighter, pinned her between his chest and the wall.

She knew she could not overpower him, but she had to get him to release her. She went soft and pliable in his arms, and, for just one moment, she let him deepen the kiss. Just long enough to slip her knee between his thighs.

She twisted her face away.

He slobbered kisses along her neck.

Sophie fought the urge to retch.

"Sir John," she said in a calm, steady voice that belied the revulsion and rage swirling inside her.

She waited until he lifted his head to meet her gaze. "I know how to slam my knee into the most sensitive part of a man's anatomy." To emphasize her words, she wiggled said knee, lodged perilously close to the male anatomy to which she had just referred. "And, I assure you, I am not afraid to do it."

A long moment passed before understanding dawned in his lust-filled eyes. He laughed. It was not a pleasant sound.

"A whore's trick? Why am I not surprised?" He dropped his hands and stepped back. "This is far from over, Sophie. I want you, and I intend to have you."

She brushed past him, quickly fixing her cap and smoothing her skirt as she hurried toward the door. She resisted the urge to scrub her lips with her apron. There was nothing she could do about the heat flushing her cheeks. She took a calming breath before emerging from the stables, then forced herself to walk slowly and deliberately to Thea's side.

Her companion eyed her suspiciously until a shuffling sound inside the stables drew her attention back to the door. A few moments later, Sir John appeared, looking for all the world like the well-mannered gentleman he pretended to be rather than the scurrilous rogue who had just accosted a defenseless woman.

"I am afraid I am undecided about the mare, after all," he said, his voice heavily laden with ennui.

"Perhaps you could return with your sister?" Thea chimed in. "I should so like to see her. Then she can decide for herself if she wants Lady May."

Sophie rolled her eyes. She knew Miss Lucy Shays would never visit the Park, not even to meet the regent himself.

Sir John nodded. "An excellent idea, Miss Washburn, but I am afraid my sister is indisposed at the moment."

Which was a polite way of saying his sister would not be caught dead paying a social call on Sophie Treneham.

He stared at Sophie. A smile that fell just short of a leer curved his lips. "With your permission, I shall make my decision and return in a day or two?"

She might need the money, but not badly enough that she was willing to allow anyone to manhandle her.

"I am afraid I have changed my mind," she said. "The mare is not for sale."

Thea stared at Sophie as if she had just turned somersaults across the drive.

Sir John's lips tightened. "As you wish. Perhaps I should inquire again in a day or two? On the off chance that you have changed your mind?"

Sophie wanted to tell him not to step foot on her property again or she would shoot him, but she refused to give society any further entertainment at her expense. What she really wanted to ask him, yet again, was if he had made any progress toward apprehending the criminal she had once employed as her steward. She held her tongue, though. She knew it was useless. She now doubted he had ever tried to catch that thief.

At her continued silence, he bowed stiffly, then turned on his heel and strode away. Thea stood beside Sophie, her eyes shining with admiration for the man who had just left.

Sophie thought she should tell her companion the wretch wasn't worth such devotion, but she knew her words would not be heard. Thea wanted a man. Any man would do.

Even a scoundrel like Sir John Shays.

Sophie sighed. She linked her arm through Thea's as they started back to the house. "Why don't I fix a nice tray of tea and pastries? Then you can keep me company while I clean."

* * *

Thea was comfortably settled on a sofa in the blue drawing room with a tray of sweets on the table before her. As Sophie attacked the mantel with her feather duster, she prayed the treats would keep her companion's mouth too busy to chatter. She needed peace and quiet and time to think.

Her available funds were running desperately low and it was only May, months before the harvest brought in any cash. Of course, if this summer proved to be as bad as last year's, the harvest would likely fail again. If that happened, Sophie didn't know what she would do.

She thought she heard a noise coming from the doorway behind her, a deeply masculine sound of a man clearing his throat, followed by the rap of knuckles on wood. It had to be her overactive imagination since the only other person in the house at the moment was Cook, and she was in the kitchen.

Her heart pounding wildly in her chest, she spun around.

A man stood just inside the drawing room door.

Sophie's breath caught in her throat. Her ears rang with Thea's scream. Her skin burned as the temperature in the room seemed to rise to a hundred degrees.

The man was dressed in black from head to toe. He was tall, so tall—at least six feet—and just as broad-shouldered, or so it seemed to Sophie as he loomed in the doorway.

His mouth was slightly ajar, as if he intended to speak, but he said nothing as he stared at Thea as she screamed. It was as if he were paralyzed by the shrillness of her shriek.

Brandishing her feather duster at his chest like a sword, Sophie rushed forward. "Who are you? What are you doing here?"

Her words seemed to snap him out of his spell.

He focused his attention on Sophie. His thick black hair emphasized his deeply tanned face. He had piercing blue eyes that sparkled with a dangerous gleam, like a pirate's eyes beholding his booty. A wicked smile played upon his lips as he looked at the weapon she held in her shaking hand.

She must appear a ridiculous twit, standing there with only a feather duster to protect her. What did she plan to do? Dust him to death? Why, oh, why, hadn't she grabbed the poker from the fireplace stand? She had no doubt that if this intruder were bent on evil intent, he could crush her with one blow of his hand. Her blood pounded in her ears. Rational thought fought with panic. She had to get him out of the house. But how?

She kept a loaded pistol in the gunroom in case of emergencies. Well, this was definitely an emergency.

She was too far away from the door. He would surely catch her if she attempted to run. Besides, she could not abandon Thea. Though she had finally stopped screaming, Thea now cowered behind the settee, holding on to it as if she didn't have the strength to remain on her feet without solid support.

Sophie strongly doubted she could depend on any help from that quarter. Still, she would not let this man see her fear.

Pulling herself up to her full five feet, she squared her shoulders and jabbed the huge black feathers at his chest.

"Who are you?" she demanded in an imperious voice that would do a queen proud. "How did you get in?"

Great clouds of dust puffed in his face.

He coughed, waved his hands. "Put that thing down! I knocked. Several times. When no one answered, I opened the door. Which, I might add, someone stupidly left unlocked. I was afraid someone might be hurt," he added, almost as an afterthought—or so it seemed to Sophie—as if he were trying to lure her into complacency so that he could have his evil way.

His left cheek was badly scarred, a wound he no doubt sustained during some clandestine raid. He held up his hands. He smiled what she imagined he thought was a reassuring smile. In truth, it sent terror spiraling down her back to her toes.

She dropped her feather duster to the floor, took a small step back, edging toward the fireplace. Reaching the fire iron seemed her greatest hope.

"I have business with your mistress and the earl," he said. His voice, low and deeply masculine, rumbled like distant thunder across the sky.

He tried to move around her, but she matched him step for step. She had to protect Thea.

He gave an exasperated sigh, quickly sidestepped around her, and turned to her companion.

"Miss Treneham. I am Jagger Remington, a friend of your brother's. Perhaps you have heard him speak of me?" His features were perfectly polite, but his voice had a sharp edge, tinged with bitterness, or perhaps it was disgust.

"I am afraid you have made a mistake," Sophie said.

Slowly, Jagger Remington turned around.

"I am Sophie Treneham." She nodded at the other woman. "That is my companion, Miss Washburn."

His gaze roamed over Sophie, taking in her dirty dress, her threadbare apron, the oversized cap upon her head, the feather duster at her feet. No hint of his thoughts played upon his face as he studied her.

She stood stiff beneath his inspection, her head tilted proudly in the air. She cared not how she appeared to him, or to anyone for that matter. He was a stranger who had entered her house unannounced and uninvited. She had to get rid of him.

Her skin grew warmer with each passing second as his gaze roamed over her. An uncomfortable tingle traveled along her arms and neck, as if he had smoothed his hands over her flesh, rather than merely looked at her with his eyes.

"Your business, Mr. Remington?" she said, crossing her arms over her chest.

His gaze followed her motions. His eyes widened almost imperceptibly, but Sophie noticed.

She looked down. The cut of her bodice was demure enough, but by holding her arms as tightly as she was, she had accentuated her bustline, pushing her fullness between her arms and stretching the cloth over the mounds.

Her cheeks heated. Her breath burned. She was ten times a fool. Why not just invite the man to rape her?

She dropped her arms to her sides.

"Your business?" she demanded, shame and anger making her voice quiver, a weakness she cursed even more than her foolishness.

"Business?" he said.

She pulled the cotton cap from her head, let it fall to the floor. Her thick mahogany curls spilled around her face. "You said you are a friend of my brother's. Do you have a message from him?"

Jagger Remington cleared his throat but said nothing.

Sophie clenched her hands into fists. "If you have come to ask for money, do not bother. You will not get it."

That seemed to startle him. His gaze roamed over her again, then he glanced around the room. It was a beautifully furnished room with settees and chairs covered in rich, blue damask. A deeper blue velvet draped the windows. Portraits and tapestries worth a small fortune hung on the walls.

Had she been able to sell just one of those pictures, she would not be in her current dire circumstances, but they belonged to the estate and the Treneham family. She was merely the current keeper of the wealth. And, as Sir John had so aptly put it, a right poor job she was doing of it, too.

Sophie cursed herself for drawing the man's attention to the treasures on the wall.

"What is your message?" she said at last, breaking the silence that had stretched between them.

He smiled at her then, a cat-ate-the-cream kind of smile that set warning bells clattering in her brain.

"Why, Miss Treneham. I have come to claim my wife."

Chapter Three

Sophie stared at him. She couldn't think, couldn't speak. She was amazed that she was still on her feet, considering her legs felt as if they had no bones. He was a madman. They were alone in the house with a madman.

His words echoed through her mind. She shook her head.

He nodded.

With an air of bored detachment, he clasped his hands behind his back. The fabric of his shirt stretched from seam to seam until Sophie thought that surely it would rip. He stood with his booted feet shoulder-width apart. His seemingly casual stance held an underlying fierceness that frightened her.

She had to get him out of the house. She would have to try to reason with him. But how did one reason with a madman?

"I believe you are mistaken," she said, keeping her voice softly soothing just as she did when she comforted Cecelie after a tumble.

"I assure you, I am not."

He smiled a smile of such masculine self-assurance, Sophie nearly screamed. Oh, he was clever.

"Did Edmund put you up to this?"

His smile vanished. "Who is Edmund?"

"If this is some sort of elaborate scheme you have devised between the two of you, you can forget it."

"Who is Edmund?" he said, advancing on her.

Sophie forced herself to stand her ground. "Do not pretend you do not know him. This is just the sort of madness he would concoct."

"I have no idea what you're talking about."

"I see I've arrived just in time," a deep voice said from the doorway.

Sophie spun around.

"Stephen," she gasped, finding it suddenly hard to breathe. She clutched her fist over her heart as if she could ease the ache in her chest. She didn't know whether to throw her arms around his neck to welcome him home or to pummel him for worrying her to death. He looked older, much older than when he had left. His shoulders drooped, giving him the appearance of someone totally worn down, defeated by life.

"Your timing is impeccable, my lord," Jagger Remington drawled. "Why, one might even be tempted to say—planned?"

The implication of his words struck Sophie like a blow to the chest. She glared at Stephen. "Do you know this man?"

He studied his feet.

His refusal to meet her gaze worried her.

"Answer me," she demanded, fighting the panic trying to wrap its icy claws around her.

Stephen grasped her elbow. "Excuse us for a moment," he said as he steered her out the door.

Sophie shook her arm free.

He tried to grab her again.

"Do not," she said, then marched down the hall and into the library. She knew he followed because she could hear his boot heels clicking on the wooden floor.

Row upon row of shelves, some crammed full of

books, others bare and covered in dust, gave the room a desolate air. A lone mahogany pedestal table stood like a sentinel to the dirt.

This once was her favorite room. Now she avoided it as much as possible. Somehow it seemed fitting to have this discussion here.

She rounded on her stepbrother. "Who is this man? What is he doing here? And, please, do not dissemble."

Stephen leaned his back against the door. "Why are you dressed like that?"

Sophie choked. "Why am I dressed like this? I haven't seen you in nearly two years and all you can say to me is why am I dressed like this? Why do you think I am dressed like this? I was cleaning the house. Where have you been?"

His face turned white. "Did you not get my messages?"

Sophie laughed bitterly. "The only message I got was the same one your creditors got. That you had fled England to escape your debts."

She tried to curb her acidic words but months of agonized worry rippled to the surface and turned to rage. "Where have you been? I thought you were dead!"

Stephen closed the distance between them. He reached out to take her in his arms.

She stepped back.

"Sophie, I am sorry you were worried. I sent word to Mr. Danvers. And I wrote you several times. Are you saying you did not receive any of my letters?"

She shook her head. "It appears the despicable Mr. Danvers was hiding your letters from me, just as he was bleeding the estate dry."

"Danvers?" Stephen shouted, clearly stunned that his estate manager would betray him. "I do not understand. He has been with this estate for as long as I've owned it."

"And he has been stealing from you the entire time. Good heavens, Stephen, did you never audit the books?"

Stephen didn't answer. His face had lost all color,

making him appear even older than he had a few moments ago.

Sophie bit her tongue to dam the flow of angry words. Honesty compelled her to admit that Stephen wasn't entirely to blame. If she hadn't sleepwalked through most of the last two years, the dastardly land agent would never have succeeded in his treachery.

"Tell me everything," Stephen demanded, his voice harsh.

Sophie laced her fingers together to keep her hands from shaking. "He has been stealing from the estate for years, with no one the wiser. Oh, he started out with such small sums, you might not have noticed even had you checked the books."

She rubbed her forefingers over her temples. "After you transferred ownership to me, he grew emboldened. No doubt because I was a female and he thought I wouldn't notice."

It galled her to admit how right the scoundrel turned out to be in his assumptions. Her stepbrother had given her the greatest gift: a home of her own. She ached with shame at how badly she'd failed in her duties as chatelaine.

She wanted to hide her face in her hands, but she forced herself to meet Stephen's gaze.

"Six months ago, I informed him I would check the accounts before renegotiating the rents. A few days later, the villain disappeared, taking all the plate and household cash—along with the rents, the servants' pay, a few of the more valuable pieces of art, leaving behind a mountain of bills that had never been paid—" Her voice cracked. The horror and worry of those first few months after the villain had disappeared was still a raw and aching wound.

Stephen fished in his pocket for his handkerchief, then shoved it into her hand.

She crushed the linen in her palm. She never cried.

Not even when her life had fallen apart and the world turned against her had she shed a single tear.

She was not about to start now.

She walked over to the window. She stared out at the garden—or rather, at the jungle of tangled branches and wandering vines in desperate need of pruning. The smaller, more delicate flowers had long since given up the fight.

Afternoon sunlight filtered through the dirt-streaked glass. She ran her hand along the windowsill. "I imagine I should be thankful the dastardly cur remained current with the taxes. No doubt he realized if he hadn't, his schemes would have been discovered long before he had time to flee."

"Why did you not write to Edmund?"

Sophie shuddered. Unlike Stephen, her other stepbrother was so evil, he could give the devil himself lessons in cruelty.

"Do you honestly believe he would have helped me?"

"You should have contacted my solicitor."

"I wrote to him. He never answered my letters."

"I shall have that idiot's head on a spike! I spoke with him two days ago. He never said a word." Stephen circled his hand through the air. "You should have sold the paintings or some of the furnishings—"

"I would never! You might have given me this house, but the paintings and furnishings belong to your family!"

"You are my family!" Stephen exploded.

She lifted her chin. "By marriage. Not by birth."

"As if that matters!" Stephen wagged his finger at her face. "I vow, Sophie, your stubborn pride will be the death of you yet! Those paintings came with the house, which, I might add, did not devolve to me through any of my family connections. I bought it many years ago. I have never even lived here, except for one brief period after I first purchased it, and then again when you moved in."

Sophie did not back down. She was not a child to meekly hold out her hand for punishment. "I did not know that. How could I know that? I sold only those items that belonged to me. My books. My gowns. My brooch—" Her voice quivered. It was the only piece of jewelry she had possessed. A gift to her at her birth from the father she had never known.

Now this man, this pirate, had arrived to claim her as his bride? It was the final indignity. She would not suffer it.

"Why is he here?" She fairly growled the words. She didn't recognize her own voice.

"Now, Sophie, calm down—"

"Do not tell me to calm down. I want to know the truth. And I want to know it now! Why is he here? What have you done?"

He hesitated a moment. "I could die, you know."

He held up his hand to stop her protests. "Just listen to what I have to say. I could die today, or I could live another twenty years. Either way, I cannot stop the title and entailed property from passing into Edmund's hands. But I can keep you out of his clutches. Would you like it if he were in charge of your maintenance?"

Sophie winced. But that did not matter to her. She was not a piece of property, a part and parcel of the entail. She had plans that would turn the finances of this estate around. Once it started to turn a profit, she would be able to live quite comfortably for the rest of her life. Plus she had a small inheritance of her own, a settlement made upon her by her stepfather at the time of his marriage to her mother.

It was the only provision her mother had ever made for her. It wasn't a large sum, but it was locked up in a trust until her twenty-fifth birthday. In three short years, she would come into her inheritance. Then she would be dependent on no one. And that's the way she wanted it to stay.

"What of Colin and Cecelie?" Stephen said.

Sophie clenched her teeth. "Colin is dead."

Oh, it was cruel of her to blurt it out like that. Her voice sounded so bland, so emotionless, no one would ever guess she was dying inside.

Stephen gasped. He stumbled backward, his hand blindly feeling for the wall.

Sophie pulled her dust cloth from her pocket. She focused all her energy and thoughts on erasing the grime from the pedestal table. She polished the wood until it gleamed.

The rag turned as black as the hole in the center of her chest where her heart used to be.

Stephen drew a sharp breath. "When?"

This was hard. So hard. She rolled her lips between her teeth. "Shortly after I saw you last. Nearly two years." Which marked her descent into darkness and sent her sleepwalking through her days. Barely able to function. Unable to care. The perfect pigeon to be plucked of her possessions by the villainous Mr. Danvers.

Sophie never let herself think about the horror of that night, let alone voice it aloud. She preferred to live in a dream world where she could pretend it never happened.

Yet the ache in her heart, the void in her life, was a constant reminder of her loss, like a blue-black swirling whirlpool sucking in the sky. Piercing ice blue, like Jagger Remington's eyes.

Why had she thought of that man's eyes?

Several long moments passed. No words were spoken. So much was left unsaid.

Stephen rubbed the heels of his hands over his eyes. "And what of Cecelie?"

"She is fine."

"That is not what I meant. What would happen to Cecelie if I should die? Her future is at stake, too, you know."

Sophie pressed her forefingers against her temples.

She couldn't think about any of this now. She wasn't about to fall into Edmund's hands. All she knew was she had to get rid of that man in the drawing room. His piercing blue eyes were haunting her mind with their vividness. Their clarity. Could he see into her soul with those eyes?

"I will not marry him," she said.

"Sophie—"

"Not another word. I won't marry him. I can't. You, of all people, should know that!"

Stephen banged his fist on the wall. Dust clouds swirled like snowflakes in the air. "I will not let you bury yourself in this mausoleum. It is time you put the past behind you."

Sophie laughed, the sound as cold and bitter as the north wind that howled in from the sea each winter. "Put the past behind me? How can you, of all people, say that?"

A sudden, awful realization dawned on her.

She could barely give voice to the accusation. "You did not tell him, did you?"

"I am thinking of your future."

"No, of course you did not or he would not be here."

"You need someone to protect you—"

"I can protect myself. I always have!"

"You are being unreasonable," Stephen growled.

Sophie sniffed. "I beg to differ. I seem to be the only one who is thinking clearly. I suppose I should be thankful you are at least not trying to foist me off upon a peer of the realm. Then again, I imagine I am in no danger of that as I cannot think of one who would have anything to do with me. So where did you dig him up?"

"I beg your pardon?"

"How far did you have to travel to find a man to marry me? He looks like a heathen with all that dark skin."

"He's as English as you are. He's merely lived abroad these few years past." Stephen's gaze shifted to the floor. "All I ask is that you give him a chance. Get to know him."

Sophie shook her head. "I have nothing to hide. I have done nothing of which I am ashamed."

Well, that wasn't entirely true. She was ashamed of allowing Mr. Danvers to rob her while she slept, but she was not ashamed of her life and the choices she had made.

"I will not marry him."

She sailed out the door and nearly collided with Thea who was standing in the hallway, as close to the door as she could.

"Did you hear everything?" Sophie asked. "Or should I repeat it for you?"

Thea lifted her shoulders and chin. "Now, Sophie, do not work yourself into a snit. I just wanted to make certain you were all right."

Sophie shook her head and walked away.

Thea trailed along behind her. "What are you going to do?"

"I am going to get rid of that man."

"How do you plan to do that?"

"I will simply tell him the truth," she said over her shoulder. "He is a proud and arrogant man. He will thank his lucky stars for his near escape and be on his way quicker than *you* can say, 'I told you so.' Care to watch?"

Without waiting for a reply, Sophie marched to the drawing room. She hesitated outside the door. She needed to collect herself before she faced that man again.

He stood by the fireplace, one booted foot upon the hearth, one hand resting on the mantel.

Sophie had to admit that he was a magnificent specimen of a man. His civilized clothes did nothing to hide the raw power of his well-built frame. The jagged scar across his cheek could not detract from his rugged good looks, his strong, square jaw, his vivid blue eyes. His thick black hair was long and hung loose about his neck, giving him the air of a pirate come to plunder what was left of her home.

As if he sensed her staring at him, he turned and caught her gaze. He smiled, a slow, sensuous curving of his lips that held her spellbound.

Her breath caught in her throat as she stepped into the room. She tried to tell herself the twinge in her stomach was anger. Nothing more. Nothing less.

She could not be attracted to this man. Could she?

He sauntered toward her.

An image from a book she'd read as a child rose in her mind. A panther on the prowl for his prey. This man was a stunning portrait of elegance and grace and unleashed power.

His gaze traveled down her body in a way that made her extremely uncomfortable, as if he had just undressed her with his eyes.

He probably had, the wretched man.

He stopped mere inches away from her. His clean, fresh scent of ocean air and masculine strength filled her senses.

Though her knees were shaking and her breath burned in her throat, she forced herself to stand her ground.

She clamped her hands together. "I am afraid you have been sadly duped, Mr. Remington. I have no desire to marry you."

His smile never faltered, but there was a look in his eye that disarmed her. A look of pity, or perhaps it was admiration. Not quite the reaction she had expected. She found herself staring at his lips, at his straight white teeth, gleaming in stark relief against his deeply tanned cheeks.

Her mouth went dry. She wrenched her gaze away from his face. He held what looked to be several legal documents in his hand. Where had they come from? She was certain he had not possessed them when he had arrived.

A shudder of premonition raced along her spine.

He held the documents out to her.

Her fingertips brushed against his as she reached for them. The heat of his hand surprised her, as did the shiver that traveled up her arm. Her self-assurance faltered, along with the barrier she usually kept wrapped around her heart.

She was drawn to this man, aware of him in a way she had never experienced before, and she did not like it.

She did not like him.

As if reading her mind, his smile vanished. "It is a pity you feel that way." He nodded at the papers in her hand. "One might wish you had discovered your sentiments before today. As these documents are legally binding on us both, all you need do is choose your wedding day. Might I suggest . . . today?"

Chapter Four

She was having a nightmare. There could be no other explanation for the bizarre events of this day.

Yet, she remembered the frustration of a long, sleepless night, lying in bed, listening to the wind rattle her windowpane. She remembered dragging herself out of bed and crawling into her clothes. She remembered waving good-bye to Cecelie as she left the house with Betsy and Timmons. Then Sir John had arrived, and she remembered every repulsive detail of his visit. Maybe she wasn't dreaming after all.

She bit her lip.

Pain flashed through her jaw. Definitely not a dream.

Her hands shook and her vision blurred as she scanned the first document. Only bits and pieces of the words penetrated the fuzzy confusion in her brain. A marriage agreement. Spelling out in excruciating detail the financial benefits this man would receive when he married her. This house—*her house*—and all the land that went with it. All the furnishings. The carpets. The paintings. The rents. What bitter irony. The pirate had come to claim a treasure trove. Instead, he was getting abandoned tenements and bankrupt accounts. She should find some satisfaction in that. But she didn't.

There was no mention of Colin or Cecelie, a betrayal more bitter than any that had gone before.

"This is a mistake," she finally managed to whisper.

She looked at Jagger. She almost thought she could see sympathy in his deep blue eyes. Normally, it would have made her furious. At the moment, she was too stunned to care.

"Do you not understand? I am past the legal age of consent. He had no right to enter into this contract without my consent. And I most certainly did not consent!"

His shoulders stiffened. Whatever sympathy she may have read in his eyes vanished, replaced by a cold mask of indifference. "You signed the documents, did you not?"

She shook her head, turned her attention back to the papers clutched in her fingers. She skipped to the bottom of the next page. Her eyes went wide as she saw her name. In her hand. There was no mistake about that.

The second document was a special license that would allow them to wed at any time, anywhere. She didn't bother to read the details but quickly flipped to the last page.

It was a document acknowledging her legal age and granting Stephen her power of attorney and the right to arrange a marriage between Sophie and the man of his choice.

Again, at the bottom, she saw her signature.

She closed her eyes. A vision floated through her mind, a vision of Stephen handing her a sheaf of papers to sign. Papers he had claimed would transfer ownership of Norwood Park to her, granting her independence and security for the rest of her life. He had appeared nervous at the time. Now she understood why.

She hadn't even bothered to read the papers because she had trusted him, believed that he loved her as a sister, even if there was no blood between them. He was the only person in her life who had ever seemed to care for her. The only one who had helped her in her hour of most desperate need. The only man she had thought she could trust, and he had betrayed her in the worst possible way she could imagine.

Impotent rage burned in her chest.

She thought she might scream.

Yes, she could definitely feel a scream building in the back of her throat.

She had to get out of there. She had to get away.

She spun on her heel, stalked to the door, and came face-to-face with Stephen who was just entering the room.

"Sophie, I must speak with you," he said, a desperate edge in his voice. "There is something I still need to tell you."

She shoved the papers at his chest, watched what little color that had returned to his face drain away, then stalked from the room and out the front door.

She had to get away. Before she killed someone.

Jagger watched her parade from the room, her shredded dignity wrapped around her like a ragged cloak, her anger clearly visible in the stiffness of her spine.

She was magnificent. No other word could describe her. And not just her looks, though he could find no fault with her there. She was lovely. Truly lovely. Not the pale beauty so common amongst the ladies of the *ton*, but a dark, rich beauty that bespoke of earthly pleasures and long hours in the sun.

Her eyes were deep brown, like melted chocolate. Huge, liquid-brown eyes beneath long, spiked lashes and gently flaring brows, all set in a round face with high cheekbones and full pouting lips that begged to be kissed. Hers was a stunning beauty, a fact that rammed home to Jagger the depth of Stephen's betrayal. She could have married any man she wanted.

What would make the earl stoop so low as to trick her into a match with a man she would no doubt rather see dead?

Faced with the same situation, Jagger imagined most women would have suffered a fit of hysterics or would have wept or swooned. Not Sophie Treneham. She held her head high and confronted her enemy with more courage than many a soldier in Wellington's army. She was truly a magnificent woman.

Jagger understood her rage. He was still grappling with his own shock, his own sense of betrayal at the hands of a man he had trusted. To make matters worse, memories of the last time he'd entered this house were trying to invade his mind.

His hands clenched into fists at his sides as he advanced on Stephen. "You lied to me."

Stephen dropped the papers to the floor. He held up his hands as he started to back out the door. "I can explain."

Jagger grabbed him by the lapels of his frock coat and lifted him off his feet. "You lied to me," he said through gritted teeth. "You told me she was agreeable to this ridiculous scheme. Now it seems as if she knew nothing about it. Give me one reason why I shouldn't throttle you."

"Put me down, and I will."

Jagger opened his hands.

Stephen slid to the floor. He glared at Jagger, but said nothing as he struggled to his feet.

"It is a long story," he said, tugging his shirtsleeves into place. He adjusted the angle of his cravat, the hemline of his coat. "I am not sure where to begin."

Jagger crossed his arms over his chest. "It does not matter. The marriage is off."

"Now, wait just a minute. You signed the contracts. You cannot back out now."

"I signed them under false pretenses. You said she was

agreeable and you lied. Therefore, the contracts are null and void."

Stephen's face turned red. "The courts will not see it that way."

"Are you threatening me?"

"I am merely stating a fact. If you renege on our agreement, I will bring suit for breach of contract. Make no mistake about it. I will win."

"You would shame your sister? Destroy her reputation?"

"Her fate is in your hands."

Jagger shook his head in disgust. He strode down the hall toward the front door. Stephen sputtered and fumed as he followed behind him, uttering nonsense words about duty and honor.

Why should Jagger worry about honor when Stephen had lied to him, betrayed him more thoroughly than his father ever could have—because he had trusted Stephen!

Jagger grabbed the knob, ripped open the door.

"Did I turn my back on you," Stephen shouted, chasing after him, "when you came to me? Begging my help. Did I turn you away?"

The words slammed into Jagger's back like a volley of bullets, spinning him around, spiraling pain through his chest.

He gnashed his teeth. "What did you say?"

Stephen was breathing hard, as if he had been running for miles. "You heard me."

They glared at each other for a long, tense moment.

Anger billowed through Jagger like noxious fumes. He wanted to tear Stephen apart with his bare hands, but long years of practice had taught him how to contain his rage.

He took several deep breaths, clenched and unclenched his fists, then crossed his arms over his chest and assumed a negligent pose. "I thought you a better man than my father," he drawled. "But I was wrong. Tell me, my lord, was your life ever in danger? Or did you slice your own wrist for effect?"

Stephen flinched, but did not back down. "I am protecting my sister."

Jagger laughed. He lifted his brows. "Is that what you call it? When I arrived, the door was unlatched with no servants to be seen."

His skin had grown cold as he'd remembered Stephen's assertion that someone was trying to kill him. Fearful of what he would find, hopeful that he wasn't too late, Jagger had entered the house and crept down the hall, only to be shocked to find two women alone and unprotected.

His shock had turned to horror as he'd faced the woman he'd wrongly assumed was his bride-to-be, a screaming banshee who appeared to be every bit the vapid female he despised most.

Jagger had not known what he had expected to feel at that moment—perhaps instant attraction, perhaps physical desire for the woman with whom he was to spend the rest of his life. He had felt nothing but distaste—until the "maid" had stepped forward and claimed to be Sophie Treneham.

The nerve of the insolent chit nearly made him laugh, but she had looked so sincere that he'd believed her—and learned the meaning of instant desire as she'd battled him toe to toe with no more than a feather duster in her hand.

The image of her dressed as a pauper and cleaning the woodwork reignited his rage. "Where was your protection while you were traipsing across the ocean spinning your lies and baiting your trap? You abandoned her to poverty and physical labor?"

Stephen pursed his lips, his expression pompous and smug. "The past is beyond my control. I am protecting her future."

"By forcing her into a marriage against her will? How did you get her to sign those papers?"

"What difference does it make? She signed them. And so did you. She will come around . . . if you convince her."

The insinuation in Stephen's voice turned Jagger's stomach. "And how, pray tell, am I to do that?"

"Given your considerable appeal to women, I am certain you will find a way."

Jagger smirked. "You want me to seduce her?"

"Of course not! I want you to woo her, to court her like any young girl deserves to be courted. Make her want to marry you. Make her love you."

"You are out of your mind!"

"Maybe I am. But that doesn't change the facts. You *still* owe me. And I have yet to be paid."

Chapter Five

Jagger cursed himself as he traipsed through the woods in search of his missing bride-to-be. Then he cursed the world in general and Lord Hallowell in particular.

His blood was running as hot as his rage. He had thought Stephen Treneham a man of honor, incapable of such a stunning betrayal, though Jagger didn't know why he was so surprised. Experience had long since taught him no one was ever quite what they seemed.

The carpet of dry leaves covering the footpath crunched beneath his boot heels. Twigs snapped and leaves rattled as a pair of squirrels chased each other through the trees. The scent of pine needles hung in the air. Up ahead, the woods grew thinner and narrow shafts of sunlight flickered over the ground.

Jagger was tempted to cut his losses and run, but that would make him as dishonorable as Stephen. He had given his word. His word was his bond. Honor demanded that he pay his debt and wed a woman who no doubt would rather see him dead.

He strode out of the shelter of the trees. Momentarily blinded by the sun, he squinted until the world came into focus again. Unlike the landscaped areas of the park, this pond was far removed from the house, untouched by human hands, shaped according to nature's plan. The wild ruggedness of her chosen refuge suited Sophie Treneham well. She was as untamed as the wilderness around her, unafraid to stand her ground.

He scanned the perimeter of the pond.

His intended was sitting on a huge boulder jutting out over the water's edge. She had her knees drawn up to her chest, her arms wrapped around her legs. Her eyes appeared to be closed.

Her long mahogany hair flowed over her shoulders, floated in the breeze. She was the perfect picture of misery. And vulnerability. The complete opposite of the feisty termagant who had confronted him with no more than a feather duster in her hand.

Sympathy welled up within him, and an odd sort of kinship. Although she didn't know it, they had much in common. A man they both loved had betrayed them. And it hurt.

Jagger breathed deeply to control his temper. She did not deserve his anger. She was as much a victim of her brother's duplicity as Jagger was. In truth, she was the only innocent victim in this disgusting situation.

She must have heard his footsteps crunching on the pebble-strewn path for she pushed her shoulders back and locked her jaw. He could almost see her drawing on her wounded pride like a knight of old drawing on a suit of armor, preparing to do battle. He walked up beside her. He stared out over the pond, rocked on his heels, and tried to think of something to say.

She grabbed a handful of pebbles from the boulder's surface, and tossed them, one by one, into the water. A pair of swans cruised over to investigate. Once they realized it wasn't food she was tossing, they swam away, and still he rocked on his heels and tried to think of something to say.

Nothing came to mind. He was tongue-tied, like a green youth trying to make his first conquest. It irritated him beyond belief. Finally, she looked up at him, and he lost himself in the beauty of her dark brown eyes.

He breathed the soft scent of rosewater and beeswax as the wind played with her hair. The mahogany strands looked so soft, so sensuous, flowing over her shoulders, he itched to run his fingers through it, to feel it wrapped around his naked flesh.

He stifled a groan as unbidden—unwanted—desire rushed through him. Good God, he felt like the worst kind of lecher.

She was beautiful. Truly beautiful. And the ugly truth churned yet again in the pit of his stomach.

She could have wed any man she wanted.

Why would her brother betray her so despicably?

"You must have been very desperate," she said, her voice huskier than he remembered, as if bruised by stifled screams.

He cleared his throat. "I beg your pardon?"

"To agree to wed a woman you had never met. You must have been desperate indeed."

He could set her straight. He could tell her of her brother's duplicity. He tried, but he found he could not heap insult onto injury. The truth would only hurt her more. He was strangely reluctant to add to her pain.

He shrugged. "I thought you were agreeable."

His words made her laugh, a melancholy sound that rippled through him. He silently cursed as he realized he wanted nothing more than to draw her into his arms and ease her heartache with his kiss.

No doubt she would claw out his eyes if he tried.

What was wrong with him? He didn't understand his strange attraction to this woman, this need to protect her. He was insane. Truly, there could be no other explanation. Other than lust, he thought with no small measure of self-disgust as he realized he was more than eager for his wedding night.

She placed her hand on the boulder and rolled to her knees.

He moved to assist her to her feet, but her glare froze him midstep. He crossed his arms over his chest as he watched her stand. She brushed the dust off her dress, tossed her luminous hair over her shoulders, and turned to face him.

He could almost see her brandishing her sword, sharpening the words she was about to say. He was surprised to find he was eager for the battle.

There was no doubt about it. Sophie Treneham intrigued him. She had spirit. She had courage. She would no doubt run him 'round the Maypole and back, but he found he rather relished the thought of matching wits with her.

He smiled as he planned his strategy. Sometimes a full-frontal attack was too obvious.

He needed something more subtle.

"I will not marry you," she said, and he could see the determination burning in her eyes.

"It appears neither of us has much of a choice," he said. "We both signed the contracts. There is no way out."

"I did not know what I was signing. I was tricked."

"Hmm. Would you testify to that in court? Label your brother a cheat and a fraud?" He read the answer in her eyes. "I thought not. You have more pride than that. As do I."

"You could cry off," she said.

He nodded. "Yes, I could. As could you. But I suspect neither of us will. Duty and honor and all that. If you know what I mean. And I can see that you do."

She rolled her lower lip between her teeth. She bit it so hard, he suspected she drew blood. He had to call upon all his self-control to keep from yanking her into his arms and soothing her bruised lip with his tongue.

"It will be the longest engagement in history," she said. "Because I will not marry you. You cannot force me."

"Your brother will fight through the courts to see us wed. Though I do not think his argument would have any legal backing, it would cause a terrible scandal and drag on for years. He is determined, though I cannot imagine why."

Sophie winced, and Jagger longed to draw back the words. She did not deserve his wrath. She was merely a pawn in her brother's devious scheme.

Jagger had no intention of wounding her further. He had to convince her to wed him. His honor demanded it.

No matter how either of them might feel.

"A prolonged engagement will not work," he said, trying to win her over with logic. "Whether you like it or not, I am now responsible for your welfare. Unless we wed, I cannot live with you here, nor can you live with me at my home."

She studied his face with an intensity that made him want to shift on his feet and look away, but he held her gaze.

"*Why* did you sign those papers?" she said. "Why would you agree to marry a woman you had never met? It is inconceivable, yet I have seen the proof."

He could dissemble. It would be the easiest escape. The kindest response. But he found he respected her too much to lie. Respect for a woman? It was a strange sensation he had thought long dead inside his withered soul.

Warning bells clanged in his mind. He should leave this place. He should run while he still had the chance.

"I owe your brother a debt of honor," he said as an emotion that felt something like guilt clenched his stomach.

She closed her eyes. The wind rustled the leaves on the trees. A hawk circled overhead. Its screech echoed off the stillness of the water. The sun caught the glistening highlights in her hair.

She thrust her chin in the air. "Thank you," she said,

meeting his gaze. "It is ugly, but I appreciate your speaking the truth."

At that moment, he would have given half his fortune to have met her under any other circumstances than these. A man would be lucky indeed to win the hand of this remarkable woman.

"What did *you* think you were signing?" he asked.

"Does it matter?" She shook her head sadly. "No. That is not fair. You honored me with the truth. You deserve the same. He told me he was giving me this estate."

She laughed, a sound full of bitterness and pain. "It seems I should have read the papers after all."

She seemed to give herself a mental shake, as if she just realized she had shown too much of her emotions.

Jagger would wager a thousand pounds that few had ever seen the softer, more dependent side of this woman.

She squared her shoulders and angled her chin higher.

Jagger braced himself for her next volley.

"I hope you are not too eager to claim your prize, Mr. Remington. The estate is bankrupt."

She threw the words at him like a gauntlet.

His gaze roamed over her, noting again the coarseness of her dress, her threadbare apron, the smudges of dirt upon her cheeks, the redness of her hands. Anger at Stephen Treneham flared anew. The bastard claimed to love his sister so much, yet he abandoned her to who knows what fate while he had traipsed across the globe, spinning webs of deceit and betrayal.

She stood stiff beneath his inspection, her head tilted proudly in the air. She cared not how she appeared to him, an admirable trait indeed.

"I have no need of money," he said, that unfamiliar feeling of guilt resurfacing its ugly head.

Every woman he knew wanted to marry for love. How bitterly disappointing for this fiercely proud woman to learn she was merely the victim between two men and a decades-old debt of honor. He suddenly realized it would have salvaged some of her pride if she believed he needed her money.

Once again, he regretted his hasty words. He was swimming in uncharted territory with no hope of rescue in sight.

"Given the so-called protection your brother has provided you, it is painfully obvious that you will be far better off wed to me." His voice came out harsher than he'd intended.

Her eyes went wide. "So you are riding to my rescue?" She made it sound like blasphemy.

"You need a man to take care of you."

She laughed. "Oh, that is rich. 'Tis a familiar refrain. One I've heard several times today. Yet, since men are the source of all of my problems, I must ask why would I choose to sink myself deeper in misery."

"Do you not want children?"

The words stunned Jagger the moment they left his mouth. He did not want children. He had never wanted children. Yet he half suspected she could make him change his mind.

She laughed again. "One hardly needs marriage for that, Mr. Remington."

She eyed him suspiciously.

He could almost see the wheels turning in her mind. What outrageous declaration was she about to make?

"I already have a child—" She crushed her fist against her lips. A horrified look passed over her face. "I will never bear another!" She fairly spat the words, as if she needed to get them out of her mouth as quickly as possible. As if they caused her pain.

Jagger stared at her, his eyes wide, his mouth agape. She'd finally managed to render him speechless. She must be desperate indeed to utter such dangerous words, so easy to disprove, yet so damaging to her reputation.

"Do not pity me," she ground out through her teeth. "I will not marry you. I do not care what society thinks.

Now go away, Mr. Remington. This conversation has grown tedious."

He wanted to grasp her arms, to shake some sense into her.

"I have an idea," he said as a notion came to mind. It was so ludicrous, it just might work.

She tapped her toe as she waited for him to continue.

"A marriage of convenience," he said.

She laughed, a deep throaty laugh that trembled down his spine. A wry smile played at the corners of her lips. "I was right. You are a madman."

"Think about it for a moment," he said. "It would solve our problem and preserve the integrity of your brother's name."

Not that he gave two figs about Stephen's honor, but he strongly suspected that she did. "It is perfect."

"It is insane."

"Why?"

"I know nothing about you. That's why. You could be a murderer, for all I know—"

"Do you honestly think your brother would betroth you to a criminal?"

"I can hardly say, given the situation I find myself in."

She was right, of course, but he had to convince her. "A marriage in name only would be perfect. We would have time to get to know one another. A temporary arrangement. In effect until such time as *you* change your mind and invite me to share your bed."

Her lips curved in a mocking smile. "You would give up your marital rights? Why do I have trouble believing that?"

"I am a man. Not an animal. I do assure you I can control myself. Your virtue would be perfectly safe with me."

Before he even finished the words, he knew it was a lie. He wanted her in his bed. The sooner the better. But he would give her time to adjust to the situation. Once she wanted him as badly as he wanted her, he would claim his husbandly rights.

She laughed ruefully. "That would make you the first man I know who wasn't ruled by his lust."

Her unexpected response spawned a fury in Jagger the intensity of which he had never experienced before. "What do you know of a man's lust?"

She just shook her head.

Anger rolled through him in waves. He advanced on her.

Her gaze never wavered as she stood her ground.

He felt a momentary admiration for her courage before rage washed it away. He wanted to shake the answer from her lips.

He had to force his hands to remain by his sides.

He clenched his teeth. "Answer me."

"I told you I have a child!"

His anger evaporated as quickly as it had appeared. "I think you an innocent babe who is playing with fire."

She was breathing quickly, as if she couldn't quite catch her breath. As if his nearness disturbed her.

As he stared at her mouth, the tip of her tongue, a perfect pink triangle of beckoning flesh, darted out to wet her lips.

A new strategy formed in his mind. He smiled as he lowered his head and closed his eyes.

There was more than one way to win a war.

He was going to kiss her.

Sophie gasped as she watched his eyes close and his lips part. She knew she should run, but her feet wouldn't obey her commands. It was almost as if they were frozen to the ground.

Part of her wanted to give in to his kiss. He was so very handsome. His voice, so seductive. His eyes, so enchanting.

She was attracted to him. She could no longer deny it,

not even to herself. But to succumb to his kiss would make her no better than a tavern whore.

As he lowered his head, she placed her hands in the middle of his chest to push him away. The wall of muscles beneath her fingertips hardened and flexed. The heat of his skin seemed to burn through his waistcoat and shirt, scorching her hands.

He slid his arms around her waist. His palms pressed into the curve of her spine, drawing her closer to the solid length of his body. His eyes closed slowly as he lowered his head until his lips were mere inches away from her mouth.

The heat of his breath sent a shiver down her spine. An exotic scent clung to his skin, a spicy cologne mingling with an underlying essence that was intoxicatingly male.

The moment hung between them as if suspended in time. The sounds of nature, the wind, the bees, drifted away along with her ability to think clearly. Her pulse quickened. Her breathing grew shallow and rapid. His hand slid up her back, cupped her neck, and drew her closer still, until they were almost, but not quite, touching chest to chest.

She felt powerless to stop him, as if she were moving through a dream, as if he were a sorcerer and she were enslaved.

A small portion of her brain still capable of rational thought cried out a warning. The rapid fluttering in her belly intensified until she thought she might double over in pain.

What was she doing? She could not let him kiss her.

She shoved him as hard as she could. The force broke his hold on her and sent her stumbling backward. She gasped as she teetered on the edge of the boulder.

For a moment, she hung there, her arms flapping in the wind as if she could fly to safety, then she fell.

She heard the loud splash as she hit the water. The water was so cold, it sucked the breath from her lungs. Her skin felt tingly and numb like the pins-and-needles feeling she sometimes got in her legs after sitting on her knees for too long.

As she hit the bottom, her hands sunk in the slimy mud. Her skirt, tangled around her legs, weighed her down like an anchor. Weeds wrapped around her ankles and wrists like chains.

She clamped her lips together to keep her mouth from instinctively opening and sucking in pond water. She clawed at the weeds, kicked her feet to free herself, but only succeeded in tightening the bonds.

Helpless and furious, she knew she was about to die.

She thought of Cecelie. A piercing pain gripped her chest.

She was such a fool.

She should have listened to Stephen.

Chapter Six

Trying desperately not to panic, Sophie tore at the weeds.

Numb from the cold, her fingers were too clumsy, too weak to rip the swamp grass chaining her in place. Her heart was pounding so hard, it felt as if it might explode.

Her lungs ached. She needed air. She didn't know how long she could hold her breath before instinct kicked in and she dragged in a lungful of water.

She heard a splashing noise, distorted through the liquid in her ears. She felt a current against her face. Something was moving toward her. She didn't know what kind of fish lived in this pond. For a wild moment, she wondered if she was about to be eaten alive. As if that mattered, given that she'd be dead mere moments from now if she didn't get free.

Something brushed her hand.

She opened her eyes to see what it was.

The murky water stung so badly, she swiftly shut them again. Oh, she was scared. She wanted to scream. To give in to the urge would be certain death as pond water would flood her lungs. She would not give up. Cecelie needed her!

Something warm and hard grabbed her wrist. She did

scream then, but the sound got lost in the tangy water rushing into her mouth. She choked. She wanted to cry.

Who would take care of Cecelie if she died?

Whatever had a hold on her wrist gripped her tighter, tugged her toward the surface.

Was it a hand? Jagger Remington's hand?

She thrashed her arm around in front of her, hit something solid. Was it a chest? Yes, it was definitely a chest. His chest. Solid and stable and surprisingly warm.

She clutched at his shirt, reached for his neck.

He batted her hands away, wrapped one arm around her waist, then turned her so her back was snug against his chest.

He slid one palm along her legs.

She forced herself to remain still. She knew if she struggled or tried to help him she would waste what precious little air remained in her lungs. As ridiculous as it seemed, she had to trust him. He was her only hope.

Agonizing moments passed as he wrestled with the weeds, then she was free and he pulled her to the surface.

The full sun hit her face, but she was so cold she thought she'd never be warm again. He kept one arm wrapped around her waist. She clung to his wrist as she coughed and gasped and finally dragged in a deep breath.

Warm air filled her mouth, rushed into her lungs. Nothing had ever tasted so sweet nor smelled so good, despite the ache in her throat and the stinging in her eyes.

With hard, powerful thrusts of his legs, he dragged her to shore, then hauled her onto the bank.

Too weak to move, she collapsed on the ground, sprawled on her stomach with her cheek pressed against the mud. The reassuring scent of swamp grass hung in the air. An insect buzzed around her ear. She didn't care. *Let it bite me!*

That despicable man lay beside her. She knew because she could hear his ragged breathing, feel the length of his leg pressed against hers. Even through her wet clothing, she could feel the heat emanating from his skin, like a furnace.

How could he be so hot when she was so cold, she felt as if she had just spent a month in the icehouse?

She rolled onto her back, let the sun warm her face.

The tops of the trees caught the light, a black canopy against a bright blue sky. Puffy white clouds floated by.

She should probably thank him for saving her life. But if it weren't for him, her life never would have been in danger. How dare he try to kiss her, then drop her in the pond?

He was a barbarian! A cutthroat pirate willing to stoop so low as to kill a woman to claim his prize.

Anger was good, she decided as warmth spread through her veins. Anger was comfortable. Anger made her push herself into a sitting position.

He was sprawled on his back with one leg bent at the knee. One arm rested on his chest. The other was flung out beside him. His wet black hair was slicked back from his face. His eyes were closed. He appeared to be sleeping and that made her furious. She poked him in the ribs.

He glanced at her through one, half-opened eye. He smiled his slow, pirate smile. "There is no need to thank me," he drawled. "But if you're of a mind to, I'd settle for a kiss."

She choked. Of all the arrogant male nerve!

She balled her hands into fists and clubbed his chest.

He tried to grab her arms, but she was a madwoman. She struck him again and again.

He wrestled her to the ground, grabbed her wrists. He lay full-length atop of her. Hip-to-hip. Thigh-to-thigh.

She caught her gasp in her throat. She was painfully aware of every inch of his body resting upon hers.

He leaned on his elbows to glare at her, his hard blue eyes as sharp as shimmering shards of ice. "I saved your life and this is how you thank me?"

"Saved my life," she sputtered. "You tried to kill me!"

"I did not."

"Of course you did. Once you realized I would not fall for your scheme—"

"What scheme?"

"—you tried to kill me."

"Why would I do that?"

"Because I would not marry you."

"You are babbling like an idiot."

"And you are pathetically transparent."

He clucked his tongue. "I think the water has muddled your brain."

"You want my land. My house!"

His forehead furrowed as he narrowed his eyes dangerously. He gripped her shoulders. "How, pray tell, would I get your land, your house, if you died before we had the chance to wed?" His voice was soft, each word spoken with painful precision.

"You threw me in the pond," she said indignantly.

"You threw yourself in the pond."

"But I can't swim!"

"How was I to know you would try to kill yourself over a kiss? Did you say, 'Please, don't kiss me. If you do, I'll throw myself in the pond and I don't know how to swim'?"

When she didn't respond, he squeezed her shoulders.

She thought it prudent to keep her mouth shut.

She bit her lower lip to stifle her words.

His gaze dropped to her mouth. Heat flared in his eyes.

Her breath caught in her throat. Her gaze roamed over his face, lingering on the puckered flesh beneath his eye, the whiteness a stark contrast to the golden tone of his skin.

Her mind wandered foolishly. She found herself wondering how he had gotten the scar and if it had hurt.

He had a well-shaped mouth, strong and defiant. A shadow of hair darkened his jaw. For a wild moment, she wondered what it would feel like to run her hands along his skin, to bury her fingers in his night-black hair, to press her lips to his mouth.

Her breasts, crushed against his chest, started to ache. Her nipples hardened as a wild fantasy ripped through her mind. She had a vision of his hands cupping her breasts, of him shoving her skirts above her waist and taking her there in the full light of day with the songbirds singing in the trees not twenty feet away. She wanted him, she realized with chagrin. She wanted him in the most elemental way a woman could want a man and she hated herself.

And she hated him for making her feel this way.

His eyes darkened. He looked even angrier than he had a few moments ago. Then he closed his eyes and lowered his head.

He was going to kiss her. This time there was no way to avoid it. No hope of reprieve. No escape.

She braced herself, expecting brutality, a kiss meant to punish, to conquer and control. His lips brushed hers in the barest whisper of skin against skin, a kiss meant to seduce and betray. She was weak and defenseless, unprepared for such tenderness. She longed to give in. His warmth spread over her cold, wet skin, kindled a desire, a yearning she hadn't felt in years. To be held. To be wanted. To be loved.

His kiss grew more urgent. His lips, more persuasive. His tongue touched her teeth, probed her mouth, and she moaned. She drifted her hand up his cheek, then through his hair. It was soft like silk and long enough to curl around her fingertips.

Without conscious thought, she arched her back, pressed herself tighter against his chest. One of his hands slid down her side, pressed her hips against his.

She could feel his erection, vivid proof that he wanted her as much as she wanted him. What a fool she was to think she could resist his seduction. She was so lonely. So tired of being alone. Could this unbidden, unexplainable desire for this man overrule reason and logic and control?

Could this longing for his touch, no matter how brief or how shallow, be stronger than pride? Could Edmund be right? Was she just like her mother, after all?

No! She was nothing like her.

She twisted her face away.

He nibbled her ear.

Delicious shivers traveled her skin. She had to make him stop, but she could not find her voice. She pulled her hands back, fisted them against his chest, pushed as hard as she could.

"Stop," she finally managed to gasp.

She hated the pathetic sound of her voice. She doubted very much that he would. Why should he? She had allowed him liberties that would lead any man to believe she was a woman of easy virtue.

To her surprise, he lifted his head immediately.

His confusion was evident in his piercing blue eyes as he studied her face. He was breathing as hard as she was. The self-control he was exerting was evident in the tautness of the muscles in his neck, the tightness around his lips.

"Get off of me," she said, afraid to move lest his carnal desire overwhelm his control.

"What is wrong?" His voice was a husky whisper.

"Please," she said. He would never know how much it cost her pride to utter that word.

A long moment passed before he rolled off her and onto his feet. He held out his hand to assist her.

She would have ignored him if he let her, but he muttered an oath, grabbed her elbow, and hauled her to her feet.

Shame spread warmth through her veins and over her skin. Her cheeks felt as if they were afire. Her neck burned with the telltale rash that covered her chest whenever she felt extreme anxiety. Her breathing was as ragged as his, though she suspected for entirely different reasons.

Silently, she stared at him. Her pride refused to allow her to look away. He wore only his shirtsleeves, no doubt having abandoned his coat and waistcoat before leaping into the pond. His wet shirt clung to his muscular chest, his masculine strength clearly visible in his sinewy arms. The bulge between his thighs gave clear proof of his desire.

She tore her gaze back to his face. She watched as his attention dropped to her chest.

She glanced down, horrified to see her hardened nipples thrusting against the wet fabric clinging to the curves of her breasts. She had long since abandoned her stays as she had no maid to help her lace them.

Choking back a cry of alarm, she turned and raced up the path. His footsteps pounded on the ground behind her. He called her name, but she did not stop running.

Her soaked gown slapped her legs and felt as if it weighed a hundred pounds. The wind chilled her skin, tangled her hair. She could well imagine how long it would take to run a comb through this mess. He was right behind her, close enough to grab her if he wanted, but he made no move to touch her or to get her to stop. Neither did he let her out of his sight.

Her mind worked furiously. She had to get rid of this man before Cecelie came home.

Too late, she realized as she reached the house and saw Betsy and Timmons walking across the lawn, Cecelie lagging behind them until she caught sight of Sophie.

The child spoke not a word, but raced across the carriage drive as fast as her little legs would carry her and flung herself into Sophie's outstretched arms.

Sophie closed her eyes and hugged her daughter. She bit back a scream. After all of her planning. After all of her sacrifices. How had it come to this?

The sound of her servants' chattering voices growing

louder and closer warned Sophie that she needed to make her escape. She needed to get back to the house before they drew near enough to discern the scandalous condition of her clothing and hair.

She faced the man beside her with her head held proudly in the air. "You must excuse me now, Mr. Remington. I need to tend to my daughter."

She turned and left him standing there, his mouth hanging open, his black hair plastered against his cheeks. She clenched her teeth against the inexplicable urge to tell him the truth, to make him understand. She would never explain herself to anyone. Least of all him.

Chapter Seven

He should never have kissed her.

Jagger sucked a mouthful of brandy straight from the bottle as he prowled the confines of the cramped attic room above the inn. It was the only room available in the whole damn village, thanks to a large party of ne'er-do-wells gathering for a weekend of debauchery at nearby Scarborough House.

Anticipation coiled within Jagger's gut. He relished the tension tightening the muscles of his legs. His moment of revenge was at hand—and he didn't even have to travel to London to confront his father. Learning that the bastard was in residence at his principal seat was the single bright spot in this miserable day.

He ducked his head to avoid hitting a crossbeam, then turned when he reached the bed, a rickety contraption draped with a threadbare cotton coverlet of some nondescript color. A lopsided, trilegged table flanked by two ladder-back chairs stood near the head of the bed.

A lone window, not much bigger than a porthole, let in the shadows of the night and added to the room's overall gloom. Jagger found his dismal surroundings suited his mood perfectly.

Another gulp of brandy set fire to his belly, but it wasn't nearly as hot as the fire still burning in his groin.

He should never have kissed her. It was the biggest mistake of his life. He could still taste the sweetness of her breath, feel the smoothness of her skin, smell the sweet scent of roses in her wet hair.

He wanted her. He couldn't pretend that he didn't. He wanted her in his bed. The severity of his desire disturbed him. But what rankled him the most was the knowledge that he was not the first. Someone had already sampled the pleasures of her flesh. To his utmost surprise, Jagger realized he wanted to kill this unknown man for touching her.

Why should he care if she had been with another man?

He slammed the bottle on the wooden table. Because she was going to be *his* wife, dammit. Whether he liked it or not.

And he did not like it. Not at all.

A loud rap sounded on the door.

Jagger smiled. Just what he needed to occupy his mind.

"Enter," he called as he strode to the bed. He grabbed the hem of his shirt and lifted it over his head. He had not bothered to change after his dip in the pond and the fabric had dried stiffly, scratching his skin.

He dropped his shirt on the floor and turned to greet the winsome serving wench with whom he'd arranged a tryst. To his supreme disgust, Stephen Treneham stood in the doorway.

Jagger chuckled darkly. "Why am I not surprised?"

"You will listen to what I have to say," Stephen said, slamming the door.

"I think not."

Jagger retrieved the brandy from the table and took a long slug. It burned in his belly, spread heat through his veins, but it wasn't nearly as hot as his temper.

He wiped the back of his hand across his mouth. "I

am expecting a guest. You know what they say: 'Two is company, but three is more.'"

"They also say: 'No fool to the young fool.'"

Jagger sat on the edge of the bed. "Uh, uh, uh. That's an old fool. As I have just turned twenty-seven, I do not believe I qualify as old." He pulled off his boots, then dropped them on the floor. "But, then again, since you have played me for a fool, I guess you win this war of words, after all."

He stood and worked the buttons of his breeches. "Now, unless you have a strong desire to see me in the altogether, I suggest you leave."

Stephen stood his ground.

Without a fireplace, the room was damp, the evening air cold. Jagger decided to leave his breeches on until his bed partner arrived and they could generate some body heat.

Stephen planted his fists on his hips. "I am not going anywhere until you listen to what I have to say."

"Why should I?"

"I beg your pardon?"

"Why should I listen to you when I cannot believe a word that comes out of your mouth?"

"I have never lied to you!"

"Nor have you told me the truth. You've led me a merry dance of half-truths and omissions, all designed to further your grand scheme. Whatever that might be."

Stephen glared at him. "What would you like to know?"

"Who is the father?"

The bluntness of the question seemed to throw Stephen off balance. He ran his hands over the back of his neck, sighed as if a heavy burden had just settled on his chest.

Jagger tensed as he waited, uncertain what he wanted to hear, or why it was so important to him. He couldn't quell the vision of Sophie in bed with another man, her legs wrapped around his hips, her lips parted in a sigh of ecstasy. It was enough to drive Jagger mad, to ignite the bloodlust in his veins, to provoke him to murder—and he didn't know why.

Finally, Stephen said, "I do not know."

Jagger raised his brows.

"She never told me."

"You did not ask?"

"Of course I asked. She refused to answer. I questioned anyone and everyone who might have a notion. No one knew anything. My father threw her out, told her never to return."

"So she came crying to you?"

"You've met her. What do you think?"

The very idea brought a reluctant smile to Jagger's lips. She was strong-willed, defiant, and, most of all, proud. He doubted very much that she cried about anything.

"She is as stubborn as a mule. A character flaw you might have mentioned before you blackmailed me into my current predicament."

"Your predicament? What have you to complain about? You have gained a valuable estate—"

"Which I did not need."

"—and a beautiful woman to wed."

"With a bastard child."

"The child is not to blame!"

"Of course she is not." Jagger sighed, his anger dissipating into the night like the fumes of the brandy.

Despite the church's teaching that all children were born with Original Sin, Jagger truly believed every child entered the world innocent of all evil. How could he think otherwise?

He had seen true evil in his life.

He did not know why the existence of this child disturbed him so much. Perhaps because she was the visible proof of his future wife's easy virtue? Should that matter?

It wasn't as if he were a virgin himself. But he had confined his carnal needs to women who knew what they were about. He had never planned to marry one.

Stephen pursed his lips. "She was heavy with child by the time I found her working in a tavern in a small village near the Scottish border. She was determined to make her own way. Nothing I said made any difference until I managed to convince her that her babe's health was at stake. I brought her to Norwood Park. What else could I do? It was the only property I owned outright, purchased with money left me by my mother."

"How very noble of you," Jagger drawled. He hated himself for his base reaction. He truly admired Stephen for standing by his sister in her time of need. But the conflicting emotions within him made it hard for him to think logically.

"Hardly," Stephen said. "It was the least I could do. I blame myself—oh, do not look at me like that! I am not the father. She is my sister!"

"Not by blood. Even so, you would not be the first."

"Shut your mouth before I punch you."

"I'd like to see you try," Jagger drawled.

Perhaps the earl should punch him. Jagger had no doubt he deserved it. His words were cruel and unjustified.

Stephen's voice shook with indignation. "She came into the family when she was eight years old. Only four years older than Cecelie is now. I watched her grow up. Do you honestly think so little of me that I would take advantage of a child?"

Jagger shrugged. "I thought you a man of honor. Yet your recent manipulations make me wonder."

If looks could kill, Jagger surely would be dead by now. He did not understand why he was being so deliberately cruel. He was acting like a spoiled child, and he knew it, but he was so angry by this deception, he couldn't seem to help himself.

"My family wronged her terribly," Stephen said. "Edmund, my half brother from my father's second marriage, treated her unkindly. Ha, that is an understatement. He was downright cruel. My father ignored her completely. He tolerated her presence merely to get her mother into his bed. And her mother, well, that is another story. As for me, I am ashamed to say, I was too busy searching for you to pay her much heed."

Jagger laughed. "Oh, that is rich. It is my fault?"

"I never said that!"

"No. But the implication was perfectly clear."

"It is not what I meant, and you know it. It is simply that I should have paid more attention to her well-being. I knew what my family was like. No child could thrive in that situation. But I was too wrapped up in my own needs to notice her loneliness. Her naiveté. But at Norwood Park, she is safe." Stephen stopped abruptly. His face flushed, as if he were embarrassed at having shown so much of his own humanity.

Jagger had to admit, if somewhat grudgingly, that Stephen had acted in the only honorable way he could in shielding his sister from society's scorn.

Stephen cleared his throat. "I love her as if she were my sister in truth. She is sweet and kind, a true lady in every sense of the word. When you get to know her, you will see the truth."

Jagger was disgusted to realize that he was hurt. That his pride was damaged. He had expected a woman of virtue. Instead, he would be shackled for life to a whore.

He thought of her kiss, of the way she had run her fingers through his hair and molded her body to his. He should have known from her response. No maidenly protests. No cry of alarm. No fear in her eyes.

Yet, there was one bright side to this dark cloud. His

father would suffer an apoplectic fit when he heard the news, and Jagger couldn't wait to carry the tale.

Questions rolled through his mind. Who had seduced this proud beauty? Why had she refused to name the scoundrel? She must have known her brother would avenge her honor. Why would she choose to suffer the scandal?

Jagger could not understand. Nor could he banish the image of the child from his mind. Even at the tender age of four, she was already beautiful. A miniature version of her mother with a wealth of mahogany hair that curled around her oval face. Deep brown eyes, so wide and so somber, as if she had already seen too much of the world. Her little rosebud lips, pursed in a frown, were pure innocence brought to life.

As she stared at Jagger through those too-somber eyes, she had clung to her mother's neck as if her very life had depended upon it. Sophie had clung to the child just as fiercely, leaving Jagger no doubt she would do anything to protect her daughter, or she would die trying.

He had to respect her for that. How different his own life might have been if his mother had shown half as much courage as Sophie Treneham. A small voice in his brain squealed in protest at his thoughts, but it was true just the same.

His mother had stood silently by while the monster she'd married abused her son.

Not that she'd had much choice, he told himself. Given the laws of the land, a man had a right to "discipline" his family as he saw fit, though Jagger couldn't help but wonder if the law had ever imagined a man would use such a heavy hand.

If he married Sophie, he would be a father. The thought sent a shiver of terror coursing through his body. He did not want children, had never wanted children. He had spent years mastering control of his emotions, but what if he turned out to be the same type of monster as his own father?

The possibility terrified him.

A knock on the door interrupted his thoughts.

"You might want to leave," he said to Stephen as he crossed the room and opened the door to reveal a buxom redheaded wench. "Unless you care to watch?"

Stephen cast him a dark look. Without saying a word, he reached into the inside pocket of his frock coat, pulled out a sheaf of papers bound with a string, tossed them on the low wooden table, then turned and strode from the room.

Jagger slammed the door. He ignored the bundle of papers.

The serving wench sashayed toward him. She slipped her arms around his chest, pressed hot little kisses against his neck.

He waited for a physical response. He'd been months without a woman. He needed to release the tension building within him, but he felt nothing.

She giggled and ran her fingernails down his belly.

"Come ter bed," she whispered in a throaty voice that left no doubt as to the state of her desire.

Her hair smelled of smoke and booze and stale perfume.

Jagger wrinkled his nose. A few hours ago he had kissed a woman who smelled of beeswax and honey and roses and dew.

"In a moment," he said. "Why don't you slip out of that dress, slide between the covers, and warm up the sheets for me, hmm?"

She made a sound of protest.

He reached up and gently tugged her arms from about his neck. "I will join you in a moment."

She sighed, nodded peevishly, then drifted over to the bed.

Oblivious to the passage of time, Jagger stood by the

window and peered into the darkness. Thoughts of Sophie Treneham filled his mind.

He should never have kissed her.

In that moment, a connection had been forged between them. Her desperate response bore witness to a soul-deep loneliness that had sparked an awareness of his own loneliness, an emotion he had managed to hide from the world, and even from himself, by burying himself in his work.

Now it was throbbing in his chest and he hated her for it.

He did not know what to think. Underlying her passionate response was an unskilled innocence, an uncertainty of where and how to move her lips or what pleasure the tongue could bring to a kiss. An innocence that belied the fact that she had borne a child outside the bonds of wedlock.

Dammit! What was wrong with him? Brooding over a kiss like a love-starved puppy. He had wasted far too much time on this insanity. He would not break his word, but neither would he force an unwilling woman to marry him. She was right. It would be the longest engagement in history. He would hire servants to protect her and give her money to support the estate, thereby fulfilling his obligations. Then he would carry on with his life as he had originally planned. But first, it was time to confront his father and spring his well-laid trap of revenge.

With careful precision, Jagger pulled on his shirt and boots. The serving wench had long since fallen asleep.

He tossed a guinea on the bed and grabbed the papers Stephen had left on the table. They were letters. In his father's hand. How had Stephen come by these?

Jagger laughed aloud as he dropped onto one of the chairs and settled down to read. It was almost enough to make him forgive Stephen for his stunning betrayal.

Almost, but not quite.

* * *

Sophie slapped the mop against the kitchen's stone floor, the sound a vicious reminder of the blow she should have delivered to Jagger Remington's cheek when he'd kissed her.

Instead, she'd behaved no better than a waterfront doxy. She'd allowed him liberties she'd vowed no man would ever take from her again. She could still feel the soft, sensual caress of his lips, the burning in her belly—and even farther below.

The desire darkening his eyes to the violet hue of dusk in summer had entranced her. Locked in his embrace, she'd lost all sense of reason, of propriety, of self-control, and self-preservation. Loathing, for herself as well as for that man, shuddered through her, as if a violent wind had suddenly swept through the room. He was a sorcerer and she was a fool.

She scrubbed at a stain on the floor, wishing she could as easily scrub away the longings he'd reawakened within her, the loneliness she'd thought long subdued, the desire for someone to love who loved *her* in return.

The scent of freshly baked bread usually soothed her. Tonight, it only added to the turmoil of her current situation.

How much longer would this kitchen be hers? How long before she would be forced to seek shelter elsewhere? Where would she go? How would she support her child?

"I thought I would find you here," Thea said, entering the room. Though it was nearly midnight, she wore a sprigged muslin frock, as if she were making a social call. "Might I join you?"

Sophie closed her eyes. She fought the urge to scream. Was she never to have a moment's peace?

She shoved the mop into the bucket, eyed the bins of vegetables on the table. Somehow she managed to drag a smile to her lips. "It is very late. Should you not be abed?"

She would peel them now, she decided, then soak them in water overnight, thus giving Cook a head start on to-morrow's pottage. She grabbed a paring knife and a potato, the dirt on the skin gritty against her fingertips.

Thea shrugged. "I could not sleep."

"Would you like me to fix you a cup of tea?" Sophie said, though it was the last thing she wanted to do.

"No. I thank you, though." Thea wandered around the table until she stood facing Sophie. She wore her usual disapproving frown. "You have flour in your hair."

"I have been baking, Thea. The arrival of that man's baggage wagons has brought seven more mouths to feed: two coachmen, four grooms, and a valet. And that does not include Stephen's entourage."

Sophie heartily resented the drain on the food supplies, not to mention she'd had to open more rooms in the ser-vants' quarters, as well as a room for that man, adding to the burden of her work.

"Could not Cook—"

"It is the dead of night," Sophie said, somehow man-aging to keep her irritability out of her voice. "Do you truly intend to give me a lecture on deportment now?"

Thea pursed her lips. "Of course not. I merely thought that you might like some company. Since I did not see you after . . ."

Sophie smiled sadly. Ever prim and proper, Thea could not seem to find polite words to describe the events of this day. For once, they were in harmony.

Thea laced her fingers together. "I thought, perhaps, you might wish to discuss . . ."

Again she trailed off, drawing a soft chuckle from Sophie.

"Why not state it for what it is," she said, scraping the peel from the potato, as she should have flayed the skin from that man's hide for daring to touch her. "My devas-tating betrayal at the hands of my brother."

Thea's eyes went wide, but she said nothing.

What was there to say?

Sophie's eyes burned, but she knew she would not sleep. Try as she might, she could not stop thinking about the precarious turn her life had taken this day.

She slammed her knife into the potato, chopping it into quarters. She shoved the pieces aside with the flat end of the knife, then reached for another.

Was she truly such a horrible person that God should punish her this way? Was Colin's death not enough? Should Cecelie have to pay for her mother's sins for the rest of her life?

Why would Stephen betray her so cruelly?

And that man? That blasted, no-good, too-handsome man. Why was he here? What did he want?

Despite his claims to the contrary, it had to be greed. Sophie could think of no other explanation. The estate was once profitable, and would be again. If it weren't for the treacherous Mr. Danvers, it would be supporting itself now. Once out of debt, Sophie knew she could have managed the estate quite nicely by herself. Now it looked as if she would never have the chance.

Tension tightened the muscles at the back of her neck. A spasm of pain shot down her arms. Stephen had lied to her. He had said this would always be her home. He had offered her security, then rushed across the ocean to God knows where and bought her a husband. He'd brought this man to her house, given him her home, and exposed Cecelie to ridicule and scorn.

Sophie would never forgive him.

"What are you going to do?" Thea asked, pulling Sophie from her thoughts.

"I do not know." She truly did not have a clue as to how to proceed. One thing she knew for certain, though: She would never marry that man.

He had said that Stephen threatened a breach-of-promise suit if either of them refused to wed. She planned to confront her stepbrother about this further betrayal as soon as she found him. No doubt he had slinked off to hide like the coward he had proven himself to be.

The death of dreams was hard, Sophie realized, as her breath tangled on a sob in her throat. She had always admired Stephen as the kindest and most honorable of men.

Now she hated him!

Thea gathered the chunks of potato from the table. She picked them up, one at a time, between her thumb and forefinger as if they were slimy worms. Then she dropped them into the bucket of water.

Sophie watched in shocked silence. Never before had she seen Thea lift a finger to perform a chore.

"Why not marry him," Thea said, brushing her hands together to remove any potato residue, "as Lord Hallowell has proposed?"

Sophie's eyes went wide. "Surely you are not serious?"

"He must be a man of integrity, or your brother would never have put forth the suggestion."

Sophie slowly shook her head. A few short hours ago she might have agreed with Thea, but not now.

"Would it be so terrible? You would still be mistress of this estate, but you would have the protection of his name."

"As if that means anything to me. You know the law as well as I. A wife's property belongs to her husband. As well as her person. I would cease to exist. He could do with me—and my daughter—as he pleased." Even beat us, she thought as a violent shudder shook her hands. She could not place Cecelie in that kind of danger. She could not marry that man.

She could not marry any man.

"He does not seem the type who would be deliberately cruel," Thea said.

Sophie laughed. It was one of the most outrageous comments she had ever heard Thea make.

"And how long have you known him? Think, Thea. Do

you honestly believe he will treat Cecelie kindly? The natural child of another man?"

She would not gamble with her daughter's life. She had to protect Cecelie, no matter the cost to herself.

"There are precious few options for women in this society," Thea said, and Sophie thought she detected a hint of bitterness in her voice. "If not a wife, then a governess, or a companion, like me, but who would hire you given your situation? The alternatives do not bear mentioning."

Those alternatives included being a rich man's mistress. Perhaps she should entertain Sir John's offer, after all, Sophie thought wildly. No. She would rather die first, which led back to the problem that had become so abundantly clear as she had floundered in the pond. *Who* would take care of Cecelie if anything happened to her?

She had always thought she could depend on Stephen. She had never dreamed he was capable of such astounding deceit.

How he must have hated her all these years!

Well, she had no intention of meekly marching to the altar. If Stephen brought a lawsuit against her, then so be it. She was under no obligation to stay here.

But where would she go?

She had no money. Nothing to sell or trade. How would she feed, clothe, and shelter her daughter?

"I am tempted to emulate Mr. Danvers, grab a painting or two, and make my escape," Sophie said, only half in jest.

"You must not speak so," Thea scolded, though Sophie heard the unasked question lurking beneath the words. *What would happen to me if you did?*

For the first time, Sophie understood how Thea must feel, forced to live off the charity of a relative, no matter the circumstances, even if it meant living in exile as companion to a woman with a scandalous past.

Sophie sighed as she shoved the potato peelings into

the slops pan. She was well and truly trapped, and Cecelie was trapped along with her. As were Thea and Betsy and Timmons and Cook. These people depended on her. She had let them all down.

She closed her eyes. Immediately, her mind summoned an image of that man.

"Jagger Remington," she said, startled as his name rolled from her lips. She had to admit she liked the sound of it, even if she didn't like him.

"He *is* exceedingly handsome," Thea said.

Sophie had to agree, though she would never admit it aloud.

"He looks like a pirate, with all that black hair and suntanned skin," Sophie said. "All he is missing is a bauble in his ear to complete the picture."

"And a parrot on his shoulder," Thea countered.

Sophie smiled. "And a wooden peg for a leg."

"And a black patch across his eye."

"To complement the jagged scar on his cheek." Which only added to his appeal, Sophie thought with no small measure of self-disgust. It looked to be an old wound, the skin bleached white by the sun, despite the tan on his face. It must have hurt at the time.

How had he gotten it? Why should she care?

She didn't, she told herself. She was curious. That was all. She dismissed the niggling fear that her curiosity might be concern in disguise. She did not care if he lived or died.

Well, that was not precisely true. She would never wish death on anyone. Not even Jagger Remington.

She simply wanted him out of her life.

What was she going to do?

She rubbed her fingertips over her forehead as if it might help her think clearly. Try as she might, she could not conceive of a single plan. It was as if her brain had turned to mush. Or was stunned into insensibility, as when he had kissed her at the pond. She wished she could confide in Thea. She wanted to tell someone, anyone, about his kiss and how it had made her feel. The power of the moment was so unexpectedly tender, so outrageously frightening. She had wanted his kiss to last forever when she should have scratched out his eyes.

He was the devil in disguise, as dangerous to her immortal soul as sin, and just as seductive.

A faint sound coming from the darkness beyond the kitchen door startled Sophie out of her reverie. Her heart slammed against her chest. "Did you hear that?"

"I didn't hear anything," Thea said.

"There it is again. That thumping sound, like a tree branch hitting the door." It was followed by what sounded like a deep moan, perhaps of a person or an animal in pain.

Thea opened her mouth, as if she were about to scream.

"Do not say a word," Sophie whispered.

She grabbed a cleaver off the chopping block. Drawing a deep breath for courage, she grabbed the knob and pulled the door wide. A man lay facedown on the ground. She stooped to her knees. A dark liquid stained the flagstones beneath his shoulders. She touched the puddle. It was warm and sticky, and smelled like . . . blood?

The knife slipped from her hand, clattered to the floor. She rolled the man over. "Oh, God. No!"

Chapter Eight

"Stephen," she cried. She cradled his cheeks in her hands as she screamed over her shoulder, "Thea, fetch help. Fetch the servants. Hurry. Please hurry."

She heard the panic in her voice. She swallowed hard to catch her breath. If she were to be of any use to her brother, she could not let her emotions overwhelm her.

Her hands shook as she smoothed the hair from his brow. His face was covered in mud. His eyes were black and swollen shut. Blood knotted his hair, poured from a gash across his temple. His lips were cut.

She ripped off her apron, wiped the blood from his eyes.

"Stephen, can you hear me?"

"I followed the light," he moaned. "Followed it home."

Sophie thanked the Good Lord that she had been working in the kitchen, otherwise the house would have been dark and he might have been lost.

His clothes were ripped and torn and stained with blood. He must have other injuries that she could not see. Terrified of what she would find, she pushed open his frock coat. His waistcoat and the shirt beneath it were slit from shoulder to waist. Blood oozed from a deep gash across his chest.

Sophie gagged on the bile rising in her throat. She shoved her apron against the wound to staunch the flow.

"Help me," she screamed.

All the angry, spiteful words she had flung at his head rose in her mind. Guilt gnawed at her stomach.

"Stephen, I'm sorry. I am so sorry."

Where were the servants? What was taking so long?

An eternity seemed to pass before Thea was back, followed by Jagger Remington's men. Earlier, Sophie had begrudged their presence as more mouths to feed, a deeper strain upon her resources. Now she saw them as a godsend.

Thea touched her shoulder. "Let the men help him now."

Sophie scrambled to her feet. The men hoisted her brother into their arms. Cook bustled into the room, her gray hair all disheveled around her face. She led the men to the stairs, all the while issuing commands.

"We need water," Sophie said, as she fought back the blackness threatening to engulf her, trying to drag her back to an earlier night when she had felt as helpless as she did now.

She needed to keep busy. She could not let the darkness take control of her now. "We need linens for bandages. And the herbals and medicines."

"I sent Timmons to fetch the doctor," Thea said.

For once, Sophie was grateful for her company.

Scarborough House was the same as Jagger remembered it. Built in the Jacobean style, the brick mansion had pitched roofs, elegantly flowing curved gables, and a graceful aspect that belied the evil lurking within.

It was still dark when Jagger arrived. Dawn was just starting to brighten the edges of the sky. No lights burned in the windows. The servants had yet to start their daily chores.

Jagger momentarily contemplated marching up to the front door, but he wanted the element of surprise. Leaving his horse tied to a tree, he crept through the gardens to an entrance cut into the side of the house, hidden from view by the shrubbery.

He remembered the day he'd discovered the secret passages threading through the walls of this house. How young and naïve he'd been. How his discovery had thrilled him as he'd contemplated the exciting games he could invent. Cutthroat pirates. Marauding Vikings. Murderous barbarians.

Until his mother had learned of his secret hideaway.

It was the only time Jagger remembered her ever raising her voice to him. Her face was as red as the flame of the candle he'd held in his hand as she'd scolded him. It was not until years later that Jagger understood her reaction.

The original owner of the house had no doubt built these passages for far less nefarious purposes, Jagger supposed as he opened the door and stepped into the hall. A lantern burned on a table near the wall. His father had company. Perfect.

Anticipation thrummed through Jagger's veins. He was a mere youth of twelve when he had left; now he was a man grown on a man's mission of revenge.

Lanterns placed strategically along the passage led the way to his father's apartments. Not that Jagger needed a map. He had every curve memorized. It was burned into his brain.

At the top of the stairs, Jagger opened the door. It swung silently inward on well-oiled hinges. He marched to the bed, kicked his heel against the mattress.

"What the hell?" His father's voice, groggy from sleep but filled with alarm. "Who's there?"

Heavy velvet curtains over the windows blocked any hint of morning light. They were red, Jagger recalled, as were the hangings on the bed and the fabric on the furnishings.

A few burning embers in the hearth gave the only light in the room. The thick Chinese carpet on the floor muffled his footsteps as Jagger crossed the room.

"Who's there?" his father yelled. "How did you get in?"

Ignoring his father's questions, Jagger wove his way through the furniture. When he reached the windows, he grabbed the draperies, then thrust them wide. Pale gray light from the breaking dawn poured into the room. "Never say you do not recognize me?"

His father shielded his eyes. "I can't see you. Move away from the window."

Jagger shoved his hands into his pockets and slowly, casually, strolled to the middle of the room.

His father glared at him.

Jagger knew the minute realization dawned in his eyes.

"You," his father growled. "I thought you were dead."

Jagger smiled. "Is that any way to greet me after all these years?"

"What do you want?"

"Why, to visit with my loving father, of course. What else would I want?" He nodded at the other person burrowed under the covers. "Still up to your old tricks, are you?"

Jagger barely resisted the urge to throttle his father. He forced himself to plant his feet and square his shoulders. His outward appearance of strength and self-confidence masked the hollow pit in his stomach that Jagger greatly feared might be lack of courage.

Nonsense. He was more than eager for this moment. He had dreamed of it for years.

His anxiety stemmed from anticipation. Not fear. Or so he told himself as he resisted the urge to shift on his feet. He would not show any hint of his conflicting emotions. He would not let this man provoke him into petty squabbles. He would not surrender his pride to this monster.

He grabbed the edge of the coverlet and yanked it off the bed. His father's companion was a youth who looked to be no more than fourteen, with light brown hair and belligerent green eyes. He was tall for his age, but his lanky body had yet to fill out. He was all arms and legs and skinny chest.

Despite the obvious tension in the boy's shoulders, he thrust his chin in the air. "M'name's Peter. And for another guinea, I'd do you both."

"Get out of here, Peter," Jagger's father roared.

Jagger clenched his fists against the urge to pummel his father as he deserved. He pulled a dozen or more coins from his pocket and shoved them into the boy's hand.

"Take care that no one sees you," he said quietly, as the youth grabbed his clothing from the floor before sprinting from the room through the hidden door.

Jagger turned to his father. He forced an indifference into his voice that he did not feel. "Tsk, tsk, tsk. 'Tis a dangerous game you play, bringing your catamite into your home. What would your servants say if they knew? Better yet, what would the authorities say? Last I heard, buggery was a hanging offense. I believe it still is. And I can't think of a man who deserves it more."

"What are you doing here? What do you want?"

Jagger smiled. "I am alive. I thought you might want to know that. And I am taking a wife. You might even know her. Sophie Treneham. Lord Hallowell's sister-by-marriage."

"The one with the bastard—"

"One and the same. Only, now they will bear your name."

His father laughed as he rose from the bed and shrugged into his dressing robe.

It was not the reaction Jagger had expected. Knocked off balance, he pursed his lips as he studied his father's haggard face. The loose skin and the dark, sagging circles under his eyes made him look like a bloodhound. He was nearly bald. What was left of his hair was gray and framed his face like a horseshoe. His emaciated hands hung out of his sleeves, the bones prominently protruding from his liver-spotted skin. Time had not been kind to the proud Duke of Mannering.

Jagger smiled. Perhaps there was a God after all.

"You promised you'd never come back," the duke said.

Jagger shook his head. "No. I said I would stay away as long as you signed the papers and allowed my mother to live in peace away from you. Now she is dead. All bets are off."

"I kept my end of the bargain. I never went near her again. Nor did I deny her. She kept the benefit of my name, whilst providing none of the comforts of a wife. I could have divorced her. But I wouldn't shame her as she shamed me."

Jagger laughed. "Really? That's news to me. Considering you had no cause."

"Oh, I had cause, believe you me."

"No, *she* had all the legal rights in the world. But that's what you were afraid of, wasn't it?"

"What are you talking about?"

Jagger ignored the question. He strolled to the bedside table. He picked up the bottle of brandy. There were no empty glasses, so he tossed back a mouthful from the decanter. The liquid warmth soothed his tightened nerves.

Putting his hands on his hips, his father thrust his shoulders forward. "A man may discipline his wife as he sees fit!"

"By beating her to within an inch of her life?"

"She should have minded her own business."

Jagger tossed back another mouthful of brandy before setting the decanter on the table. "She was trying to protect her son. Your son, for all you cared about me. Why did you do it?"

Jagger couldn't believe the pitch of his voice, the high and petulant whine of a child trying to understand the incomprehensible notion that his father hated him. Fury ripped through him, fisting his hands, hardening the muscles in his arms and legs. He was no longer that child.

He cared nothing for this man.

The duke merely laughed.

Jagger crossed his arms over his chest. It sickened him to remember how much he had longed for some small sign that his father cared about him. He lost count of how many nights he had cried himself to sleep, sore and bruised from chin to shin. Still he had dreamed that his nightmare would end, that his father would love him. Even now, knowing the depths of the man's depravity, it shamed Jagger to realize that some small part of him still craved his father's acceptance and longed for his approval, despite the man's sins.

What did that say about him?

"I used to wonder why you did it," Jagger said.

"Did what?"

"Agreed to stay out of her life. At first, I thought it was because you hated me so much, you would do anything to get rid of me. Then, I thought perhaps you feared for your life, that you feared I would come back and finish the beating I started that night, as I threatened to do should you not agree to my terms. But now I know better."

"You don't know anything."

"You didn't want the truth to come out. Hanging does appear a particularly gruesome way to die."

"Tell the world. I don't care. All you have are rumors and speculation, which mean nothing, when all is said and done."

"Ah, but such rumors can ruin a man."

"You have no proof!"

"Do I not?" Jagger let his words hang in the air.

The duke shifted on his feet. Sweat pooled on his brow. His cheeks puffed out, as if he were about to explode.

Jagger moved in for the kill. "I have come into possession of a certain number of letters. Love letters, if you can imagine that. Written by a man and addressed to, well, to you."

"That proves nothing."

"They were quite explicit. Amazingly so."

The duke's expression turned ugly. "That is not proof. I can't help it if the man was in love with me."

"The man? He was just a boy, you sick son of a bitch, and you seduced him into believing he was in love with you. And he lived with you, for Christ's sake," Jagger shouted. "In the same house as my mother. You shamed her in ways no woman should have to endure. Her own brother?"

The duke laughed. "Why do you think I married her? The stupid cow. She looked like a gypsy with that long black hair and those piercing blue eyes. Devil's eyes. Just like yours. 'Tis a pity he died so young."

"But she was smarter than you thought."

"Smart? The woman couldn't string two sentences together to save her life."

"Really? You might be interested to know that I have recently acquired a number of other letters. Fifteen of them, in fact. Also of a startlingly explicit nature. In your hand. Written to—well, I'm certain you know to whom. It seems you must be capable of love after all. What else would compel you to put such damning words into writing?"

The duke raised his clenched fist. "That stupid bitch! She said she would burn them if I left you alone. I should have killed her when I had the chance!"

Jagger froze. His gaze riveted on his father's fist. The vehemence of the old man's words barely penetrated his brain. All he could see was the massive ruby ring on his father's finger. It caught the morning sun pouring through the window and swept Jagger back to when he was just a boy.

Memories he had tried to hide. Memories he could no

longer deny. Lying in bed. Night after night. His body broken and bruised. His mother's arms around him, soothing his wounds.

"Why does he hate me so much," Jagger cried.

She wiped his tears away and whispered words of love. But she never intervened. She allowed it to happen. And Jagger had hated her, almost as much as he'd loved her. But something different happened that last night. Something changed. The details of which had been blocked from his memories for so long.

But now he remembered. He remembered everything.

His father had entered his room.

Huddled under his covers, Jagger tried to make his breathing slow and deep, as if he were asleep.

His father's heavy footsteps tramped across the floor. He leaned over the bed, clumsily touched his hand to Jagger's cheek. "I know you're not asleep."

His hot breath reeked of strong spirits and rotting teeth.

Jagger didn't move. He heard a sharp cry of alarm. Then his mother was there, grabbing his father's arm, trying to drag the much bigger man from the room.

The duke swung around and clubbed her hard across the face.

Jagger jumped from the bed. His nightshirt wrapped around his legs as he leaped onto his father's back.

It was the first time Jagger had ever fought back.

"Leave her alone," he cried.

The duke shrugged his massive shoulders, tossing Jagger through the air. He landed in a heap, his head bouncing on the floor. The room seemed to spin in rapid circles around his eyes. He could vaguely make out the image of his father kicking his mother in the ribs.

Jagger stumbled to his feet, charged across the room, rammed his shoulder into his father's stomach.

"Leave her alone," he cried in his high-pitched voice,

a remnant from childhood that had yet to change. He landed blow after blow into the monster's chest.

His father merely laughed, then sent that massive ruby ring crashing into Jagger's face.

The next thing Jagger remembered was waking up. Blood was gushing from his cheek, which was split open, exposing the bone.

He scanned the room. His father was gone.

He crawled to his mother. Despite the pain in his ribs, he swept her into his arms, staggered down the hidden stairs, and out of the house. He couldn't stand to look at her face. He stared at the ground as he tramped through the woods in his bare feet and nightshirt. The air was damp. Jagger was unsure if the moisture running down his cheeks was blood, tears, or rain.

By the time he reached Norwood Park, he was covered with sweat and gasping for breath. His mother was unconscious still, her breathing shallow and low, her pale cheeks swollen and purple. The night mist coiled her long black hair, which hung over his arm, nearly reaching the ground.

He clutched her against his chest as he stumbled up the stairs of the house he had visited occasionally as a boy— until he was ten and his father and godfather had started their own private war. Over what, Jagger had no clue.

Afraid to shift his arms for fear of causing his mother pain, he kicked the door. Several moments passed with no response. He kicked it again. And again.

The vibration shot up his bare toes and ricocheted through his knees. Lamplight appeared in the windows flanking the door, and still Jagger kicked and kicked the heavy wood until it finally opened to reveal the Earl of Hallowell's stunned face.

The rest of the night passed in a blur of anguished emotions. Stephen vowed he would protect Jagger's mother with his life, no matter the consequences, despite the law granting the duke total control over his wife.

Stephen promised he'd provide for her until such time as Jagger was able to shoulder the responsibilities himself. He swore he'd never allow the duke near her again. It was a debt of honor Jagger knew he would never be able to repay.

Sometime in the early morning, just as the sun began to lighten the sky, Jagger had returned to his father's house.

He'd found the bastard cowering in his room. In no uncertain terms, Jagger spelled out the price the man would pay should he ever tread near Jagger's mother again. He'd made his bargain with the devil. Then, after he was certain his mother was safe, Jagger sailed from England, stashed aboard a frigate bound for he knew not where.

He only knew that if he stayed in England, his father would wield his influence and prevent Jagger from earning the money he'd need to support his mother for the rest of her life. His only comfort came in knowing Lord Hallowell would keep her safe.

That was fifteen years ago.

Fifteen long years he had waited to make his father pay. And now, at his moment of triumph, he was too stunned to move.

He could hear his father's ranting voice, but he couldn't make out the words. All this time, he had thought he'd saved his mother's life. But in reality, she had saved him in a way Jagger had never imagined, even when he'd first heard rumors of the man's dirty secret.

As he realized the awful truth, his stomach lurched.

"You were going to rape me," he said in stunned disbelief. "You were going to rape your own son."

His father laughed bitterly. "That is the cruelest irony of all. Don't you understand? I never fucked her. You are not my son!"

Chapter Nine

The unexpected blow ripped through Jagger's chest like an arrow launched from a crossbow. Only years of controlling his emotions kept him on his feet.

He locked his knees in place, tightened his arms at his sides. His mind screamed in denial, yet, logically, it made perfect sense. It explained so much, answered so many questions—almost as many as it raised.

Jagger dragged in a ragged breath as he stared at the duke. He laughed, feeling freer than he had in years. "Cruel irony? I must disagree. In fact, I think it the best news I have ever heard. And imagine, while you are rotting in your grave, the bastard you were forced to claim will wear your coronet."

The duke sputtered. His eyes widened as if he were about to explode. "I'll be damned—"

"No doubt you will," Jagger agreed cheerfully.

The duke thrust his clenched fist in the air. "I'll be damned if you inherit anything from me. You will never wear the title. I'll disown you today. I'll discredit your name and reveal your mother for the whore she was."

Two steps brought Jagger nose to nose with the man he had thought was his father, the man whose love he had craved, the man he had come to hate with a passion that went beyond rage.

He grabbed the lapels of his dressing gown and hauled him off his feet.

"You are twenty-seven years too late to deny me," he growled through his teeth. "I earned that title at your fist, and I intend to wear it. Oh, what sweet revenge it will be."

Jagger tossed the man on the floor. Towering over him, he called upon all of his self-control to keep from murdering him where he lay. "I will never let you sully my mother's name. I will kill you first."

But Jagger wasn't finished with the man yet. He wanted him alive. He wanted him to suffer as much as his mother had suffered. "Though I am certain I would have no difficulty dredging up the requisite witnesses to testify to your buggery at trial, perhaps I'll simply publish these letters in the *Times* and leave you to face society. It might not be as gruesome as hanging, but it would prove far more entertaining."

His face drained of all color, the duke curled into a ball on the floor. A look of pure terror contorted his features.

Jagger stiffened the muscles in his legs against the overwhelming urge to kick the bastard in the ribs as the monster had kicked Jagger's mother all those years ago.

He had a more effective weapon to launch. "You may not realize this yet, but I own you, body and soul. And I am about to call in your debts."

Without another word, Jagger strode from the room and down the hall. The house was quiet, save for the soft patter of the housemaids' footsteps as they scurried from room to room with their buckets of ash and cleaning utensils.

No one paid Jagger any heed as he headed for the door. He had to get out of this house. He had to think over all that had happened this day. His stomach was queasy. The pounding in his head felt as if someone were hammering his brain.

As he strode out of the house, he nearly collided with a man making his way up the steps.

"Watch where you're going, you insolent scallywag!" the man shouted, waving his cane at Jagger's chest.

The day could not get much better than this.

Jagger sketched a bow. "I am pleased to see you, too, Uncle."

Anthony's eyes went so wide, they looked like pale blue moons surrounded by his bleached white face. "Good God, can it be? Can it really be you? We thought you were dead!"

Jagger touched his forefinger to his brow, then snapped it away in a parody of a salute. "So I've been told. Sorry to disappoint you, old chap, but it seems the title will not fall to you, after all. Now, if you will excuse me, I'm afraid I must run."

His uncle followed him down the steps, all the while shouting at him, "Wait. Wait, I said! Where have you been? Where are you going? How can I get in touch with you? I don't have your direction."

Jagger almost pitied the man.

He retrieved his horse and rode down the drive without a backward glance. The irony of his situation was not lost on Jagger. His father had never wanted him, and neither did his future wife. If the duke only knew, he would laugh all the way to his grave.

Jagger's barely leashed temper snapped when he reached the stables at Norwood Park and found no one there to tend his horse. Sophie Treneham might not have well-trained servants in her employ, but Jagger's men knew better than to abandon their duties. He paid them well. He treated them well. He expected their loyalty and hard work in return.

The fact that he was still reeling from his encounter with his father only served to increase his rage.

After seeing to his stallion's needs, he strode to the door. He knocked, but no one answered. He turned the knob. He heard the click as the door swung free. Once again, she had left the entryway unlocked and unattended. How unsurprising.

The stupid fool. Did she not care about her safety? Not to mention that of the child? She was asking for trouble, and by God, he was going to give it to her.

He stood in the hall, trying to decide where to search for her first. Before he could move, she appeared at the head of the stairs. She had changed into another dress that was as woefully out-of-fashion as the last one and an ugly, swamp-gray color to boot.

"Oh, it's you," she said, her voice surprisingly flat.

"You were expecting someone else?"

He hated the challenging tone of his voice. Was she awaiting her lover? The father of her child?

She grasped the railing. She seemed to sway on her feet.

Jagger rushed up the stairs.

For the first time, he noticed the state of her clothing, the disarray of her hair, and the stains on her bodice that appeared to be blood. "Good God, what has happened?"

She drew a deep breath, rolled her lips between her teeth.

"What is it? Tell me." He wanted to shake the answer from her. He may have only known her for a few hours, but he felt as if he had known her forever. She was strong and proud and courageous. Something truly dreadful must have happened for her composure to be shaken so badly.

"It's the earl," she finally said. "He was attacked. By footpads, we believe, but we do not know for certain as he has succumbed to unconsciousness. The doctor is with him now."

She turned and walked down the hall.

Feeling numb and overwhelmed, Jagger followed her to Stephen's rooms. He fought the urge to burst through the door. Instead, he stood in the hall and waited with her.

He wanted to take her in his arms, to offer her comfort, but he knew she would resist.

"I hoped you were the magistrate," she said, her voice sounding as if it were being dragged over broken glass. "I do not know what is taking him so long to get here."

Jagger squeezed the knuckles of his fists. He could feel the bloodlust rushing through his veins. He wanted to find whoever was responsible for this vicious attack. The devil himself would not be able to help the villain when he did.

The door opened and the doctor emerged. He looked at Jagger suspiciously.

Sophie pursed her lips. "How is he, Mr. Taylor?"

The doctor sighed, as if unsure what to say.

"Please, do not dissemble," she said, straightening her spine and lifting her chin. "I am no delicate flower in need of careful handling. I want the truth."

Jagger would have laughed, if he weren't in danger of ripping the man's throat apart.

"His Lordship is grievously wounded," Mr. Taylor said. "In addition to multiple contusions, he has several stab wounds. To the chest. The back. The thighs. Very deep and very dirty. He has lost copious amounts of blood, as evidenced by his clothing and his color. I have given him decoctions to try to ward off infection and fever, but I do not have much hope. Were I you, I would send for the vicar."

Sophie nodded slowly, her face turning as white as the plastered frescoes on the wall behind her. "I thank you for your honesty."

The doctor patted her hand. "I am sorry."

"You will stay?"

It was more a command than a question, a general lining up his troops for battle. Jagger admired her composure. She had obviously gained control of her emotions. He wished he could say the same. He felt like a little boy, lost and alone in the woods, who knew he had to be brave, but didn't think that he could.

"Of course," Mr. Taylor answered.

She tried to smile, but it was a miserable attempt. "I will show you to your room."

"I would like to see him," Jagger said. He would push his way in if she refused, but she merely nodded her head.

The room was overly hot, thanks to numerous lamps and candles and the roaring fire in the grate. The air reeked of blood and imminent death.

Jagger strode to the bed. He didn't know whether to sit or stand or what to do with his hands.

He leaned over the earl. "Lord Hallowell. Can you hear me? Who did this to you?"

The earl moaned. His eyelids fluttered open, then closed.

Jagger heard his earlier words taunting him. He had dismissed the earl's claim that someone was trying to kill him. He had thought it all part of the man's treacherous scheme.

How he wished he had listened. It was his fault Stephen now lay near death. Jagger should have protected him, just as he should have protected his mother all those years ago.

He grasped Stephen's hand. He was shocked to feel hot tears in his eyes. "I will not rest until I find the man who did this to you. This I vow. On my life and my honor."

Jagger released the earl's hand and spun on his heel, intent upon finding his men and starting the search for the villainous cur who had dared this vicious attack.

He was halfway to the door when it opened and Sophie

entered the room, followed by the doctor and another man Jagger assumed was the magistrate. It was about time.

The man appeared to be in his early thirties, with blond hair and blue eyes. His elegantly tied cravat, deep blue frock coat, charcoal waistcoat, and buff pantaloons were more suited for a night about Town than an attempted murder investigation. Jagger despised him at once, and that was before the man set his lascivious gaze upon Sophie.

All her attention was focused on her brother. She appeared not to notice how close the man stood to her or how he ogled her with rapacious intent.

She bent over the bed, spoke softly near Stephen's ear.

"My lord. Sir John is here. He needs to ask you a few questions."

The earl moaned, but didn't open his eyes.

Sophie pressed the back of her hand to her lips in an uncharacteristic gesture of weakness, or perhaps it was simply fatigue. Jagger strode to her side, slipped his hand around her elbow, and eased her to a chair by the wall. She made no protest, which increased Jagger's concern a hundredfold.

Sir John flicked an annoyed glance at Jagger, then dismissed him as if he were a beggar not worthy of his notice. He made a perfunctory examination of the earl's condition.

The room was silent, save for the light tap of rain on the windowpane and the earl's occasional moan.

When had it started to rain?

"Lord Hallowell," Sir John bellowed into the silence. "I must ask you a few questions."

Stephen did not stir. With every passing moment, he appeared to grow weaker, his breathing more labored. His hands moved restlessly over the blanket. Fever reddened his cheeks.

The medical man felt his pulse. "I fear he cannot hear you, sir. You will have to wait for your answers."

Jagger wanted to rail at the incompetent fools. "Might I suggest we move this discussion into the hall," he said through clenched teeth.

Sir John raised his brows in mocking query. "And who, sir, are you?"

As if drawing on her inner strength, Sophie pushed to her feet. "I beg your pardon. Sir John, might I present to you, my brother's friend, Mr. Jagger Remington?"

Sir John looked down his aristocratic nose at him.

Jagger was not about to play games with this man. He opened the door, strode into the hall, and waited impatiently for Sophie and Sir John to join him.

He turned on the magistrate. "Crucial moments are slipping away. In case you haven't noticed, it has begun to rain. If we have any hope of finding the miscreant who attacked the earl, we must begin the search immediately!"

"Do not presume to tell me how to perform my duties," Sir John snarled. As if he were a rabid dog marking out his boundaries, he circled around Jagger, then strode to Sophie's side. The predatory gleam in his eye was disgusting, given the circumstances that had drawn them together, the terrible purpose with which they were charged.

A sudden suspicion rose in Jagger's mind. Could this man be the father of her child?

The thought was repugnant in the extreme, given that the man was the justice of the peace and sworn to uphold the law. Seducing a young girl and abandoning her to scandal were vile acts made more despicable given his power and position.

Jagger did not doubt the man capable of such villainous deeds, but Sophie seemed to want no part of him. She stepped back, then moved to stand near Jagger. The revulsion he read in her eyes spoke to him as clearly as if she had said the words aloud. She despised this man, but she did not fear him.

"Mr. Remington is right. Where is the constable? Where are your men?"

Sir John could not seem to raise his gaze above her chest.

Jagger wanted to smash his fist in the man's face.

"Miss Treneham," the magistrate said, "I assure you, there is no need for you to worry yourself over this matter. I have everything in hand. It is obviously the work of footpads."

"If so," Jagger said, barely restraining the urge to throttle the man, "all the more reason to get the search under way—before they flee without a trace."

Jagger debated telling the man about Stephen's suspicions that someone was stalking him. One glance at Sophie's pale face told him to wait. There was no reason to worry her further.

"I will meet you outside in ten minutes," he said.

Sir John started to protest, but Jagger silenced him with a glare known to have made grown men quiver.

Grumbling under his breath, Sir John bowed stiffly, then strode down the stairs. A moment later the front door slammed. The sound echoed off the walls.

They were alone for the first time since their kiss by the pond. So much had changed in those few short hours. The feisty feline who had fought him toe to toe was now a pale ghost of herself. He took her hand in his. Her skin was cold.

"I promise you this," he said, holding her gaze with his. "I will find the man who attacked your brother. He will not escape my vengeance."

She nodded solemnly. "I know you will."

He wanted to drag her into his arms, to possess her lips in a kiss born of anguish and fear. He settled for briefly pressing her hand to his lips, before he turned and strode down the stairs and out the front door.

Before he closed it, he turned. "Make sure you lock this—and do not open it for anyone you do not know!"

* * *

Stephen moaned. "Bury me beneath the flames."

His words hurt Sophie more than a physical wound. She wished he would stop talking about dying, but she knew he could not help himself. His were the rantings of a fevered mind.

The table beside the bed held a tray of herbal concoctions and medicines and a basin of water.

Sophie dipped a cloth in the tepid liquid, then wiped his fevered brow. "Hush, my lord. You must rest."

"The vicar knows where to bury me." He coughed. Spasms racked his entire body, shaking the bed.

He opened his eyes. He stared at her, his face as white as the linens beneath his head. "No heraldic funeral," he said. "No mourning. No black. Promise me."

Sophie clutched her hand over her heart. "I promise," she said as she watched him close his eyes and drift off into what she hoped was a peaceful sleep. She placed her forefinger between her teeth to stifle her screams. She thought she might lose her mind. She could not go through this one more time.

He opened his eyes again, stared at her as if he couldn't see her. "Catherine, I can't find him."

His voice was filled with so much pain, it tore at Sophie's thin layer of self-control. A trembling started beneath her skin, rolling in waves down her arms and legs. "Please rest, my lord. Save your strength."

Her words seemed to clear the fog from his mind. He grasped her hand. His palm was hot and wet with sweat. "I must make my wishes clear, before I die."

"You will not die. I will not allow it," she said, as if she had the power to change the future.

He smiled at her then, but she could see the resignation in his eyes. "Send no invitations. They shunned you while I was alive; I will shun them in my death. Promise me—" Another fit of coughing shuddered through him. He wheezed. "I am in pain."

She dosed him with laudanum, then held his hand as he drifted off to sleep. She felt useless and helpless and on the verge of losing control. Memories she fought every waking moment threatened to overwhelm her.

She focused her thoughts on the trivial details of her life. Of what rooms needed cleaning. Of what supplies were running low. Of what meals to plan for the upcoming week.

She heard a soft knock on the door before it opened and Jagger Remington entered. Yesterday, she had thought him merely devastatingly handsome. Today, though he wore the ordinary clothes of a gentleman, he was the picture of pure masculine power, of raw, brutal strength, a rampaging god of war on a mission to find the criminal behind Stephen's vicious attack.

He carried a tray in his hands. He glanced toward the bed.

"He is sleeping," Sophie said.

Jagger nodded. His face held a haunted look. Dark circles shadowed his eyes. He pulled up a chair, placed the tray on the table. He held out a steaming bowl to her. "I brought you some soup."

She shook her head. "I am not hungry."

"You must eat. You must keep up your strength if you are to be any help to your brother."

His hair was wet.

"It is still raining?" She had not noticed.

"Yes."

He said it with such vehemence, she widened her eyes.

"The ground has turned to mud. It makes it impossible to track the—"

"I understand." She did not want to hear the details. She could not worry about anything else. She had to keep her mind focused on the here and now.

Then, as if she couldn't help herself, she asked, "You have called off the search?"

"No. My men are scouring the road between here and the village, but the rain has washed away any footprints or signs of struggle, which might have given us some clues."

He swirled the spoon through the soup, studying the contents of the bowl as if he could find the answers he was seeking within the steaming liquid. "They are questioning anyone who might have seen or heard anything. They will move into the woods, the footpaths. I will join them again in a few minutes. I wanted to check on the earl."

She closed her eyes, rubbed her fingertips across her forehead, as if she could wipe away the image of this man sitting mere inches away from her. She did not want to admire him. She did not want to like him.

"Earlier, he was raving," she said. "At times his words were coherent, then it became nonsense."

"It is the laudanum." Jagger scooped some soup into the spoon and held it to her lips as if she were a child incapable of feeding herself.

Too tired to argue, she opened her mouth. The broth was hot and spicy, warming her from the inside out. She had to admit that it felt nice for a change to have someone concerned about her welfare, which was so selfish. Her brother was fighting for his life and she was happy to have this man feed her soup?

She grabbed the bowl from his hands. She needed no help from this man. She needed no help from anyone.

They sat in silence. His brooding gaze seemed to bore a hole in her as she ate. What did he think when he looked at her? She resisted the urge to fidget on her seat. She did not like the way he made her feel, uncomfortable in her own skin.

He took another bowl from the tray, held the spoon to Stephen's lips. Instinctively, her brother opened his mouth, but half the liquid dribbled down his chin.

Jagger patiently wiped the spill, then repeated the process until the bowl was empty.

What a contradiction this man was. He was rugged and strong, arrogant and heavy-handed, more handsome than any man she had ever met, yet he spoon-fed her brother as if he were a babe, whispered soft, soothing words, wiped Stephen's brow, clasped his hand. His love for Stephen was painfully obvious.

There was so much Sophie wanted to ask him, so much she wanted to know. She bit her lip to stop the flow of questions. This was not the time or place.

She needed to focus on saving her brother's life.

"His skin is afire," Jagger said. "We must bring his fever down. Help me."

He drew back the covers to Stephen's hips. Stephen was naked save for the linens dressing his wounds. Sophie fought the urge to avert her eyes. This was no time for modesty.

The bandages were soaked in blood. He was not healing.

Earlier, she had shredded sheets into thin strips. She grabbed the bundle and held out one at a time as Jagger stripped off the old bindings and replaced them with the new.

He took the washcloth from the basin, twisted it over Stephen's skin. The water evaporated nearly as fast as it landed on his heated flesh.

"I will lift him so that you can cool his back," Jagger said, gently rolling Stephen onto his side.

The cloth felt like hot coals in her hand.

"The surgeon wanted to bleed him," she said. "I would not allow it. It seems ridiculous, when he has lost so much blood already, is losing blood still."

"The man is an idiot. There is not one among them worth their salt. You are right."

His approval eased the guilt she had experienced over her decision. After all, she was a mere woman. What did she know about medicine?

They eased the earl onto his back. Sophie tucked the coverlet up under his chin.

"My men are more than capable of searching without me for a few hours," Jagger said. "I could sit with your brother while you rest."

She looked at him then as if seeing him for the first time. A day's growth of beard darkened his chin. The sleeves of his frock coat were damp. His neck cloth and waistcoat were stained with mud. His hands were reddened and chapped by the wind and rain. Yet, he had never looked more appealing.

He smiled at her slowly, almost tenderly.

She quickly glanced away. She wanted to hate this man for barging into her life. For awakening hopes and dreams she had long since forgotten.

She found she could not dredge up the emotion.

"I am not tired," she said, though it was a lie. She was as weary as if she were a thousand years old. "But I would not mind the company, if you would care to stay."

Sophie knelt by Stephen's bed. She clasped his hand in hers. She was vaguely aware of people coming and going, the vicar, the doctor, Betsy, and Cook—but all she could focus on was her brother. He was dying. As much as her mind screamed in denial, she had to accept the truth. He was dying.

Three days had passed. There was no hope. He had bled too much. His fever was too high. His fluid-filled lungs could no longer sustain him. There was nothing more she could do except hold his hand and wait with him until he passed.

She felt hollow inside, numb with fatigue and grief. There was so much she wanted to say. So many angry words she longed to take back. Now she would never have the chance. He was too weak; he needed to save what little strength he still possessed to breathe, not to listen to her tortured confession.

The brace of candles on the bedside table accentuated the sharp angles of his face, the hollows beneath his eyes. He had lost so much weight, he looked like a skeleton wrapped in a flesh-colored shroud. His chest barely rose and fell as he dragged in short, wheezing breaths.

Sophie stifled her scream with her fist. A horse would never be allowed to suffer so. A single shot would put it out of its misery. Not so for a man, who was forced to suffer unbearable agony until God in His infinite wisdom saw fit to carry him home.

Merciful God, either spare my brother's life, or, please, take him home. Do not let him suffer so.

The sound of running feet on the steps caught her attention. She glanced at the door, her heart pounding in her throat as Jagger Remington came into view.

His long, black hair curled wildly about his face. A dark growth of beard covered his chin and cheeks, accentuating the puckered scar beneath his eye, making him appear more than ever the cutthroat pirate.

Sophie would have been afraid except he stood in the doorway looking for all the world like a little boy lost in a foreign land, not knowing the language or which way to turn.

Slowly, she rose and walked to his side. She couldn't bring herself to speak his name. "Any word?"

He shook his head. He hadn't slept in three days as he searched for the villains who had attacked her brother.

She walked back to the bed. She knew he followed because she could hear the soft thud of his boots on the rug.

They stood side by side.

He looked nearly as haggard as Stephen.

Sophie whispered in her brother's ear. "Stephen, Mr. Remington is here to see you."

His eyes fluttered open. They no longer appeared blue.

Now they were a dull, flat gray. "James?" he said in a voice so soft, she had to bend close to his lips to hear him.

Sophie stroked his brow. "No, my lord. It is Mr. Remington. Jagger Remington."

"Jagger. I forgot."

Jagger knelt and clutched Stephen's hand in his fist.

Stephen gasped. "You must . . . promise me. Wed . . . Sophie."

Jagger closed his eyes, as if in prayer. When he lifted his gaze to Stephen's, his blue eyes burned with fierce determination. "You have my word, my lord. If she will have me."

Stephen looked at her then. She could see the pleading, the desperation in his eyes.

Her breathing grew shallow as panic attacked her. Could she do this thing? Could she marry this man, this stranger, if for no other reason than to grant her brother's dying wish?

She touched one hand to her cheek. She would lose so much. Her freedom. Her right to make her own decisions about her life. Not to mention her property, which would legally transfer to this man the moment they wed.

Her heart beat frantically as she thought about her daughter. Could he accept Cecelie? Treat her with kindness? Perhaps even love? Could Sophie take that chance?

She knew nothing about him. Yet, in the days since Stephen's attack, she had witnessed the genuine love he had for her brother. His sorrow was evident in his shadowed eyes. His determination to find the miscreant who had done this terrible deed spoke of loyalty and courage and honor.

Jagger was staring at her, his clear blue eyes narrowed with grief and conviction.

"Might I have a word with you," she said quietly before her nerve deserted her.

He followed her to a secluded corner of the room. It was darker here, the candle by the bed too far removed to cast more than a dim glow. The shadows gave her comfort and the courage to lift her chin and face him without shame.

She drew a deep breath. "I know what you must think of me. What everyone thinks of me. But I will have your word of honor as the gentleman Stephen believes you to be. You will not harm my daughter—or me—in any way. Not verbally. Not . . . physically." There, she had said it, even though her heart felt as if it were stuck in her throat.

He would never know how hard it was for her to voice her deepest fears, but from the look on his face, he was none too pleased. She watched his jaw grow rock-hard and unforgiving, yet he did not speak.

They stared at one another for an interminable moment.

The only sound in the room was Stephen's breath rattling in and out of his chest.

Sophie refused to back down, though her knees felt weak, as if they were on the verge of collapse.

"Swear it," she said.

His eyes narrowed. A muscle twitched in his jaw. "I assure you, from this day forward, should you choose to become my wife, your daughter will be my daughter and I will protect her with my life. This I swear on my honor and your brother's dying breath."

She could have loved him. She realized it then. Despite his arrogance, she could have loved this man had they met before such foolish hopes and dreams were ripped from her soul like so many useless pieces of trash.

Still, she believed him. Despite the churning in her stomach and the words of warning racing through her mind, she agreed. "With one added condition," she said before they returned to Stephen's side.

Jagger cocked one dark brow in silent query.

She licked her lips. How could she word such an intimate remark without blaring the details of her life to the various people gathered in the room? How could she not?

"I do not want children."

He studied her carefully. "There are methods to prevent the conception of children."

She had not known that. Somehow she found the words disconcerting and sad. She could tell by his answer that he misunderstood her meaning.

She shook her head. "By the pond. You made me an offer," she said, referring to his suggestion that theirs could be a marriage in name only. "Do you remember?"

He nodded stiffly.

"On those conditions, I will wed you."

"Enough," Stephen gasped.

Sophie and Jagger turned to face him. A spasm of pain crossed his face, but he clenched his teeth and leaned forward.

"I know. I am dying," he said. "I would see you wed before——" He fell back against his pillow. An agonizing sound gurgled in his throat as he struggled to catch his breath, his small reserve of energy drained by his outburst.

Jagger turned to Sophie, his anger obvious in the slant of his eyes. "I agree on all points."

"Thank you," she said, surprised that her voice sounded so calm, so much like herself, when she felt like a stranger in her own body. "I suppose I should be thankful for one thing. At least you are not a member of the nobility."

Jagger narrowed his eyes. "I beg your pardon? Why would marriage to a peer of the realm be anathema to you? You are, after all, the sister of an earl."

Sophie merely shook her head. She had no intention of telling this man the intimate details of her life.

She called for Betsy to attend her. "Would you please fetch Cecelie?"

"But, miss," the nursemaid said, waddling toward her. Although short and plump, Betsy was pretty in an unobtrusive sort of way, with brown hair, green eyes, and a stubbornness of will matched only by her fierce loyalty to Sophie. "'Tis two o'clock in the morning, miss. You're certain you want me to wake her?"

"Yes," Sophie said, although she wasn't certain about anything anymore. She scanned the room. The only other person present at the moment was the doctor, and he was snoring in a winged chair near the grate.

"Please fetch the vicar, also. I believe he is in the study."

"Should I wake Miss Washburn, too?"

Sophie chewed her fingernail. Thea would be furious at her for disturbing her beauty sleep. "Yes, fetch her."

Jagger strode to Sophie's side.

She didn't look at him. She couldn't. But she was very aware of his presence, of his much bigger shadow on the floor next to hers. The scent of damp night air clung to his clothes.

His body seemed to emanate heat. Thank God, for Sophie was cold, deep inside, as if it were the middle of winter and she had ventured onto thin ice and fallen through to the frigid water below. She sidled closer to the man who would soon be her husband. She wanted his heat to warm her skin.

The events of the next hour took on a preternatural atmosphere, as if Sophie had stepped outside herself and was watching the proceedings through a haze thick as smoke. She saw Thea enter the room, hastily dressed and bitterly grumbling. Cecelie was the last to arrive. Her mahogany hair hung down her back in a single thick plait. Her white nightgown and robe made her brown eyes look huge and frightened. She ran into Sophie's outstretched arms.

Sophie buried her nose against her daughter's neck, inhaled the almond-sweet scent clinging to her baby-soft skin.

Oh, God, what was she doing?

After tonight, nothing would be the same.

No, she could not do this, after all. She could not place Cecelie in harm's way.

As the panic built to a scream in her throat, she caught Stephen's gaze. Though she knew it was impossible, he looked as if he had aged ten years and lost ten pounds in the last five minutes. He was looking at her, pleading with his eyes, silently begging her not to change her mind.

The fog around her lifted. Only she could give her brother the gift he most desired. By marrying this man, she could ease Stephen's worries about her future, and grant him the peace he deserved as he drifted into his eternal sleep.

She set Cecelie on her feet, but kept her daughter's hand in hers as she nodded at the vicar to begin.

"I trust you have the necessary papers," he said.

Another ten minutes were wasted as Betsy was dispatched to the study to retrieve the special license.

Sweat dampened the hair at the base of Sophie's neck. Now her greatest fear was that Stephen wouldn't live long enough to witness the ceremony. With each passing minute, he seemed to shrink. Each breath he drew increased his pain.

Then Betsy returned, and the next thing Sophie knew, she heard the vicar saying ominous words like "Those whom God hath joined together, let no man put asunder" followed by the chilling "I pronounce that they be man and wife together."

Chapter Ten

The room seemed to be swirling around her, leaving Sophie light-headed and dizzy. It was all she could do not to sway on her feet. Her new husband touched two fingers to her cheek, the rough pads of his fingertips searing hot against her too-cold skin. He eased her mouth to his for the ceremonial kiss.

It lasted less than a heartbeat, yet Sophie was breathing so quickly, she thought she might faint.

Betsy's soft weeping filled the room.

Thea stood strangely silent near the door.

Moving as if she were in a dream, Sophie placed her palms on Cecelie's shoulders and turned her to face Jagger.

She drew a deep breath. Her voice came out raspy and low. "Cecelie, I would like you to meet your new papa."

Jagger bent on one knee. The expression on his face was inscrutable. "Hello, Cecelie. I am honored to make your acquaintance."

Cecelie flipped her right hand over and stuck her little finger in her mouth. She raised her left hand and rubbed her thumb along her upper lip, all the while staring at Jagger through solemn brown eyes.

"Would you like to call me Papa?" he said.

Sophie could detect no hint of bitterness or anger in his voice. In fact, he sounded almost tender.

When Cecelie didn't reply, he glanced at Sophie. "She does not speak?"

Sophie wanted to snatch her daughter into her arms, but she forced her hands to stay by her sides. For better or worse, this man was her husband now, and Cecelie's father.

"She is shy," Sophie said swiftly. Too swiftly, it seemed, for his eyes narrowed as if he knew she were hiding some secret. "You are a stranger to her, after all," she added defensively.

Jagger nodded, then pushed to his feet. "Let's say good night to your uncle, shall we? Then it's off to bed you go."

Cecelie pulled her finger out of her mouth just long enough to slap a sloppy kiss on Stephen's cheek, then she left the room, hand in hand with Betsy. Seeing a chance to escape, Thea rushed after them. The doctor ushered the vicar from the room, leaving Sophie and Jagger alone with Stephen.

He smiled weakly. "Thank you."

Sophie couldn't speak past the knot in her throat. She nodded quickly and kissed his brow.

His eyes glazed over. "James," he cried.

Sophie looked at Jagger. She had no idea who James was or why Stephen kept calling for him.

Jagger clasped Stephen's hand to his chest.

In a sudden burst of strength, Stephen slid one hand behind Jagger's neck, then pulled him down until his lips touched Jagger's ear. He said something. Sophie didn't know what. All she could hear was the shaky rumbling of his voice.

She knew the exact moment Stephen died. The tension drained from his face. His hand, which only moments before had clung to Jagger's neck, fell to the bed. His eyes closed. A soft smile curved his lips.

A moment later he was gone.

Sophie told herself it was for the best, that Stephen no longer suffered, but cool reason did nothing to ease the aching emptiness in her chest, or the hollowed-out pit in the middle of her stomach, or the trembling of her legs.

She left the room. She knew she should remain and keep company with the body, but she couldn't. Her memories of Colin's death and her vigil by his side were too raw to allow her to stay. Besides, Stephen's valet would have to assist the undertaker to prepare and clothe the body. She would be of no use to them.

She walked around the house, stopped the clocks, drew the blinds, covered the mirrors, and slammed the door on yet another part of her mind. A room filled with grief and regret—and memories she would rather forget.

She thought of the day ahead of her. Somehow she would have to tell Cecelie that her uncle had died. She had no idea if Cecelie would understand or not. The burden of guilt Sophie bore weighed so heavily on her shoulders that many times she found it difficult even to be in the same room with her daughter, whom she loved more than life itself.

Sitting at Stephen's desk in the study, she pulled out paper and pen. Her hand trembled as she dipped the quill's tip in the inkpot and began to write. She heard the door click open. She knew who it was without looking—the man who was now her husband. Good Lord, what had she done?

She ignored the sound of his footfalls on the carpet. She kept her gaze fixed firmly on the paper before her.

When he reached her side, he crouched down on his heels.

"What are you doing?" he said gently.

Too gently. Her eyes started to sting.

She clenched the quill between her fingers.

She would not cry. She never cried. She blinked away the pain and continued her task.

"I am writing the death announcements," she said, amazed at the lack of emotion in her voice. She might just as well have said she was sending out invitations to a ball, rather than writing the final chapter of her brother's life.

She wrote until her fingers cramped, all her thoughts and energy focused on the words taking shape on the paper, and not on the man kneeling by her side.

She would have to open the dining room and the reception hall to accommodate any mourners who called to pay their last respects to Stephen. She would have to plan a funeral adhering to Stephen's last requests. She would have to keep busy in order not to lose her mind.

She sealed her letters, placed them on the desk before her. She grabbed a fresh piece of paper. She was acutely aware of the man kneeling beside her. She wished he would go away.

He ran his fingertips along her arm, the warmth of his skin a sudden shock to the chill in her bones.

He freed the quill from her grip, dropped it on the desk, then took her hand in his.

She wanted to turn to him, to bury her face against his chest. The urge to seek comfort in his arms was nearly overwhelming. Somehow she managed to remain in her chair.

She looked at his face, saw a reflection of her own pain etched in the harsh lines about his jaw, in the deep circles under his eyes, in the wild disarray of his black hair.

Unable, or unwilling, to meet his gaze, Sophie turned her head. She did not want to feel sympathy for this man.

Her husband!

Panic clawed her throat, quickened her breath.

How could she have entrusted her daughter's welfare to this man, to this complete stranger?

The dull haze of morning light creeping through the

draperies let her know she had survived another night. But how was she to survive the rest of her life?

He rubbed his thumb over the palm of her hand, shocking Sophie into the realization that she had never pulled away from him. She shot to her feet and stepped around the chair. She needed to put as much distance between them as she could.

Slowly, he stood. He wanted to pull her into his arms and soothe her heartache with his kiss, but he made no move to touch her. Instead, he thrust his hands in his pockets.

He did not know how to comfort her. He had no idea what he should say. Everything had happened so quickly. He had barely begun to process the fact that the man he'd always thought was his father was not. Now Stephen was dead.

She clasped her hands before her.

"I would ask you a favor," she said stiffly, letting Jagger know in no uncertain terms that it was the last thing she wanted to do. "I would ask that we keep our marriage a secret. At least until after the funeral."

His first instinct was instant denial. He could see no reason to hide the truth. Did she think he would disappear? Abandon her to society's wolves as had the father of her child?

"As you can well imagine," she said slowly, "I have been the center of a good deal of scandal."

She never lowered her eyes as she made that admission, and, once again, Jagger found himself admiring her courage.

"As such," she continued, "the swiftness of this marriage will cause much speculation and rumor. I would not have my—situation detract from the honor Stephen deserves."

He was an idiot. A pompous fool. She had just lost her brother and here he was thinking her guilty of any number of selfish motives. He could only blame his reaction on his own sense of shock, his own grief and the guilt he bore for his complicity in Stephen's death. Had he not been sulking in the village, Stephen would never have followed him, would never have met with the deadly assassin on that fateful night.

She kept her gaze fixed on him. Jagger found himself suddenly ashamed. No doubt she was cut off from all good society because of her indiscretion. She wanted only to honor her brother's memory, while Jagger wanted only to possess her. His thoughts disturbed him.

"It is impossible," he said gently. "While I do not think the vicar would talk out of school, the doctor has already left, no doubt eager to spread the news."

Sophie pursed her lips as she held his gaze. What thoughts were hiding behind her dark brown eyes? She was young, but she seemed soul weary, and sad, and alone. They had so much in common, though they were separated by miles.

She was the first to look away. "Of course. You are right," she said, staring at the wall. "This juicy tidbit should carry Mr. Taylor into every drawing room in the parish."

The candle on the desk flickered, casting her in an ethereal light. He could feel the beat of his heart, hear the sigh of her breath, smell the rosewater on her skin.

"There is something else," she said softly, but distinctly. "During the three days of his illness, my brother spoke of you often. Incoherent words, mostly, but the affection in his voice was unmistakable. I gather you were friends?"

Her voice faltered. It was the first time she had shown any emotion at Stephen's passing.

Jagger wanted to yank her into his arms. Instead, he waited patiently for her to continue.

She looked at him.

"That is true," he said. "I have known Stephen since I

was very young." He expected her to ask him questions he was not prepared to answer, but she did not.

She simply nodded. "Would you care to make the arrangements for his funeral? I believe it would have pleased him greatly."

His throat felt thick and dry. Words escaped him.

"He wished to be buried in the parish churchyard. He made me promise. He said the vicar would know the spot. It seems he has saved this particular patch of earth for Stephen for years . . ."

Her voice trailed off. Jagger strained to hear her next words. "Though I cannot imagine why. He should be buried at his family seat with all the pomp and ceremony due his station."

Jagger was moved beyond words. He took her hand in his. "It would be my honor."

She made no attempt to pull away. Her fingers felt small and fragile in his much-larger hand. As he stared into her eyes, an overwhelming truth hit him like a sledgehammer.

He was a husband now. A father to her child.

The muscles in his arms and legs clenched against a fear so great, it left him weak in the knees. What the hell did he know about being a father or a husband?

"Would you be so kind as to post my letters," she said, her voice trembling slightly. "Usually Betsy handles the mail, but as you will be visiting the vicar, I thought perhaps you could save her a trip to the village."

She swallowed, as if it were taking all of her self-control and conscious thought to form her words.

Jagger nodded, unconsciously rubbing his fingers over her skin. Her wrist was soft, but her palm was rough with calluses.

He stared at the evidence of her poverty and he cursed.

The momentary sense of closeness they had shared shattered.

She pulled her hand from his, thrust her shoulders

back, and lifted her chin. "There is no shame in hard work," she said stiffly, then marched from the room.

Damn it all to hell and back. What an insensitive fool he was.

He followed her. "Would you like to accompany me to the village?"

She stared at him from over her shoulder, her expression one of shocked surprise, as if he had asked her to chop off her head. He would have laughed if he didn't feel more like dragging her to bed. Why the hell had he ever agreed to a marriage in name only when it was the last thing he wanted?

He wanted to bed this woman—his wife—with whom he was going to spend the rest of his life.

"I thought you might care to help with the arrangements," he forged on manfully. "For the funeral."

She shook her head, then turned and marched up the stairs.

An hour later, Jagger strode out of the parsonage. His emotions were raw. Though six months had passed since he'd learned of his mother's death, Stephen's demise had ripped open the thin layer of skin covering that wound. Jagger felt the loss of the two people he'd loved most in the world as a physical ache, as if someone were carving a hole in his chest.

Now that he'd settled the details of the funeral, he turned his focus back to the investigation of Stephen's murder. He wanted to question the villagers again. He wanted answers to the how and why of Stephen's attack. He was unwilling and unable to believe that no one had witnessed the deed.

Slivers of sunlight poked through the shifting storm clouds hanging over the sky. Though the rain had finally stopped, the damage was done. Any evidence pointing to

the location of the attack that took Stephen's life had
melted into the mud.

Jagger sloshed through a puddle as he headed for the
inn. He questioned the innkeeper and all of his help. No
one had seen anything. Not even Mary, the redheaded,
big-busted wench with whom he'd intended to tryst less
than a week ago.

She followed him out of the inn. "Beggin' yer pardon,
sir, but, where yer new to the neighborhood, mayhap ye
didn't know. Sir John Shays, he be the magistrate, he already questioned everyone hereabouts."

And he had chalked it up to footpads, Jagger thought
in disgust. The man was an incompetent fool.

Jagger refused to believe it was the work of thieves,
not with the fact that Stephen had suspected someone
was trying to kill him, a fact the magistrate had dismissed out of hand as nonsense. Jagger had wanted to
strangle the man.

He grabbed the reins of his horse from the post boy.
"Thank you, Mary, but I prefer to conduct my own in-
quiry. If you should hear of anything that would help me,
please, contact me at once."

"Of course, sir." She glanced at the door to the inn. Her
voice dropped. "Will ye be comin' back, sir? Ye know, to
claim what ye paid for?"

When he'd ridden into the village a week ago, Jagger
had harbored every intention of slaking his urgent physical need with this eager and more than willing wench.
Now he found himself uninterested. Strangely enough,
the only woman he was interested in bedding was the
woman who was now his wife.

He wanted Sophie with an intensity he had never felt
for any other woman. No doubt it was because she
wanted nothing to do with him and that must intrigue
him, he thought with no small measure of self-disgust.

He shook his head, but offered no explanation.

She placed her hand on his arm. "I hear from me brother

yer lookin' fer help at the big house," she whispered. "Do ye think ye might hire me? I can cook. I can clean. I can do anything. Anything ye might need, sir."

She placed a slight emphasis on the word *need*.

Jagger had no difficulty understanding that this would be a disaster of the worst magnitude. His new wife might not want anything to do with him, but if he knew anything about women—and Jagger was certain he knew at least this much about women—she would not want him cavorting with any other woman, especially one of the serving maids in her own home.

"Y'see, sir," Mary continued. "I'm with child—"

"Good God, you're not going to try to pass it off as mine?"

She laughed. "Of course not. Since we ne'er did the deed, that'd be right impossible, wouldn't it? But Mr. Harrington, he's the innkeeper, sir. He's all moral and disapproving. I had to sneak up the back stairs to be with ye that night. I only did it a few times. To earn a few extra shillings, fer me ma. When Mr. Harrington finds out my condition, he'll sack me, sir. Me not being married and all. Then what'll I do?"

"Do you know who the father is?"

She set her chin stubbornly. "No, sir. And I have no intention of living 'pon the parish, neither."

He admired her courage, but it would be a tremendous mistake. "Perhaps you haven't yet heard," he said softly. "I have recently wed. With Miss Treneham."

Mary nodded. "I heard it from me brother, who heard it from the bonesetter, but don't ye see, sir. It's perfect. Miss Treneham, I mean Mrs. Remington, she'd have a right understanding of my situation. What with her having had babes of her own and no husband—"

"Babes?" Jagger said, feeling as if someone were pressing a hot branding iron against his chest.

"Of course, sir. Twins, she had. But the boy, he died. Two years ago, it was."

"We need a housemaid," he said. He was surprised his voice sounded so normal since he felt as if the world had tipped onto its side and was spinning backward. Twins! He didn't know why he was so surprised. Or why it bothered him. What was one more secret in a lifetime of secrets and lies?

Chapter Eleven

The next week passed like a bad dream, excruciatingly slowly, seemingly without end. Sophie dragged herself through the days, her thoughts haunted by all the horrible words she'd thrown at her brother's head before he died.

How she wished she could take them back. He was the only one who had ever truly cared for her, even when she was a lonely child and he was a man grown. Whenever he'd visited, he'd brought her a gift, as if she were his sister in truth, rather than the unwanted offspring of the Italian whore who had trapped his father into marriage, as her other stepbrother, Edmund, used to taunt her. But Stephen hadn't cared about her mother, or her dubious parentage on her father's side.

He had loved her like a sister. He'd read to her, sang with her, taught her to dance. But, most of all, he had stood loyally beside her through her greatest folly.

And how had she thanked him?

She'd accused him of betraying her.

A small part of her mind protested that he *had* betrayed her by tricking her into signing those papers, but it no longer signified. Despite the anger she'd felt at the time, she knew he hadn't done it to hurt her. In some strange way, he had thought he was protecting her.

Her emotions were all tangled up. She sensed she was in danger of slipping into melancholy, or madness, or a rage so great she would turn into a bitter shrew, but she could not let that happen. She had to remain strong. For her daughter.

The coroner called a jury to investigate the death, as was his duty under the law. After examining the body, Stephen's death was ruled a murder. Unfortunately, the precise location of the attack remained a mystery. As there were no witnesses to the crime, no suspects could be named and no warrants for arrest issued. The case remained unsolved and under investigation.

Sophie held no hope that the murderer would ever be apprehended. She was certain the villain had fled as far from the parish as possible. Perhaps he had even left the country.

The tenants and villagers paid their respects to Stephen by viewing his body as it lay in state, but Edmund had failed to arrive, despite numerous letters dispatched.

Hardly surprising, Sophie thought bitterly as she stood on the steps with Cecelie by her side. She watched the funeral procession wind its way down the carriage drive, the torches glowing eerily in the twilight, like a river of fire. Storm clouds covered the moon. The threat of rain hung heavy in the air. The gloomy darkness suited the occasion perfectly.

As the last of the torches disappeared from sight, Sophie took Cecelie by the hand and returned to the dining room.

The walls and table were hung with black. The chairs, also draped in black, were pushed up against the walls. Sophie had decided there would be no separation of mourners by rank. Anyone who honored Stephen's passing this day, be they the lowliest beggar or the highest peer of the realm, would share the same meal.

She surveyed the feast on the table. She had planned enough food to feed a battalion of ravenous men, but she had no doubt that very few people would return to the house after the burial. If it were not for the tenants, who cared more for Stephen than for propriety, no one would have paid any heed to his passing. But Jagger, she grudgingly had to admit, seemed genuinely devastated by the loss, though Sophie still had no idea how he knew Stephen, or what their relationship had been.

She could ask him, she supposed, if she could bring herself to speak to him. But to acknowledge him would be to acknowledge his place in her life as her husband.

As much as she wanted to deny it, she was married to this all-too-handsome stranger, with his rugged smile and the deepest blue eyes she had ever seen. Eyes as deep as the ocean—and just as unfathomable.

Her name was Mrs. Jagger Remington now. If she were still in the schoolroom, she would roll the name over her tongue, relishing the sound, the taste, the shape of the words. She would scrawl her name across a paper a thousand times, trying to perfect the *J*, to elaborate the *R*. But she was no schoolgirl miss. She was a woman grown with a child of her own to protect.

The irony was too precious. She was finally married, her schoolgirl dream achieved, but she was married to a man who wanted as little to do with her as she wanted to do with him. Whenever their paths crossed, they were perfectly polite to one another and as distant as the sun from the moon.

A gentle tug on her gown reminded Sophie not to step away from the table too quickly. She glanced at her daughter who stood at her side, sucking on her finger while tugging on Sophie's gown. Having gained her mother's attention, she thrust her arms in the air.

Forcing a smile, Sophie scooped up the child and walked to the window. Black billowing clouds floated like balloons across the sky, pushed by the gathering wind. A spattering of rain tapped the glass. Through the twilight, she could just make out the steeple of the village church, behind which Stephen was being laid to rest. Sophie shivered.

She felt a pressing ache in her throat. She kissed her daughter's cheek. "You don't understand, do you, my love?"

Cecelie didn't respond. Not that Sophie had expected her to speak. She hadn't uttered a word since the day her brother had died. It was one more spike of guilt piercing Sophie's heart.

Cecelie wiggled her way out of her mother's arms. She climbed onto the window seat and drew figures in the mist on the glass. Sophie was tempted to sit with her for a moment, but she knew she had to keep busy or she would go insane.

A woman Sophie did not recognize came through the servant's door. She was dressed in a rough cotton frock of a dark blue color. Her red hair seem as bright as the fire burning in the hearth. She carried a tray loaded with pitchers of what Sophie assumed was the mulled wine she had ordered.

The woman's face paled as she caught sight of Sophie. She set the tray on the table, dipped a quick curtsy. "Mrs. Remington. I didn't know yer'd be here. I'd a waited."

It was the first time anyone had addressed her by her married name. Sophie fought the bubble of hysterical laughter threatening to escape from her throat. "Who *are* you?"

"M'name's Mary, ma'am." She dipped another quick curtsy. "The new housemaid."

Sophie lifted her brows. "I beg your pardon?"

"Mr. Remington hired me. He said ye needed help. I mostly been workin' the scullery these few days past. To stay outta yer way. Yer being filled with grief and all."

Sophie half expected her mouth was hanging open at this outrageous speech. Of all the arrogant nerve! Who did that man think he was, to mingle in her household affairs and hire servants behind her back? She smothered her scathing reply, which was meant for another target completely and not this poor woman who was caught like a rabbit between two warring dogs.

"I am afraid Mr. Remington was mistaken," Sophie said.

The woman's face paled. She groped for the table, doubled over at the waist.

Sophie rushed to the woman's side. "Breathe deeply," she said, brushing the woman's hair from her face as she helped her to a chair. "I will fetch you a glass of water."

Mary shook her head. "Thank ye, ma'am. But there be no need. 'Tis better now."

Sophie frowned. "I am sorry, Mary. I did not mean to upset you. But I have no need of a housemaid at the moment."

The lie tasted bitter on her tongue. She did need the help. She simply couldn't afford to pay the woman's wages.

Mary looked at her pleadingly. "I'm a hard worker, ma'am. Ye wouldn' be sorry to have me."

Sophie's heart went out to the poor woman, but that didn't change the fact that she could not take on any help until she turned the estate around. "Perhaps at a later date—"

"Ye don't have to pay me, not right away, if that be what yer worryin' about. Everyone knows that devil ran off with yer blunt and all, and yer strapped, just like the rest of us." She held up her hands. "I'd be happy to work for food and me bed."

Sophie stared at the woman's palms. They were as work-worn and callused as her own.

"All right," she said, surprising herself. She could no more afford to feed another mouth than she could afford to pay the woman.

"Thank ye, ma'am." Mary jumped to her feet. "Ye won't be sorry. I promise ye that. Thank ye. Thank ye."

She ran from the room.

Sophie was sorry already.

"This is the last one," Betsy said as she came through the door bearing a huge platter of roasted beef. The steam drifted across her face, staining her cheeks a pretty pink.

The scent of the roasted meat drifted across the room.

Sophie's stomach rumbled, reminding her that she hadn't eaten anything all day. She walked over to the window seat and sat beside her daughter.

Betsy sighed as she placed the platter on the table, then turned to Sophie. "Shall I take the little miss upstairs? She looks as if she could use a nice, long sleep."

"In a moment," Sophie said, tilting her head against the window. The condensation on the glass soothed her work-worn skin. She closed her eyes as she waited. Then she heard it. The Death Knell. The final tolling of the parish bells as Stephen was laid to rest.

She should be there. She should have damned societal strictures, which dictated that, as a woman, she would have been too overwrought by emotion to attend her brother's burial.

Only this time, she greatly feared society might be right. As much as she hated to admit it, Stephen had spoken the truth. She was a coward, too afraid of what people would say. If it weren't for Sunday worship, she would never leave the estate.

She handed Cecelie to the maid.

"Do not worry, miss," Betsy said. "I'll keep this little one right and tight while you do what you must. Do you think Lord Hallowell will arrive today?"

Sophie shuddered. She would never get used to the sound of that title linked with Edmund's name. It belonged to Stephen!

"I have no idea," she said. "He should have been here days ago. Are you sure you posted my letters?"

"That I did, miss. But don't you worry none. He'll be here. You'll see."

That wasn't what Sophie was worried about. But the maid's concern comforted her. It was nice to know she had at least one friend in this world, even if she were only a nursery maid, as Thea would say.

It was the perfect night for a funeral. Gray and gloomy. The clouds heavy with rain. As the vicar mouthed the final blessing, a fine mist began to fall, filling the air with the scent of mud. The men edging the grave bent their heads.

Jagger eyed the meager crowd. Villagers, mostly, and a few of the tenants he had met during the previous week and a half. Could one of them be the murderer?

The lack of suspects and clues was maddening. The local magistrate and constable were incompetent fools, more intent on their next meal and their drink than finding the agent of this despicable deed. On the night of the attack, Jagger had dispatched one of his men to London to hire investigators from Bow Street to track the vermin who had assaulted the earl. Nearly a fortnight later, he had yet to receive any word.

It was time to travel to London for an update. Jagger planned to leave at first light. As he also planned for his wife to accompany him, he supposed he ought to mention it to her tonight. His wife. What a laugh. She avoided him as much as possible and spoke to him only when necessary.

Jagger thought perhaps ten sentences, if that, had passed between them in the week since they had wed. He slept in a guest room down the hall from hers, and, from what he could tell, she never slept at all. He heard her roaming the halls at all hours of the night.

At first, he'd thought someone had broken into the house. When he'd risen to investigate, he'd found her waxing the marble floor in the entryway. He'd started to protest, but the look in her eyes warned him to hold his peace.

Another night, he'd followed the tantalizing scent of freshly baked bread to the kitchens and found her chopping vegetables and meats for a stew. He had wanted to talk to her, to offer her some comfort, but she hadn't so much as looked at him, let alone acknowledged his presence in the room.

How tightly she held her grief disturbed him. She had yet to weep. She moved through her days as if nothing had happened, cooking and cleaning and working like a maid.

Could one of these villagers be the father of her child?

The scent of wet soil stung his throat. The mourners began to disperse, but anger rooted Jagger in place.

The gravediggers ambled forward. Their shovels scraped the earth. As he listened to the thud of dirt and stones hitting the wooden coffin lid, Jagger closed his eyes. An unaccustomed lump lodged in his throat. The thought that he might actually cry made him furious.

He never cried. Not even as a young boy when his body was so battered and bruised he couldn't stand up. All those years of silent anguish. All those years of longing for the man he'd thought was his father to offer him one kind word, one gesture of love. He had never understood how his mother could have stood silently by and watched her son suffer so much brutality.

Part of him wanted to rail at her, and part of him understood, in theory at least, that she'd had no choice. A man had absolute control over his wife and any children produced in the marriage. Even had she wanted to leave, she would have been trapped by the law. While his mind knew this was true, the little boy inside his heart would never understand, could never forget the misery of his childhood.

Especially when the truth of his parentage would have come as a welcome relief, rather than a spot of shame.

Unanswered questions raced through his mind. Was the duke telling the truth? If so, who was his father? Why had his mother kept such a secret from him, even when he was a man grown?

Jagger clenched his fists as he thought of the night Stephen had died. The last thing Jagger had expected was for Stephen to demand a vow of silence before offering his deathbed confession. The earl's voice had been so weak, Jagger had managed to make out only a word or two. In the end, he had not been able to decipher the meaning of the earl's dying words.

Now he would never know what Stephen had tried to tell him. He only knew it involved his mother and the man he had once called Father. Jagger wanted ten more minutes with Stephen. Ten bloody minutes to demand the truth.

Oh, he supposed he could go to the duke. No doubt, the bastard would relish the chance to tell the tale. But Jagger would not demean himself so. He had the monster right where he wanted him, down in the dirt, cornered by his greed and vices, and that was where Jagger wanted him to stay.

As Jagger turned to leave, he caught the name chiseled into the tombstone beside Stephen's grave. Catherine Remington. The rest of the words were lost in the driving rain.

Jagger had never tried to locate her grave. He had simply assumed she'd been buried in her family crypt. He had planned to pay his respects as soon as he'd paid his debt to Stephen.

He started to laugh. He laughed so hard, his eyes started to water, the droplets mixing with the rain slipping down his cheeks. If Jagger didn't know better, he might suspect he was crying, but he wasn't. He was laughing.

He laughed until his sides ached and his eyes stung. He laughed at the secrets and lies he'd been told his entire life.

He did not know what to believe anymore. Nor did he care, he decided, as he turned and stalked toward his carriage.

It was time to put the past behind him and look toward the future with his wife.

Sophie stood in the dining room, her lawfully wedded husband by her side. The man with whom she was to spend the rest of her life offered to fetch her a glass of lemonade. The concern in his eyes seemed genuine, as did his grief at Stephen's death, and all she could do was wish he would leave her and never return.

Just as she wished the people milling through the room would leave. Most were villagers, but a few of Stephen's peers had lowered themselves to pay their respects, regardless of the lack of invitations. Not that they cared that her brother was dead. They came to gape at her and gossip about her future.

At least Cecelie was tucked safely in her bed upstairs.

The room was full of men. Not a wife or sister to be seen. All too good to mingle with the likes of Sophie Treneham, she supposed. Even Thea was noticeably absent from the gathering. On the day Stephen had died, Thea had taken to her bed with the headache and had yet to be seen again.

Jagger bent to whisper in her ear. "Perhaps you would care to sit down?"

His warm breath caressed her neck, sending shivers down her spine. She hated him, and she gave him a look that she hoped conveyed the depth of her hostility. This was her house. He had no right to hire servants when there was no money to pay their wages. She would wait until tomorrow to confront him, though. She did not need any more heartache today.

Nor did she need him to take care of her!

To her disgust, he didn't seem the least disturbed. In fact, he smiled at her, a sympathetic, I-understand-how-you-feel kind of smile that made Sophie want to scream.

Instead, she abandoned her husband to suffer through the vicar's long-winded and one-sided version of conversation.

As she turned, she bumped into Sir John. The loathsome toad had snuck up behind her. She lifted her chin and looked down her nose at him, a somewhat difficult feat considering he stood at least ten inches taller than she did.

"Kindly step back and put a proper distance between us," she hissed, hooking her hands on her hips as she glowered at him. What did it matter if she created another scandal? She was already an outcast. What more could society do to her?

His blue eyes narrowed in a predatory gaze. He leaned toward her, the nostrils in his hawkish nose flaring as if catching the scent of fresh meat.

"I am prepared to make you a very generous offer," he whispered. "Now that your brother is dead, you will need a protector."

His breath smelled of anchovies and ale.

Sophie gagged. She rolled her lips, held the back of her hand to her nose. "Perhaps if you did not smell of the pigsty, you might have better luck with your conquests."

His eyes widened until they nearly blocked out all the other features of his face. "You insolent slut."

Despite the venom of his words, he kept his voice low, no doubt fearful of dragging Jagger Remington's attention his way.

She could tell by the way he clenched his fists that he wanted to do her physical harm. Perhaps she should be afraid. But she was not. She had lived in fear for far too long. It was time to reclaim her life.

"I wish you to leave, Sir John. Do not dare to step foot on the Park again unless it is business of the realm that brings you here. Do you understand me?"

She did not wait for his reply. She turned toward the door with every intention of seeking the privacy of her room, only to find herself face-to-face with a ghost from her past.

The room seemed to spin, as if she had taken too much wine.

"Miss Treneham," the young man said as he bowed.

Henry Holliston. His thick brown hair was fashioned à la Byron. A single curl fell artfully across his forehead. His stiff white cravat framed his aristocratic face, highlighted his dark brown eyes. He was not quite as handsome as his elder brother, but he was just as rotten inside.

Sophie clenched her hands together in a death grip to keep from reaching out and smacking the bounder in the face.

She moved toward the door. She had no intention of talking to this man. She had better things to do. Like checking on Cecelie. Sudden panic twisted in her gut. Was that what brought him here? She had to the fight the urge to run to Cecelie's room and hide her away.

He strode along beside her. "I see you remember me."

He sounded surprised. Did he honestly think she would forget the role he had played in her ruination? The cad!

She didn't bother to reply.

He pushed himself in front of her.

"Please," he whispered. "Might I have a moment of your time? I must speak with you."

As if there were anything he could say that she could possibly want to hear. Did he have no shame?

Didn't he realize the pain she had suffered due in no

small part to the perfidy of his actions? Obviously, he didn't care.

"My brother is dead," he said.

Sophie drew in a slow breath as she waited to feel some response, some emotion to these words. She felt nothing.

He was standing too close to her, much closer than propriety allowed. The toes of his boots actually cradled her slippers. He reached out, as if to take her hand in his.

She scooted out of his reach, leaving his hand hanging in the air between them.

Slowly, he lowered his arm to his side. "When I learned of Lord Hallowell's death, I, well, I—I know you won't believe me but I would like to make amends."

Sophie chuckled. "As if such a thing is possible."

"I have taken a room at the village inn. I would like to meet with you tomorrow."

From the corner of her eye, she saw Jagger scowl as he strode toward them. The fierceness of his features declared his intentions. Sophie did not want him prying around in her past.

"Do you see that man walking toward us?" she said in a low voice, so as not to be overheard. "The one who looks like a pirate?"

Henry Holliston glanced over his shoulder. When he turned his attention back to Sophie, his face was white.

"He is my husband," she said, nearly choking on the words. "I assure you, he is quite a jealous man. Were I you, I would be on my way."

She supposed she had acted the coward, hiding behind a man she would never recognize as her husband in any way but name only, but she was too weary to care. She just wanted Henry Holliston to leave.

He studied her for a moment, his struggle over whether to stay or turn tail and run clearly evident in his face. "Madam, I had not heard of your good tidings. I have much I wish to discuss with you. I will remain in the village for a sennight. You may contact me there. I wish you great joy in your marriage. God knows, you deserve it," he added as he bowed stiffly, then hurried from the room as if he were a contestant in a foot race who had just found a sudden reserve of energy.

Was that regret she heard in his voice? Had he come here seeking forgiveness? The abominable cad!

Jagger reached her side. "Who was that man?"

Before she could think of a lie, a booming voice sounded from the entryway. Although the words were indistinguishable, the tone and tenor suggested an argument. Then the front door slammed against its frame.

A moment later, Edmund entered the room. He was dressed as if he were attending a presentation at court, in white breeches with white silk stockings and shiny black pumps. His white waistcoat was intricately embroidered in gold thread. His only concession to the death of his brother was a black band wrapped around the upper arm of his deep blue frock coat.

Sophie had not thought the day could get any worse, but she had been wrong. Edmund strode through the room, acting like the lord and master of the manor, greeting the guests as if he were at a grand ball rather than a funeral gathering, and all the while he ignored her completely.

Oh, once or twice he glanced at her with a smirk on his lips and a glint in his eyes. No doubt he had plans to throw her out of the house at the earliest possible convenience. She would relish the moment he learned the truth.

It sickened her to hear him addressed as "my lord" and "Your Lordship." Those titles belonged to Stephen, but, legally, since Stephen had died without issue, the title passed to Edmund. She would have to learn to live with it. Just as she would have to learn to live with Jagger, the man whom the law now recognized as her lord and master, even if she did not.

Gradually, the mourners left and the room emptied,

save for Sophie, Jagger, Edmund, and a man Sophie recognized as Stephen's solicitor. She supposed she should
introduce Jagger to Edmund and get it over with—they
had been casting suspicious glares at one other since
Edmund had arrived—but she did not want to.

She did not want to say the words.

Edmund took the decision away from her. "I must ask
you to leave, sir, as the family has business to discuss."

"Business?" Sophie echoed. "We buried our brother
tonight. What business can we possibly need to discuss
that cannot wait for the morrow?"

Edmund smiled his hyena smile. "Why, the reading
of the will, of course."

Sophie thought her legs would collapse beneath her.
She had always known that Edmund was heartless, but
she hadn't known to what depth his callousness ran.

"Forgive me," she said, barely keeping her sarcasm
in check. "Our brother isn't even cold in his grave. I
refuse to lower myself to such a mercenary undertaking
today."

"Sophie, Sophie," Edmund said in a voice that sounded
almost jovial. "Unfortunately, that decision isn't yours to
make. I am the new earl and I need to see to the estates at
the earliest possible moment, especially considering that
Stephen was so long away from England. Feldman sees
the logic in this. Don't you, Feldman?"

The solicitor steadily gazed at Sophie. His hazel eyes
seemed to plead with her to trust him. "I do believe it
would be for the best."

On the few occasions she had met Mr. Feldman,
Sophie had found him to be quite congenial. His gray
hair framed a wrinkled face that conveyed a sense of
honesty. Of course, these were her impressions before
he helped Stephen betray her with those documents
and ignored her pleas for help.

She wanted them all to leave. If this were the only
way . . .

"Very well," she said.

"In that case," Jagger drawled as he strolled over to Sophie and linked her arm through his, "I believe I will accompany my wife."

Chapter Twelve

The library was unnaturally quiet, as if all the other occupants were having as much difficulty as Sophie was understanding what they had just heard. She could not bring herself to look at Jagger who was sitting in the padded leather chair next to hers, so she concentrated on keeping her back as straight as if she were strapped to a posture board.

She crossed her feet at the ankles, then tucked them under her chair. She laced her fingers together on her lap. The stiff tension in her knuckles sent an awareness of pain up her arms but she did not release her grip. She kept her attention pinned on the solicitor as he carefully shuffled the pages of the will he had just finished reading into a neat pile on what used to be Stephen's desk.

Smoke curled away from the sputtering candles in the wall sconces behind him. The air seemed oppressively hot, though no fire burned in the grate. The velvet curtains, drawn against the night, added to the stifling atmosphere in the room.

She should leave this instant. She had a dozen or more tasks to complete before she retired for the evening. She wanted to kiss Cecelie good night. She could not even remember the last time she had spent more than ten minutes with her daughter. Certainly not since Jagger had arrived with his preposterous claim to her hand.

She could not move, though. Her feet felt heavy, as if they were anchored to the floor. She now knew more than she had ever wanted to know about the extent of Stephen's betrayal, which went far beyond tricking her into marriage with a complete stranger. Now she realized she had never known Stephen. It was this betrayal that hurt most of all.

She glanced at Edmund. He gripped the arms of his chair as if he were attempting to keep himself from leaping over the desk. The lines around his mouth appeared white above his rigid jaw. The tendons in his neck bulged. He was breathing so hard, his nostrils flared. Sophie half expected him to scrape his foot along the floorboards like a bull about to charge.

"This is preposterous," he finally bit out. He spoke so softly, Sophie had to strain to hear his words, but she did not miss the lethal menace in his tone, nor the threatening manner in which he leaned forward, drew his brows together, and narrowed his eyes until he was glaring at the solicitor through mere slits. "Do you seriously expect us to believe this document is legitimate? That this marriage is legitimate?"

The solicitor calmly folded his hands on the desk. "As I drew up all the documents myself, I assure you, my lord, this will is perfectly legal, the marriage contracts are perfectly legal, and the marriage was properly executed, properly witnessed, and properly recorded in the parish registry."

Edmund jumped to his feet. He towered over the desk. "You expect me to believe that my brother left me nothing other than a few thousand pounds to maintain the entailed estate? That he left everything else—all the property, all the money, all the furnishings—everything—to a man unrelated to this family in any way except by some sham of a marriage to this whore who has not a drop of Treneham blood and a bastard to boot—"

Moving as swiftly as a lightning bolt across the sky, Jagger lunged from his chair. He curled his fists into the fabric of Edmund's frock coat and hauled him off his feet.

"The lady of whom you speak is my wife," he said in a dangerously low voice. "Her daughter is my daughter. If you value your life, you will beg her pardon. Now."

Edmund's face turned red, whether from anger or lack of breath, Sophie couldn't tell, but he finally mumbled, "Your pardon" and Jagger dropped him.

They glared at each other like two cocks in a pit, each silently daring the other to make the first move.

Sophie almost laughed to think that a man was finally defending her honor. Yet, despite all the pain and betrayal she had suffered through the years, she was shocked to realize a small part of her still longed for a man to sweep her off her feet, a knight in shining armor to wrap her in his strong arms and keep her safe from those who would do her harm.

Even more shocking was the yearning, the hope, that *this* man, her husband, might learn to care for her, perhaps even grow to love her, despite all the mistakes she had made in the past, despite her lack of dowry and social significance.

Of course, whether or not she had a fortune no longer signified as he had just inherited everything that Stephen had owned that was legally his to give away.

Sophie cursed her foolish dreams, her foolish hopes, her foolish heart. Now Jagger Remington's actions made such perfect sense. Until that moment, Sophie had stupidly thought it was merely Norwood Park that he wanted. While it was a beautiful estate, it certainly wasn't worth marrying a complete stranger to gain. But to win the remainder of Stephen's fortune and estates, a man might do anything, even stoop so low as to marry a woman about whom he knew nothing. A woman ostracized from society because she had an illegitimate daughter and the reputation of a common whore.

The last gossamer strands of her illusions ripped to shreds. Sophie understood for the first time that no one had ever loved her and now she realized that no one ever would.

With as much dignity as she could muster, she rose from her chair and left the room, leaving Jagger and Edmund to thug it out on the library floor.

Jagger wanted to follow her, to offer her the comfort he knew she must need and for which she would never ask, but he could no more move his feet than an oak tree could lift its roots from the ground. His thoughts swirled around in his mind like a thousand needles, pricking him with unanswered questions, torturing him with lightning-fast flashes of memories.

Jagger was vaguely aware of Edmund blustering around the room like a thunderstorm, lashing the solicitor with his accusations, vowing to fight the terms of the will, yet Jagger could not bring himself to speak or move. Only one reason could explain Stephen's actions, from forcing Jagger into marriage with his sister to the contents of his will.

Suspicions that had formed in Jagger's mind at the graveyard coalesced into certainty, and it sickened him.

Edmund turned his fury on Jagger. His face was red, his eyes bulging in their sockets. He was foaming at the mouth.

"These documents are forgeries, and I will see you in hell before you spend one farthing of my money," he said, jabbing his finger at Jagger's chest. Then he turned on his heel and strode out the door before Jagger could gather his dulled wits enough to beat the daylight out of the man.

The solicitor smiled kindly at Jagger as he came

around the desk. He held an envelope, which he offered to Jagger. "I believe this will answer most of your questions, my lord."

Jagger took the letter. Part of him wanted to rip it open and tear through the contents. Another part of him, he realized with chagrin, was afraid of what secrets might lurk within. Like Pandora before him, his curiosity might unleash unspeakable horror upon his newly acquired family.

Jagger wasn't certain he was willing to take that chance.

One thing he did know, though. He'd had surprises and betrayals aplenty these many weeks past. Whatever secrets this letter contained could wait until tomorrow.

Right now, he wanted to find his wife.

Midnight came and went before Sophie climbed the stairs to check on Cecelie. Her chambers were a bright cheery suite of rooms attached to Sophie's by a connecting door. It was another faux pas that set Sophie outside fashionable society and their belief that children belonged in the nursery, hidden amongst the servants, rather than nestled among the family.

A few glowing embers in the grate was all that remained of an earlier fire. Through the shadows, Sophie could see a rag doll tossed on the rug-covered floor. Another doll was propped on a chair at a child-sized table, as if preparing to pour tea from the miniature tea set before her. This usually seemed such a comforting room; tonight the shadows appeared menacing.

Sophie wanted to scoop her sleeping child into her arms, to protect her from the world and the dangers around her. Instead, she brushed aside a few strands of curly brown hair that had escaped from Cecelie's nightcap.

She pressed a kiss against her daughter's cheek, inhaled the soft scent of lotion and soap. So much love for her daughter ached in her heart, sometimes Sophie thought she might perish beneath the force of it. Along with the love came the pain of knowing what a terrible mother she was.

The sound of Betsy's soft snoring floated from the second, smaller bed tucked into the corner of the room. Dear, sweet Betsy who, for the past two years, had seemed more of a mother to Cecelie than Sophie had.

Sophie spun on her heel and fled the scene of her most recent failure. She could face no further turmoil tonight.

Passing through the connecting door, she entered her bedchamber. The fire roaring in the grate made her pause.

The settee and chairs, which usually flanked the fireplace, were pushed aside. Positioned before the hearth was a hipbath filled with steaming water. On the table beside the bed was a bottle of wine—and two glasses?

"I thought you might enjoy a bath."

She recognized Jagger Remington's resonant voice. It came from the shadows near the windows. In her room!

Sophie spun around, her heart pounding painfully in her chest. "What are you doing here? Get out!"

He sauntered toward her, all lazy elegance and masculine appeal. His blue-eyed gaze traveled over her— a slow, thorough perusal that brought a blush to her cheeks and sent fire licking along her skin. His ebony hair was wet and slicked back from his face. His cheeks were clean-shaven, the puckered skin beneath his eye a firm reminder that he was a rogue, a pirate bent on ruining her life. A moment later she registered the fact that he wore no shirt. Her hand flew to her throat as if to catch her shocked gasp before it escaped her lips.

She had never seen a man's naked chest before, not even on the night her children were conceived. His shoulders were broad and well-rounded, his arms thick tree trunks of sinewy strength. Dense black hair swirled over a wall of chiseled muscles.

If he were a Greek god, she would think him Adonis,

a man so beautiful that Persephone had wanted to keep him forever and with whom Aphrodite had fallen madly in love.

Now Sophie understood why.

His stomach was flat and rippled with muscles. Though she tried to avert her gaze, a quick glance reassured her that at least he still wore his breeches.

She yanked her gaze to his face. "Get out of my room," she said in a voice shaking as badly as her arms and legs. She had reached her limit. This was *her* private sanctuary. The dusky rose tones of the bed hangings and striped silk wallpaper gave the room a peaceful air she found nowhere else.

He was trespassing. If he didn't leave immediately, she could not be held responsible for her actions.

Intent on grabbing a weapon, she sidled over to the fire irons. In one fluid motion he was at her side. He swept her off her feet and into his arms.

She opened her mouth to scream.

"Be quiet," he growled. "Unless you truly wish to bring the house down upon us before we have a chance to speak."

She held herself stiff in his arms, afraid to move, afraid to touch his naked flesh, lest she incite his carnal desire. Or was it *her* carnal desire that kept her frozen in his arms?

"Put me down," she said through her teeth.

He carried her to a chair beside the bed. Slowly, he lowered her to her feet. Her legs slid down his muscular thighs before finally touching the floor. She stood mere inches away from him, her eyes parallel with his naked chest. The heat of his flesh surrounded her, beckoned her to abandon reason, to surrender to temptation and danger. She dragged her gaze to his lips, shocked to realize she wanted him to kiss her.

She truly was insane. She knew what dangers lurked in

that direction. How cruel to realize Edmund was right and she was wrong. She *was* just like her mother after all.

"Sit," he said, his voice low and seductive. "We need to discuss what has happened this evening."

She ran around the chair, retreated like the coward she now knew she was. "What are you doing here?"

He poured a glass of wine, thrust it into her hand. "Your brother thinks this marriage is a sham."

"And he is right," Sophie hissed.

"Yes, but do you want him to know he is right?"

"What difference does it make?"

"It makes a world of difference, if you would only take a moment to think it through." He poured another glass of wine, then took a long sip. "This is wonderful. You should try it. It might help you relax."

Wine sloshed onto her hand as she slammed her glass on the table. "Oh, you would like that, wouldn't you?"

He raised his brows.

"You would like me insensible from drink so you can take advantage of my condition."

He smiled. "You know, I hadn't thought of that. But now that you mention it . . ."

Heat curled through her stomach, spread through her fingers and toes. "Beast! Get out of my room—and put your shirt on."

His smile broadencd, as if it pleased him greatly to learn she was disturbed by his near-nakedness. If only he knew it was his smile that set the insides of her stomach to fluttering.

"I have no doubt your brother will contest the will."

"And you stand to lose all that lovely money."

Was that sarcasm she heard in her voice? She was never sarcastic. She thought it inordinately rude. Yet, she was certain it had just escaped from her lips.

"Yes, that would be a shame," he said, placing his glass on the table. He sat on the edge of the bed. "But I was thinking about you."

Stunned senseless by his actions, Sophie watched as he yanked off first one boot, then the other.

"I imagine he will try to claim undue influence on my part, or that Stephen's solicitor was incompetent, that he made errors in drafting the documents, or that they were improperly witnessed, or some such nonsense."

His stockings followed his boots, revealing powerful calves sporting the same dark hair that covered his chest.

"The matter could be tied up in court for years."

The muscles in his back rippled as he bent and stretched.

"I do not know if his claims have any legal merit."

Tiny beads of water clung to his shoulders.

"I need to set my solicitors to the task of investigating the possibilities."

It was obvious he had recently bathed.

"We will leave for London first thing in the morning."

Sophie gasped as she suddenly realized that he had been naked—completely naked—here, in her room.

What if she had returned a few minutes sooner?

She might have caught him in the bath.

The nerve of the arrogant man! She grabbed a pillow from the chair and flung it at his chest. "Get out of my room."

He caught it easily and tossed it to the floor. "Haven't you heard a word I said?"

She could hardly admit that she'd paid more attention to his flexing muscles than to his words. "Of course I did," she lied. "Though I do not see the significance."

"I imagine he will attack the credibility of the solicitor, thereby casting doubt on the legality of the documents, or he will try to prove them forgeries."

"What has that to do with me?"

"The solicitor drew up both the will and the marriage settlements—at the same time. And the same men witnessed them. Both documents will be called into question."

"All the better," Sophie said, suddenly realizing there might be a way out of this marriage after all.

Jagger lowered his voice as if he were trying to reason with a simpleton. "I know you do not believe that I have no vested interest in this estate, but I thought that *you* did. I thought it would upset *you* if Norwood Park reverted to your brother."

Sophie sucked in her breath. "What do you mean?"

"If I am not mistaken, you received this estate through the contracts of marriage your brother drew up."

Sophie nodded. "But now it is yours."

"No, it is not," he said gently. "I merely have a life interest in the income generated by the property."

"Do not split hairs with me."

He looked as if he wanted to shake some sense into her, but he kept his hands firmly by his sides. "Try to reason the chain of events that will be set in motion if your brother somehow manages to prove his point and the contracts and will are declared forgeries, therefore null and void."

"I do not know what you mean."

"What do you think would happen?"

Sophie shrugged her shoulders.

"This estate would revert to Stephen's holdings and his prior will and testament would be in effect. As I understand it from Mr. Feldman, according to that document, all of Stephen's properties would devolve to the new earl at Stephen's death. Do you now understand what I am saying?"

Sophie closed her eyes. The room seemed to spin around her. For a brief, wild moment, she actually felt as if she might faint. Or heave her dinner all over the floor.

Jagger grasped her elbow, guided her to the chair. She put up no struggle or protest, but sank gratefully onto the seat.

Holding her hand in his, he bent on his knee before her. The warmth of his fingers calmed her shattered nerves. The scent of his soap soothed her like a lullaby. His eyes were so dark and filled with concern, Sophie wanted to throw her arms around his neck and beg him to protect her.

Her world was spinning out of control. She could only hang on and hope not to crash. She hated this weakness, this loss of control she had suffered since this man had walked into her life. She hated the pity she saw in his eyes.

But more than anything, she hated the desperation with which she clung to his hand, yet she didn't let go. "Do you think he has any hope of succeeding?"

"I do not know," Jagger said, his fingers smoothing circles on her palm. "I have only outlined possible plans of attack, based on his ranting in the study. He is the earl now, and, as such, has influence and power in his favor. But the courts move slowly and will tie up this matter for years to come. I will set my solicitors to the matter at once. In the meantime, I do not want you to worry. I will protect you."

His words swept over her like a summer breeze, full of hope and promise for a future she knew she could never have.

She shoved his hand away, stood up, and, as gracefully as she could, hid behind the chair. "What do you mean?"

"We must endeavor to convince those around us that this is a marriage in truth," he said. "A love match, as they say."

"Whatever for?"

"Given the haste with which we married, and the uproar your brother seems determined to create, there is bound to be talk."

"There is always 'talk' where I am concerned. In case you haven't yet realized, you married a scandalous woman." There it was again. That sarcasm. She almost did not recognize herself.

"You are my wife now," he said forcefully. "I will not abandon you to society's hags—"

He broke off abruptly. She could tell there was more he wanted to say, but for some reason, he stopped himself. His body was rigid with barely leashed tension. Or perhaps it was anger. His deeply tanned chest rose and fell as he breathed.

How had he gotten that golden glow to his skin? Could he be in the habit of spending hours out-of-doors with no shirt on?

Sophie found the thought as tantalizing as it was shocking.

"It will cause a scandal of outragcous proportions," he said, his words crashing around her like ferocious waves pounding the rocky shore.

Sophie ground her knuckles into the back of the chair. "Why should I care? I am no stranger to scandal."

"You are my wife now," he said through his teeth. "I will allow no one to drag your name through the mud."

"Is it my name you're worried about, or your own?"

He drew several deep breaths. He flexed and opened his hands, as if trying to gain control over his emotions, as if he could find words to convince her. "Stephen has done all in his power to rectify your reputation. Will you allow him to have sacrificed in vain?"

"Sacrifice? By playing on my sense of duty and thrusting me into a marriage I did not want mere moments before he died? I am the one who was sacrificed!"

"He provided you with a proper husband—"

"Ha! That is debatable."

"And a fortune to boot."

"He left that fortune to you."

"I beg to differ, my dear. He left that fortune to us while making provisions for the children of your body. That includes Cecelie, as well as any future children of this marriage."

"There will be no 'future children of this marriage,'"

Sophie cried, nearly hysterical at the thought. "I will never bear another child. Never!"

"Good Lord, woman. Attend to the matter at hand. In one fell swoop, Stephen has made you, through me, one of the wealthiest, most powerful women in England. He made your daughter an heiress in her own right. Society will overlook much in the pursuit of consequence and riches."

Sophie's head was spinning, as if she had twirled herself dizzy as she had as a child.

Jagger crossed the room. He grasped her hand. She tried to snatch it away, but his strong fingers wrapped around hers.

"Look at me," he said. He would not continue until she met his gaze. "I care naught for the properties and the money. It can revert to your brother for all I care. But I will allow no one to besmirch your name. We will convince the world this is a love match and that is the end of this discussion."

She felt almost wild, as if her hair was sticking out all over her head and she belonged in an asylum. When had she lost all control? "No one will ever believe it."

"Of course they will. I can be very convincing. Moreso considering I'm halfway in love with you already."

Of course, he was jesting, yet her heart skipped a beat.

She would not be mocked. She thrust her chin in the air. "Ha! That's what all men say to gain their evil way."

"I assure you, madam, I am not the monster you think I am. Nor am I the cad who seduced you, then abandoned you when he should have married you."

His voice was low and controlled, yet beneath the surface lurked a deadly menace that was frightening. "Unlike that bounder," he said evenly, "I am here to stay, and I will protect you with my life. Even if that means sleeping in the same room and declaring myself in love before the world."

Sophie was so angry, she wanted to scream, yet she could not get the words to roll off her tongue.

She clenched her jaw. "You promised you would not claim your marital rights."

"And I will keep that promise," he said.

She did not believe him. She was such a fool.

And now she was trapped.

"I do not wish to argue with you," he said as he strode to the bed and slid between the covers. "Now, let us get some sleep."

Chapter Thirteen

I'm halfway in love with you already.

Through her mind echoed his words. Dangerous words that taunted her. Called to her like a siren's song, daring her to forget logic and reason, beckoning her to come hither and succumb to foolish dreams until she crashed upon the rocks.

He was jesting. She knew it. By his own admission, he was playacting for the benefit of those around them. Yet some secret part of her heart longed for his words to be true.

She was pathetic, she realized as she stared at the man in her bed. He lay on his side, one arm supporting his head, the covers slung low on his hips. His naked chest rose and fell to the rhythm of his breath.

He stared at her through eyes as black as the darkest night. The air in the room fairly crackled with tension. He spoke not a word, but he called to her just the same. He *was* the siren, she suddenly realized, if there was such a thing as a male siren. He beckoned to her without words, dared her to abandon her fears and take a chance on love.

Stifling a cry of alarm, she spun on her heels and stalked to one of the settees near the fire. She would no

more sleep next to that man than she would chop off her
own foot.

She curled onto her side, wiggled her bottom closer to the
back. She'd be much more comfortable if she could kick off
her shoes, or undress her hair, but she'd be damned if she
would bare even her toes in this man's presence.

She never slept much, but tonight she knew she would
not even get her usual hour or two of rest. Damn that
man.

Damn that impossible man.

Jagger watched the feisty woman who was now his
wife as she flung herself onto the settee and wiggled herself into what looked to be the most uncomfortable position possible for sleeping. What a stubborn wench she
was. She rolled onto her back, sighed heavily, then rolled
onto her belly. She punched one of the pillows, crushed
it beneath her face, then sighed even louder and rolled
onto her back again.

Cursing under his breath, he rose from the bed. He
ignored her cry of alarm, scooped her into his arms, and
threw her onto the bed. Before she could make her
escape, he grabbed her ankles and tugged off her shoes,
leaving her socks to satisfy her modesty, then he crawled
into the bed beside her.

"Be quiet," he growled as he hauled her back against his
chest, chaining her in place with his arm. "I have no intention of forcing myself upon you. Nor do I plan to lie awake
all night listening to you toss and turn on the settee."

She wanted to pummel him; he could tell by the stiffness of her spine and the tension in her arm. Or was she
afraid?

Why would she be? She had born a child—or rather,
two children—as Mary had informed him. Twins.
Though one had died. Which meant she knew the ways

of the flesh. But she acted as if his very touch caused her pain.

Who had hurt this woman in the past? Had she been raped?

The thought filled Jagger with so much fury, he had to force himself to breathe evenly until the moment passed. More likely her seducer had been a clumsy oaf who had shown her no pleasure, only pain. Had she loved the father of her child?

Was she in love with him still?

He wanted to shake the truth from her, but she had yet to ply him with questions about his past, his family, and his connections. He would show her the same respect.

Besides, there was more than one way to gain the answers to his questions, and he knew exactly where to start.

It seemed as if an hour passed before she finally fell asleep. An hour of the most unbelievable torture a man should never have to endure, lying thigh to thigh, shin to shin, with the most desirable woman in the world, breathing her sweet scent of roses and warm flesh, and honor-bound not to touch her.

As she drifted off to sleep, the tension melted from her body. Her breathing deepened. She snuggled a little closer to Jagger. Curving her back against his chest, she pressed her legs lightly against his thighs. Her stocking-covered feet rubbed against his shins.

He hardened instantly as desire rocked through him.

It was going to be a long night.

He slowly pulled the pins from her hair, releasing the tight knot she had worn at her nape. He dropped the pins on the bedside table, spread her hair over her shoulders, rubbed the silky softness against his cheek. As he ran his fingertips along her arm, his earlier words rang though his mind.

I'm halfway in love with you already.

Whatever had possessed him to think such a thing, much less speak such sentiments aloud? It was insane.

He hardly knew her. And yet, he felt as if he had known her forever.

She was a beautiful, desirable woman, but there was so much more to Sophie Treneham than her physical attributes. She was strong, but not overbearing, fiercely proud and independent, but not arrogant and waspish. She knew what she wanted and she was not afraid to work hard to achieve her dreams.

But perhaps her most desirable attribute was her devotion to her daughter. Her absolute determination to protect her child with her life, no matter what society might think or say.

He thought of the child she had lost, of the pain and betrayal she had suffered at the hands of some bounder.

She shouldered so much suffering, yet she held her head high, as if daring the world to condemn her. Eventually, Jagger would discover the identity of the scoundrel who had destroyed her future and he would make the bastard pay.

He must have fallen asleep, for when next he opened his eyes, the dim gray light of dawn filled the room. He was on his back with one arm curled around Sophie. Her cheek nestled into his neck as she snuggled against his side. Her hair flowed tantalizingly over his naked flesh.

He stifled a groan. He knew if he stayed in that bed one moment longer, he would roll her onto her back and have his wicked way with her before she knew what he was about.

With a sigh, he gently pulled himself out from under her sleeping form. He repositioned a pillow beneath her cheek, then pulled the covers over her shoulders and tucked them under her chin. He turned onto his side to roll from the bed and found himself staring into the somber brown eyes of his wife's child.

His child now.

He was a father.

Jagger had stared down Indian mughals and marauding

privateers on the high seas, yet the sight of this child had him quaking with fear all the way down to his toes.

What the hell did he know about being a father?

No time like the present to find out, he thought, wondering if he should rise and put on his shirt, or stay in the bed as he presently was with the covers pulled up to his chin.

The appearance of the child's nurse at the connecting door saved him from his dilemma, though she shrieked at the sight of Jagger in her mistress's bed.

He held his finger to his lips to silence the twit.

Her cheeks turned scarlet as she scurried forward and hustled the child from the room.

Jagger rose, quickly dressed, and followed them into Cecelie's chamber. The child stared at him through too-wide eyes, but she did not seem afraid. The nurse looked about to protest his presence, then seemed to remember that he was the master of the manor now.

She dipped a quick curtsy. "Sir?"

"What is your name?"

"Betsy, sir."

"Betsy, I wish to become better acquainted with my daughter. You may have the morning to yourself."

"I do not know, sir. Miss Treneham, I mean, Mrs. Remington does not like me to let Miss Cecelie out of my sight."

Mrs. Remington. He rather liked the sound of that. Almost as much as he liked the woman who wore the name. "Mrs. Remington is asleep. I do not wish her to be disturbed. I fear she gets precious little rest as it is."

The maid nodded vigorously. "You are so right, sir. Works her fingers to the bones, she does. But children must have their routine. Mrs. Remington would want me to wake her. She wants to know where the little miss is at all times. And we have a schedule—"

"I will leave Mrs. Remington a note informing her that Miss Cecelie is with me. You may resume your schedule at the noon hour." He summoned up a stern frown. He would not have the servants nay-saying him. "You are dismissed."

He waited for the nurse to leave the room before he crouched before Cecelie. "Would you like to join me for breakfast? Or have you already eaten?"

She stared at him, but said nothing.

He had no notion how well a child this young should speak, but it seemed as if she should be able to say something. "Can you not speak? Or are you teasing me?"

She stuck her finger in her mouth.

"You are a trifle old for that behavior, don't you think?" he asked reasonably.

She continued to suck on her finger, a defiant gleam in her eyes, daring him to stop her.

Jagger smiled. She may not speak, but the little minx understood everything he said to her. She had a proud, stubborn tilt to her chin, reminding him of her mother.

He was tempted to turn coward and run, but he had never hidden from a challenge. How hard could parenting be?

An hour later, Jagger was ready to concede defeat.

Breakfast was a disaster.

"Sit still in your chair," he said for what felt like the thousandth time.

She smiled at him sweetly, then kicked her feet so fast she spilled her milk. She grabbed her slice of ham with her hand and gnawed off a huge bite.

For a moment, Jagger feared she might choke, but she swallowed vigorously, then took another bite.

He glared at her sternly to let her know he meant what he said. "Young ladies must use their forks when they eat. Do you need help cutting your meat?"

The little imp stared him in the eye and purposely dropped her fork on the floor. She spilled the remainder of her milk on the table. She smeared blackberry jam all over her face as she ate her tart. All the while she stared at Jagger with a challenge in her eyes.

He no longer wondered why children were banished to the nursery. They needed to be locked up until they reached a far more civilized age.

He threw his napkin on the table as he walked to Cecelie's side. He dipped her linen in her glass of water, then knelt and wiped her hands. She watched him silently, her deep brown eyes curious, but not hostile. He was about to wipe her face when she leaned forward, threw her arms around his neck, and pressed a quick, sticky kiss against his scarred cheek.

By the time she sat back on her chair and smiled at him, Jagger was hopelessly in love.

Sophie awoke slowly. For the first time in months, or perhaps it was years, she felt rested, as if she had slept deeply and without dreams. She was loath to move, to banish this sense of serenity and peace, however fleeting it might be.

Memories of the night before drifted through her mind. Jagger Remington, her husband in name only, had cradled her in his arms. He had protected her from her demons, allowing her to drift off to sleep, secure and unafraid.

Wrapped in his protective embrace, she had never felt safer. Her lack of discretion should scandalize her, but it did not. Instead, she found herself longing for his presence, for the comfort of his arms.

Stretching languidly, she became aware of a slight stiffness in her shoulders and neck. How long had she slept?

She opened her eyes. Given the brightness of the sunlight in the room, she judged it to be late morning. A quick glance at the clock on the mantel confirmed her suspicions.

Her heart started to pound in her chest. Where was

Cecelie? Why hadn't she awakened her? They always ate their morning meal together. It was part of their routine, their ritual before Sophie started her chores for the day.

Trying to contain her panic, she leaped out of bed. She was still wearing the same simple black dress she'd worn the evening before, but she didn't bother to change her clothes.

"Cecelie?" she cried as she ran through the door that led to her daughter's bedchamber.

The room was empty. A quick glance told Sophie something was dreadfully wrong. All the dolls were picked up, the books neatly stacked, the tea set precisely arranged on the table.

"Do not panic," she scolded herself as her breathing quickened. "There is a perfectly reasonable explanation."

Then where is she?

Her inner demons reared their ugly heads, lashed her with their scathing accusations. *You should never have slept. Now you've lost her. Just as you lost your son.*

Sophie ran down the servants' stairs to the kitchen. She looked frantically about. No one was there.

The new housemaid emerged from the scullery. She carried a sack of potatoes in her arms. She took one look at Sophie's face, dropped the sack, and rushed across the room. "What is it, ma'am? What's wrong?"

Sophie could well imagine how wild she looked at the moment. She felt wild, like a feral animal ready to attack.

"Have you seen Cecelie? Have you seen my daughter?" Her words rushed from her throat, shrill and fast, but not nearly as fast as the beating of her heart.

"No, ma'am. But I—"

"Gather Mr. Remington's servants. I want my daughter found!"

"The men, they're out already, ma'am. They're searching still for the scoundrel that done the earl harm."

Stifling a cry with her fist, Sophie turned and ran down the hall. She tried to tell herself that there was a perfectly reasonable explanation. That Betsy had taken Cecelie on an outing to the village, or perhaps a stroll through the park.

But Betsy knew she was never to leave the manor with Cecelie without first telling Sophie where they were going. It was the primary rule of Betsy's employment. Sophie might not spend as much time with her child as she would like due to the demands of running an estate of this size with so few servants, but she always made certain she knew where Cecelie was.

She looked in the morning room, the blue salon, the dining room. Her worry turned to horror as an insidious thought burst through her consciousness. She ran to the front door.

"Sophie, what is wrong? You look a dreadful fright," Thea said as she descended the stairs. It seemed she had finally decided to emerge from her room just in time to issue a scathing rebuke on Sophie's continued lack of proper decorum.

Sophie was too worried to care. Blood rushed to her head.

She swayed on her feet as she grasped Thea's hands. "Have you seen Cecelie?"

Thea's expression rapidly changed from one of stern disapproval to one that looked very much like worry and concern. It plunged another knife of guilt through Sophie's heart. Had she misjudged Thea all this time? Did Thea care about this makeshift family, of which she was a part, after all?

Thea wrapped both her hands around Sophie's. "Cecelie is missing?"

Sophie nodded. "I cannot find her. I know I am worrying over nothing. I know she must be with Betsy, but I do not know where they are. I do not understand it. Betsy knows that she is never to leave this house without telling me."

Thea's fingers tightened around Sophie's. "I saw Betsy

over an hour ago, from my bedchamber window. She was speaking with your brother, Lord Hallowell. They were walking down the carriage drive. She held a basket over her arm, as if she were going to the village."

Sophie nodded. "And Cecelie was with her?"

Thea shook her head. "No. She was not. Come. I will help you search."

"The stables," Sophie said as memories of another night, another frantic search, tried to steal her ability to reason.

Together they ran out the door and down the steps.

Sophie was grateful for Thea's company. She was terrified of what she might find.

Nonsense, she scolded herself. Cecelie was in perfect health last night. Why would she be in danger today?

They nearly bumped into Mary as she came running around the corner of the house. "How can I help?"

"Run into the village," Sophie said. "If Betsy is there, bring her home. I want answers."

Mary nodded and raced down the carriage drive.

Sophie lifted her skirts and ran. By the time she reached the stables, she had a cramp in her side. Her legs were shaking so hard she could barely support herself. She searched each stall. They were empty. The village youth who helped with the horses must have turned them out early today.

Sophie stumbled out of the stables. She collapsed against the wall, bent over to catch her breath. Blackness dimmed her vision. Despair threatened to choke her.

Could Cecelie have gone to the pond?

The thought tore through Sophie like a blade. What if she'd fallen into the water? What if she'd drowned?

She pushed off the wall, stumbled toward the wooded path across the lawn. A sound caught her attention. It sounded like a shriek of alarm. A very feminine, childish shriek.

Sophie lifted her head, straining to hear from which

direction it came, trying to still the panic gripping her chest.

She glanced to the left. Coming around the corner of the stables was Jagger Remington. He was walking beside Jack, the Welsh pony, leading strings firmly grasped in his hands, and on the animal's back sat her daughter, looking for all the world like a ragamuffin. She was covered in dust. She had what looked to be jam on her face, but what froze Sophie in place and sucked the breath from her lungs was the picture of pure joy on her daughter's face and the childish squeal of laughter emanating from her mouth.

They had yet to notice her. Sophie stood paralyzed as she watched Jagger drop the reins and hold his hands up to Cecelie. She watched as her daughter threw her arms around Jagger's neck and leapt into his arms. She watched as he swung Cecelie around, her feet flying out behind her, her shriek of laughter floating on the gentle breeze. The sound was more precious to Sophie than the crown jewels to the royal family.

She felt Thea's hand encircle her arm in a firm grip of reassurance. Sophie must have made a noise, for both Jagger and Cecelie turned to look at her in unison.

An expression of astonishment, or perhaps it was shock at her disheveled appearance, crossed his face. He walked toward her with long, purposeful strides. This handsome man with her child in his arms. Her laughing child. Her darling daughter, who, for two long years, had not uttered a sound.

Chapter Fourteen

Jagger thought the steward's office a dull, uninviting room. *Closet* was a better word to describe it, given its small size, lack of windows, and distance from the main chambers of the manor. The single candle on the corner of the desk gave off more smoke than light. A lone rickety chair faced the desk.

The air was hot and thick. The lumpy, upholstered chair upon which Jagger sat behind the desk was not level with the floor. Every time he moved, it tilted back and forth like a boat tossed about by the waves.

As he closed the last of the account books, Jagger sighed. Given the sad state of the manor, he had expected bad news, but even he could not have anticipated the extent to which this property had been mismanaged.

Rubbing his hands over his face, he rocked back on his chair. He should be well on his way to London by now, but after this morning's debacle, he could not bring himself to leave. Nor could he erase from his mind the image of Sophie's terror-stricken face as he had come upon her at the stables.

Never had he seen an expression so filled with sorrow, with desolation, with suffering and fear. Never had he witnessed such depth of emotion, such a deep and abiding love of a mother for her child. While Jagger knew that his mother had loved him as best she could, she had stood, complicit in her silence, to the brutality his father had heaped upon him on a daily basis.

Jagger had no doubt that Sophie would never allow anyone to hurt her child, just as he now believed that she had refused to name her seducer to keep the bounder away from her child. It was the only explanation that made any sense. Rather than put her daughter's life at risk, she had chosen a path that left her ridiculed and scorned by all proper society.

Of course, he could be wrong in his assumptions, but, given his new understanding of how deeply a parent could love a child, how deeply he loved her child, Jagger didn't think that he was.

The depth of Jagger's feelings stunned him, as did the rapidity with which Cecelie had stolen his heart. He knew without a doubt that he would kill anyone who attempted to harm his wife or his child. They were a family now. His family.

God, how he liked the sound of that.

From the moment he had met Sophie, he had admired her courage and her indomitable strength of will. His admiration had grown with each passing day, but now Jagger realized he was dangerously close to falling in love with her. Perhaps he was in love with her already. He wasn't quite certain because he didn't know how it should feel. He had never even believed it existed, much less expected to find it in his life.

How had this happened?

As a child, he learned to guard his emotions. As he grew to a man, he learned to depend solely upon himself. Oh, he had his share of friends and business associates, but he kept everyone at a distance, careful not to allow anyone past his defenses. To care was to suffer. Now his chances of suffering had increased dramatically, for he very much feared he was, indeed, in love with his wife.

"What do you think you are doing?"

The object of his affection came marching into the room. Gone was the vulnerable woman from this morning, replaced by a proud warrior prepared to do battle to protect her territory.

She wore a simple black dress that accentuated her beautiful brown eyes. At the moment, those eyes were narrowed in a fearsome scowl. Her mahogany hair was neatly pulled into a knot at her nape. Her cheeks bore a rosy glow, no doubt from the wrath she was about to unleash upon his head.

God, she was magnificent in her fury.

She marched to the desk. "I asked you a question. What are you doing here?"

He rose from his chair. He wanted to take her into his arms and kiss her into insensibility, but the angle at which she held her chin, the slant in her eyes, and the stiffness in her posture warned him now was not the time.

She slapped her palms upon the desk. "Who gave you permission to rummage through my papers?"

He breathed deeply. He would not allow her to provoke him into an argument, though she seemed clearly bent on having one.

"You could not even wait until Stephen was cold in his grave, could you?" Her voice was scathing.

His brows shot up. "I beg your pardon?"

She crossed her arms over her chest. "A fortune hunter through and through."

Jagger stifled the urge to laugh. So, they were back to that argument, were they? "Were I a fortune hunter, madam," he said quietly, "I would have done better to marry any other spinster in the country. Your books are a mess and your 'fortune' is nonexistent."

She made a low sound in her throat that resembled a growl. "You do not know what you are talking about."

"I know that half your tenant farmers abandoned their properties last year."

"There were reasons."

"I know that you reduced the rents of those who remained to practically nothing and forgave the debt of those in arrears."

He came around the desk, hitched his hip on the edge. "A particularly amazing gesture considering there is no money in the household accounts, which, in and of itself, is a mystery, given the sums your land agent claims to have collected. Where is that man? I have more than a few questions to put to him."

Sophie sniffed. "That might be a trifle difficult, as he has absconded with the rents and the servants' pay, amongst other nefarious deeds. A typical male. He swore fealty while practicing deception."

"Why has he not been arrested and your funds returned to you?" Jagger held up his hand. "Do not bother to answer. Let me guess. That incompetent fool of a magistrate cannot find him. No doubt he could not find his own arse were it not where he stores his brain."

Sophie stared at him, her eyes wide, then she laughed.

It was the first time Jagger had heard her laugh, spontaneously and with genuine mirth. It was a sweet sound, like wind chimes tinkling in the breeze. He was inordinately proud of himself for having amused her.

"That is the most ridiculous phrase I have ever heard," she said, still laughing. "For it does not make any sense."

She should laugh more often, he decided, even if she were only laughing at him. "It was the best I could do on such short notice and with no access to my manly manual of witty phrases. I have never been known for my eloquence."

"Oh, I highly doubt that," she said, obviously trying to contain her grin. "Though you should not curse in front of me. It is impolite."

Jagger sketched her a courtly bow. "I am heartily sorry to have offended you, madam."

She dropped into a deep curtsy, as if she were being presented to the king. "I forgive you, kind sir."

She was teasing him. They were making progress.

He took her hand in his and raised her to her feet. Staring into her eyes, he lifted her fingertips to his lips.

Her smile vanished. Her eyes seemed to darken as she gazed at him. She did not protest as he turned her hand and kissed the underside of her wrist. Her skin was soft and warm and held the delicate scent of roses. He wanted to pull her into his arms and kiss her with all the fervor of his desire, but he did not want to scare her away.

She took a step back, as if putting distance between them would break the spell of their mutual attraction.

"Mr. Remington," she said, her voice breathless and low.

He rubbed his thumb over her palm. "Must we stand on such ceremony? After all, we are married. We will spend the remainder of our lives together. Could you not call me Jagger, at least when we are private?"

She pulled her hand from his grasp.

He held his breath.

A long moment passed.

"Jagger," she said, her voice husky with what he hoped was desire. His name had never sounded so sweet to his ears. He wished she would say it again. He wanted her to moan his name as he possessed her body, as he possessed her soul.

He wanted her to love him.

"May we not cry peace?" he asked gently. "May we not work together as partners in this marriage, rather than adversaries out to do each other harm?"

She pursed her lips and raised her brows in an I-don't-know-you-and-I-don't-trust-you look. Any other woman would appear a shrew, but her expression only added to her allure. If he kissed those lips, would she swoon or slap his face?

They had shared a kiss by the pond, a kiss like no other kiss he had ever shared with any other woman.

Had she not regained her control, he had no doubt he would have ravished her right there, soaked to the skin, surrounded by mud and flies, with the hot sun beating on his backside.

Bloody hell! Why had he ever agreed to a marriage in name only? It was the last thing he wanted, especially when she was staring at his lips as if she could read his mind.

"You make it sound easy," she said.

"It is easy." He held out his hand. "If we each surrender some of our pride. If we take the first step."

She hesitated, then reached out her hand.

He shook it as if he were sealing a business arrangement.

"Partners," he said.

She smiled tentatively. "I rather like the sound of that."

"As do I." He grinned at her. "We are treading on dangerous ground, you know."

She quirked a brow.

"We might actually find ourselves crying friends."

"I do not believe we are in any danger of that," she said archly. Then she laughed.

Jagger let the soft, delicate sound wash over him. He was acting like a lovelorn fool, but the knowledge didn't stop him from grinning like an idiot.

He knew two things for certain. He was definitely falling in love with his wife, and he wanted her to love him, too.

He would have to win her love. No doubt he would have to woo her and court her. There was only one problem with his plan. He didn't know the first thing about wooing and courting.

As he'd never intended to marry, he hadn't bothered to learn the fine art of flirting and flattering. Now he wished he'd paid more attention to the twittering debutantes and marriage-minded misses who flooded into Calcutta each year.

Reluctantly, he released her hand to pull the chair from behind the desk. He arranged the two chairs so that they faced one another, then guided her to the taller of the pair.

He waited for her to sit before taking his seat. Placing his hands on his knees, he leaned forward to bring himself to her eye level. "Let us discuss the estate."

She stared at him suspiciously, as if he were setting a trap. "What would you like to discuss?"

"For one thing, I would like to understand why you so drastically reduced the rents. With your lack of ready money, it doesn't make any sense."

"I could not let my tenants starve." Her voice implied that she held his intelligence to be lower than a toad's.

He pursed his lips to keep from grinning. "How, pray tell, would paying rents in keeping with the value of their land cause them to starve?"

She folded her hands on her lap. "From what my tenants have told me and my audit of the books, I have now deduced that, through the years, Mr. Danvers manipulated the rents and made charges against the estate for improvements to tenant farms that were never implemented. Then he pocketed the difference."

"Not such an uncommon scheme," Jagger murmured, wondering why Stephen would not have caught on to the embezzlement before too much damage was done.

"I certainly know that *now*. However, the tenants had reached a point where they could no longer afford their rents and make a profit on their farms—not to mention last summer's disastrous weather that wreaked havoc on their crops, and the variability of market prices. Many of them were falling behind with no hope of catching up."

She paused. He took her hand in his, gave her fingers a reassuring squeeze. "Go on."

"Most of my tenants are tenants-at-will. As you've already noted, several of them abandoned their farms to seek work in the factories."

"So you forgave the others their rents in arrears to entice them to stay?"

She nodded. "Yes. Then I lowered their rents for the upcoming year. I will still receive enough to pay the taxes on the estate and provide for absolute necessities. It is a temporary arrangement, agreeable to all parties. Once my tenants recover their footing, we will renegotiate the rents more in line with the value of the land, and the estate will turn profitable again. I knew I would have to struggle for a year or two, but the long-term benefit outweighs any inconvenience I might suffer now."

If Stephen Treneham were still alive, Jagger would thrash the man. How could the bastard have left the country and abandoned his sister to such a desperate situation?

Jagger didn't speak for fear his anger would reverberate in his voice and she would mistakenly think it directed at her.

"You must not blame my brother," she said, as if she had read his mind. "He was unaware of Mr. Danvers's treachery."

"I cannot imagine how that is so."

"I gather he bought this estate on a whim, but he never really cared for it. He simply let Mr. Danvers continue on the job as he'd always performed it and never checked the books. Then, when he gave the estate to me . . ."

She trailed off, but Jagger heard the shame in her voice. She thought she was to blame for this debacle.

Her hands seemed so small and fragile compared to his, yet her palms were work-worn and covered with calluses. She was too young to have suffered so much.

She tilted her chin in the air, a gesture that was becoming as dear to Jagger as it was familiar.

"I do not require nor welcome your sympathy, Mr. Remington," she said.

"We are back to formality, then, Mrs. Remington?"

She shuddered. Was it the use of her married name?

Did she hate his name as much as she seemed to hate him? Or was it something else? She had yet to remove her hand from his grasp.

Perhaps she didn't hate him as much as she claimed.

"It is true that I have had to economize," she said briskly. "I dismissed most of the servants—especially the men, as they are taxed—and I closed off most of the house, which certainly was no hardship, and made the cleaning easier. And I was not completely without 'ready money.' I sold some of my belongings, though nothing to which I was overly attached."

The swiftness with which she uttered her last words convinced Jagger that she had parted with something very dear to her heart.

"My tenants were extremely happy."

"I do not doubt it," he said, trying to attend to her words, but more interested in the subtle shades of emotion flitting across her face as she spoke.

"Several of my tenants offered to tend a smaller portion of the home farm, for a share in the profits. Since I could not afford to pay the workers, and I could not tend the fields myself, I thought it a reasonable request. The remainder of the fields will lie fallow this year, thereby increasing its yield next year. We will all benefit, provided the harvest is good. Although I must confess, I did indulge and retain the dairymaids. I had no desire to milk the cows."

She scrunched up her nose as she said it. "Not that I am incapable of milking the cows, mind you."

It was such an unexpected and entirely missish confession, that Jagger laughed. "I do not doubt it for a moment."

When she smiled at him, she looked so utterly feminine and attractive and desirable, it was all he could do not to drag her into his arms and kiss her breathless.

Somehow he managed to keep himself firmly settled on his chair. His mind might not be functioning at full capacity, but in his new campaign to win her love, he knew he must bide his time. What would she do if he kissed her?

"Brilliant," he said, and she smiled so brightly, it was as if the sun had fallen into the room.

She was a most desirable woman, and not completely averse to him. He had learned that when first he'd kissed her by the pond. Many times since, he had longed to reignite the passion of that moment. He longed to hold her in his arms, to make her moan beneath him as he thrust to the deepest center of her womanhood. He had promised her chastity. Now he burned with desire. The solution was obvious. He only hoped he had the patience to proceed carefully so as not to scare her away.

"I must travel to London on business," he said. "I have put it off as long as possible. We leave at first light."

"We?"

"Of course. I would like you to accompany me."

"Absolutely not." She pulled her hand from his and shot to her feet as if her chair had suddenly caught fire.

So much for not scaring her away.

Chapter Fifteen

Jagger rose from his chair. "Why not? It would give us a chance to become better acquainted." He raised his hand to ward off her argument. "While I conduct business, you could visit some of the fashionable shops."

"I have no desire to shop. There is nothing I need. Even if there were, I can find it in the village."

"You could visit a mantua-maker and commission a new wardrobe," he said as he remembered his business associates' constant grumbling about their wives and their clothing bills. Besides, she seemed to own nothing but rags, and those were not even suitable for the lowest scullery maid.

She clasped her hands together, held them at her waist. "There is a perfectly good seamstress in the village."

"But does she have the latest fashion plates?"

He longed to see her in something elegant. Something soft and creamy to caress her skin the way he wanted to run his hands over the contours of her flesh. Damn and hell, he had an erection.

And she was heading for the door.

He pushed himself in front of her.

She stared at him as if he were a bothersome insect she wanted to swat away. "I cannot go to London."

"Of course you can.

"I cannot leave Cecelie."

"I never suggested you leave her. Naturally she would accompany us. We are a family now."

We are a family now.

Thank goodness he did not know how seductive those words were to her. Like forbidden fruit, they beckoned her, dared her to throw caution to the wind and plunge headlong into darkness and danger. She would not, could not, follow that path.

"I could insist," he said in that deep husky voice of his that sent shivers of awareness and need down her spine.

Sophie tried to dredge up some of the anger she'd felt toward this man mere days ago, but she failed miserably.

All she could see was her daughter sitting on the pony's back, smiling and laughing at the man who now called himself Cecelie's father.

Still, Sophie would not stand idly by while he presumed to order her around. She crossed her arms over her chest. "Yes, I suppose you could. You could fling me over your shoulder and toss me into the carriage against my will. You are, after all, the man, and I am merely the woman, with no identity of my own. How silly of me to forget. I have not yet learned to meekly accept my new position and your authority over me."

"Sarcasm does not become you," he said quietly and more gently than she deserved.

Her shoulders sagged as the steam flowed out of her as quickly as it arrived. She owed this man more than he could possibly imagine for breaking her daughter's prison of silence. But, more than anything, she owed him the truth.

"I am sorry," she said, forcing her shoulders back and straightening her spine. Inside, she might be an emotional wreck, but she refused to allow anyone to know it. "I truly did not seek you out to argue with you."

"Why did you seek me out?"

The dratted man smiled at her again, setting her insides to quivering and her heart to racing. If only he knew how susceptible she was to his smile. How it beguiled her, tempted her to trace his lips with her fingertips, to cradle her palm against his cheek, to draw him near and kiss him. How she longed to know his secrets, to soothe away old wounds and disappointments, to build a future with this man.

As much as she wished it weren't true, he was her husband. She was his wife. He was right. Their futures were intertwined. They could continue as enemies, or they could be partners. Perhaps even friends. All she had to do was take a chance. She knew this was true. Then why was she so afraid?

As she stared into his perceptive blue eyes, she wished she could read his mind.

"Why did you seek me out?" he asked again, breaking the lingering silence.

This was her moment to decide. She could take a chance, commit to this marriage, build a future with this man. Or she could continue down the path she had treaded these four years past. Years of loneliness and despair.

Yet, he had no notion of what it was he was seeking, of who she was, of what she had done. Perhaps it was time to share a few of the less sordid, but more shameful, details of her life.

She took a deep breath. "This morning, when I could not find Cecelie, I panicked."

Jagger swore under his breath. "Did you not find my note?"

"I did not take the time to notice it. Cecelie comes into my room every morning. I pretend to be sleeping. She jumps on the bed to awaken me. It is our morning routine."

He winced. "I am sorry. I asked the maid to let you sleep. I told her I would leave a note."

"Which I found when I returned to my room—"

She pressed her hand to her mouth. Could she find the courage to confess her deepest sin?

She closed her eyes, turned her thoughts to the darkest night of her life, thoughts she fought to suppress every moment of every day. After all this time, it amazed her how unprepared she was for the pain.

Her stomach ached. Her knees felt weak, as if she would double over or fall into a faint, but she squared her shoulders and forced herself to remain on her feet.

He wrapped his hand around her arm, silently offering his strength. When she opened her eyes, she saw the concern darkening his eyes and creasing his brow.

"Whatever it is, you need not say it."

She drew a deep breath. "Yes. I must. I owe you a debt of gratitude."

His brows shot up. "I cannot imagine what I have done to earn your gratitude after scaring you half to death."

"You made my daughter laugh."

He furrowed his brow as if her words confused him.

"Mr. Remington—Jagger—I have not heard my daughter speak, or laugh, or cry, or make any other sound that normal children make, in over two years."

She held up her hand to keep him from speaking. She needed to say this as quickly as possible. "Perhaps you may have already heard—I have had not one child, but two."

He squeezed her arm reassuringly, but he did not reply.

Of course he had heard. No doubt the villagers had eagerly told him the tale.

"I had twins," she said. "A boy and a girl."

She took a step away from him, pulled her elbow from his grasp. This was hard enough without his sympathy.

She rubbed her hands up and down her arms.

Twins! Sophie had not believed her good fortune. She'd thought God had doubly blessed her, despite her sin and the failings of her faith. But she was wrong.

She bit her lip, rolled her hands into fists. "My son

was a weak child from the moment of his birth, mere minutes before his sister's entrance into the world."

He had merely whimpered, whereas Cecelie had burst upon the scene screaming loud enough to scare the birds from the trees.

"What was his name?" Jagger asked, his voice rough with sympathy. Or was it condemnation she heard?

"Colin."

She rubbed her fingertips over her forehead as if she could ease the pain of her memories. "Cecelie raced through the milestones of infancy. Her first tooth. Her first steps. Her first words. By her first birthday, she could carry on a conversation worthy of a society dame. But not Colin. He walked late, talked late. His eyes seemed somewhat vague, and he often did not appear to understand what I said."

"But you loved him."

"Of course I did. What kind of mother would I be if I did not?" From the moment of their birth, she loved them both with a passion of which she had never imagined herself capable, a passion that could never be described in words.

"Despite her advanced capabilities, Cecelie clung to her brother. They looked to each other from the moment they first opened their eyes each morning. They babbled to one another in a language only they could understand."

"They were two halves of the same whole," he said simply.

She nodded, amazed at his words, amazed that he seemed to understand. "Shortly before Stephen left England, he presented them with a Welsh pony, which Cecelie promptly named Jack because Jackstraws was Colin's favorite game."

The memory brought a sad smile to her lips. "How he loved that pony. 'Ride' was the first word out of his mouth in the morning and the last word before he went to sleep each night. Even in the midst of the fever that killed him, even when delirium set in, he never stopped talking about that pony."

She laced her fingers together to keep her hands from trembling. "For three days, I kept vigil at his side." She had bathed him, spooned broth and medicines into his mouth. "But he never awakened. I never heard the sound of his sweet voice again—"

She choked as a violent shudder coursed through her.

Jagger reached out to take her in his arms.

She flung herself away, crossed to the other side of the room. She turned to face him, her back pressed tightly against the wall. "That night, I fell asleep. I awoke to Cecelie tugging on my hand and an empty bed before my eyes. I called Betsy to tend Cecelie so I could search the house, but Cecelie thrashed against the servant and would not calm down. She grabbed my hand and tugged me toward the door."

Sophie wrapped her arms around her waist as if she could somehow ward off the chill seeping into her bones. "I followed her to the kitchen and out into the garden. The night was dark and cold. No moon. No stars. A freezing rain. Cecelie pulled on my hand until I finally understood what she was trying to tell me. I dropped Cecelie's hand and started to run. When I reached the stables, the door was open."

For a moment, she had simply stood there and stared at the door as it swung to and fro, buffeted by the wind, as if performing some sort of macabre dance. She could still smell the damp hay. She could still hear the wind as it howled through the rafters.

"I could just make out the shape of Jack lying on the hay. The next flash of lightning revealed the body of my son nestled into the warmth of the pony's flesh."

Surprisingly, Sophie had found herself unable to move. She had stood as stiff as a marble statue. It was as if time had stopped and she was watching the world pass by her in a dream.

"Cecelie raced into the barn." Her soaked nightdress had clung to her tender skin. Her thick brown hair had escaped the confines of its plait. It whipped across her face.

Amazingly, the pony had remained on the straw, as if trying to shelter Colin from the storm.

"Cecelie knelt beside Colin. She took his hand, turned her tear-streaked face to look at me, silently imploring me to save her brother's life. But he was already dead."

Someone had screamed. Sophie thought it might have been her, but she couldn't be certain. She had felt so detached from the commotion around her. She had stumbled forward, fallen to the ground. The stone floor must have hurt her knees, for she'd had cuts and bruises that lingered for weeks, but she hadn't felt it. She'd felt nothing but her overwhelming sense of loss and her greatest failure.

"While my son was fighting for his life, I fell asleep—"

The screams and sobs Sophie continuously fought to suppress came dangerously close to escaping. Her throat ached with the tension of gritting her teeth. If not for her daughter, Sophie was certain she would lay down and die. But she couldn't.

She had to struggle her way through every day. For Cecelie. For her daughter. Her only surviving child.

She lifted her gaze to his. "So you see, Mr. Remington, I owe you a great debt. Cecelie has not spoken a word or made a sound since the night that Colin died. That is—until today."

Jagger's first instinct was to gather her into his arms, but he forced himself to remain motionless. He sensed if he moved, she would bolt from the room.

He watched as she fought to regain her composure. She straightened her shoulders, rolled her lips between her teeth, drew a deep breath. She had suffered too much in her young life. Jagger clenched his fists as fury ripped through him. He wanted to pummel all those who had failed to protect her.

She lifted her chin. "'Tis a poor bargain with which my

brother has saddled you, Mr. Remington. I am as unfit to be a mother as I am to be a wife. Not only that, in my grief, I allowed my estate manager to rob me blind."

"You blame yourself for your son's death." It was not an accusation or a condemnation, but a statement of fact.

She nodded once. "Naturally."

"How so?" He forced a casual indifference into his voice that he did not feel. He had no doubt that if he showed any signs of the raw, aching emotions tightening his chest, she would shut down this conversation and retreat into the safety of silence. "We have already established that you loved your son."

"Of course I loved him. How could I not?"

"Many a mother does not, I assure you. Did you neglect him?"

"No."

"Fail to feed him, or clothe him, or nurse him?"

"Certainly not."

"Then what is your crime?"

"I fell asleep!"

"After three days of constant nursing."

"You do not understand."

"I understand more than you think I do." He understood the power of guilt. He had spent years wallowing in the muck at his failure to protect his mother from his father's cruelty.

"I failed them both! First I let Colin die, then I caused my daughter to lose her ability to speak!"

His brows shot up. "You 'let' Colin die? 'Tis a mighty arrogance you have indeed if you believe you control who lives and who dies. I thought that was the job of the Almighty."

He could almost see the steam gathering behind her eyes.

"You are an exasperating man. You are deliberately misinterpreting what I have said."

"Do you want to know what I heard in your story?" His

voice cracked as his emotions seeped through his defenses. But he faced her without shame. His heart ached for all that she'd suffered. For all that she suffered still.

"No. I do not," she said, staring at her hands.

"I heard the agony of a mother whose child has died. I heard the pain of a woman who is struggling to make sense of this tragedy, and the only way she can do that is to blame herself. It was not your fault."

Her face twisted into a mask of bitter agony. "How can you say that? Of course it was my fault. I fell asleep when my son *needed* me!"

"By your logic, am I now to believe that you are also responsible for your brother's death? After all, you nursed him through his injuries, yet he died just the same."

She flung her hands out. "Do not twist my words. It is not the same situation. Stephen was killed by footpads."

"And your son suffered a fever. As I understand, it is a common childhood ailment, and many children die from it."

She closed her eyes. She shook her head.

Jagger had never seen such a look of utter despair, of utter defeat and inconsolable suffering.

"You do not understand," she said as she opened her eyes and looked directly at him, and directly through him. "Or you are being intentionally obtuse."

She crossed her arms over her chest. Jagger could almost envision the protective armor she was drawing around her, the weapons she wielded against her pain. Her pride and her indomitable spirit. Her self-avowed independence.

"I owe you my thanks for freeing Cecelie of her silence," she said in a voice devoid of all emotion. "I can now only hope that she will soon speak again. You may rest assured as you leave here that you have more than admirably fulfilled your obligations to my brother."

He almost smiled. "And where am I going?"

She lifted her chin. "To London, of course. To resume your life as you lived it before my brother so underhandedly snatched it away. While there, you may seek out an annulment."

"Why would I want to do that?"

"Mr. Remington," she said, "do not trifle with me. I have no intention of holding you to the promises my brother blackmailed out of you."

"Ah, but there we differ, *Mrs. Remington*. I have every intention of holding you to the vows you made before God and several prominent witnesses."

"Whatever for?"

Because I love you, he wanted to shout, and he knew deep in his heart his words would be true, just as he knew now was not the time to declare himself. She would never believe him. He would have to prove his feelings to her while winning her love.

"Because I believe we suit each other perfectly," he said.

She harrumphed. "You deserve a wife who wants you, not a woman dragged into the match through treachery and deceit."

"You want me," he whispered in a husky voice, filled with all the desire in his heart.

She blushed. This proud, spirited beauty actually sported bright patches of color on her cheeks, a fetching sight indeed. The moment passed quickly, and her features closed tightly.

"You must want children, Mr. Remington. Every man wants children of his own blood to carry on his name and inherit his worldly possessions."

"It has never been a high priority on my list."

"You are not listening to me. I will not give you children. I cannot."

"You already have. You have given me a wonderful daughter, whom I love as if she were my own—"

"No," she cried. She started to shake. She clutched her

hands together. Her eyes turned glassy. "You do not understand," she whispered brokenly. "I will never bear you a child. I will never bear another child. Never."

He did give in to temptation, then. He pulled her into his arms. She balled her fists against his chest, pushed with all of her strength, but he planted one hand in the middle of her back. He slid his other hand into her hair. He cradled her head against his shoulder.

"It was not your fault," he whispered against her ear.

She shivered in his arms, as if cold to the bones. She banged her fists against his shoulders, made a half-hearted attempt to twist free of his grasp.

"It was not your fault," he said, running his hand up and down her back.

She stood stiff in his arms, as if she were afraid to move lest she unleash her unbearable grief. She made a choked sound. Her shoulders heaved with her desperate attempt not to cry.

"It was not your fault," he whispered, pressing a kiss against her temple, rubbing his cheek against her brow.

Her soft skin was wet with silent tears that soaked through his shirt and burned his chest. The silent sobs racking her body hurt him more deeply than a punch to his ribs. He wanted to ease her pain, to take her sorrow into himself, to free her from her senseless guilt, her desperate remorse.

All he could do was hold her as she cried.

Chapter Sixteen

Sophie did not protest as he scooped her into his arms and headed for the door. Shivering in his embrace, she buried her face against his neck, burrowed into the warmth of his hard, unyielding chest. There was something oddly comforting in the spicy, exotic scent that he wore, in the heat of his neck against the coldness of her skin.

He carried her up the stairs as if she weighed no more than a candle, but he was the light at the end of her darkness, her sanity in the midst of this terrible storm.

She should put up a struggle, she told herself as he pushed open the door to her room, but her sorrow was trying to devour her, to sink her into madness and despair. She wanted the comfort he offered, even if it lasted no more than this moment.

Her darling child, her son, had died as she'd slept.

He'd died alone. In the dark. In the rain.

She had carried the guilt of that moment locked in the deepest part of her mind. She had known the pain of these memories would devour her should she ever unleash them.

Now they were out in the open. Though the pain was tremendous, the strength that Jagger Remington offered glimmered like a beacon of light through the shadows of hell.

He knelt on the bed, gently slipped her back against the pillows. She felt his arms slide out from beneath her.

She clutched his shoulders. "Please."

She hated the pathetic whimper in her voice, but the thought of him retreating left her empty and cold.

He stretched out beside her, dragged her into his arms. "I want you to say it."

"I don't know what you mean." She turned her face into his shoulder, burying her eyes in his shirt.

He would not let her hide. His hands gripped her hair. He stared into her eyes. "It was not your fault. I want you to say it."

Her vision blurred as tears gathered once again. It was hard to believe that, until this moment, she had never cried. Now she could not seem to stop.

"Say it," he growled.

"It was not my fault," she whispered brokenly.

"Again. Say it louder."

"It was not my fault."

"Say it as though you believe it."

"It was not my fault. It was not my fault. It was not my fault." She finally screamed the words.

She stared at him as he caressed her cheeks. He used his thumbs to wipe away the trail of her tears.

"It was not my fault," she whispered as if hearing the words for the very first time and finally believing them.

It was not her fault. She had loved her son. She had fought to keep him alive. She had bargained with God to take her life and to spare her son's, but Colin had died and she had lived and sunk into darkness, blinded by pain.

She cradled her cheek against his shoulder. She snuggled closer into his side. She cried until she was certain she couldn't possibly produce any more tears, then she cried some more. She cried until her head ached and her throat throbbed, and all the while, he held her in his arms, kissed her forehead, rubbed her back, and whispered words of comfort and hope until the storm finally passed.

Sophie slowly opened her eyes and found herself staring into the clear blue gaze of her husband. She wanted to close them again, to hide from the shame of her behavior, but she had never been a coward.

"I fell asleep," she whispered, her voice sounding hoarse from the dry ache in her throat.

He nodded and his thick black hair fell into his eyes.

She stretched out her hand. She hesitated a moment, then brushed the silky strands from his brow.

He caught her wrist, cradled her palm against his cheek.

The day's growth of beard darkening his chin felt rough against her sensitive fingertips. She studied his face, the solid outline of his jaw, the high planes of his cheeks, the puckered skin beneath his eye. How had he gotten that scar?

With a sudden sense of shame, she realized there was so much about this man that she did not know, had not cared to ask or bothered to learn. Where did he come from? Was there a woman he loved? Had Stephen's ruthless scheme stolen his dreams? He was as much a victim of her brother's treachery as she was, and she had treated him shabbily, like a beggar on the streets.

Concern furrowed his brow. "How do you feel?"

She could well imagine how horrible she looked, eyes as puffed up as a frog, nose as red as hot coals. She tried to smile, but knew it was a poor attempt.

"Thirsty," she said. "And drained."

He rolled off the bed. His frock coat was rumpled, his cravat crushed beyond repair, but he had never looked more handsome. He poured a glass of water from the pitcher on the bedside table, then held it to her lips.

Wrapping her hand around his, she drank in great

gulps of the cool, soothing liquid. When the glass was empty, he set it on the table, climbed onto the bed, and gathered her into his arms. They lay on their sides, face-to-face, eye-to-eye.

Her hair had escaped its pins. It puffed around her face, tickling her cheeks. Her eyes ached from the ferocity of her tears. Tears she had buried inside her for two long years.

Why had she surrendered her control to this man? How had he penetrated her defenses so easily? She was not ready to probe for the answers. She was afraid of what she might discover lurking in her mind.

"How long have I slept?"

"An hour. Maybe two."

And all that time, he had cradled her in his arms.

She tried not to read more into his actions than common concern, but she knew it was a lie. She saw the fire burning in the depths of his eyes. She felt the strength of his support in the power of his arms wrapped around her like protective bands, securing her at his side, shielding her from harm.

"Thank you," she said. She rubbed her palm over his cheek, rubbed her thumb over his lips. They were moist and soft.

She remembered the heat of his mouth against hers, the power of his kiss to render her spellbound. She was playing with fire. She should remove her hand. She should put a proper distance between them. A safe distance. But she couldn't move.

As if reading her mind, or perhaps reacting to her touch, his eyes darkened. His gaze remained fixed on hers, but he did not move. Slowly, she inched closer to him until her breasts pressed tightly against his chest.

He inhaled sharply. She moistened her lips with the tip of her tongue. His gaze dropped to her mouth. Sensual heat flared in his eyes. Still he remained motionless, but a low sound escaped his throat. Or perhaps it was hers.

Instinctively, she knew that he would neither help her nor hinder her. She and she alone controlled this moment. If she kissed him, she would do so of her own free will, with no recriminations and no regrets.

Suddenly, he rolled to his side.

She caught her cry of protest in her throat mere moments before she realized the door had snapped opened and Cecelie was flying across the room. She leapt onto the bed, her childish laughter bouncing off the walls and filling Sophie's heart with aching tenderness. Cecelie flung her arms around Jagger's neck, pressed a quick, sloppy kiss to his cheek, then bounced off his chest and landed half on Sophie, half on Jagger, as if she didn't want to favor one over the other. Laughing all the while, she wiggled and bounced until Jagger scooted aside, allowing her enough room to stretch out between them.

Sophie stared at her daughter, a heart-rending ache building in her chest. Once, she had despaired of ever hearing her daughter's sweet voice again.

A fresh batch of tears blurred her vision. After the torrent of grief she'd unleashed in Jagger's arms mere hours ago, Sophie would never have imagined she had any more tears to shed, yet a steady stream of liquid trailed a path down her cheeks, despite her efforts to stop the flow.

She did not want to frighten her daughter. She did not want to stop the laughter that was sweet music to her ears. She glanced desperately at Jagger and found him watching her, his eyes somber even as he laughed at Cecelie's antics.

He scooped the child into his arms, turned so she faced away from the bed. "Madam, I have promised our daughter an adventure. The afternoon is fine and I hope you will join us."

Our daughter. His words sent a treacherous shiver of longing though her core. Could he truly love Cecelie as if she were his own? Could they be a family in truth, in spite of the lies and manipulations that had thrust them together?

She pressed her shaking fingers to her lips. She breathed deeply until she was convinced she could speak without choking.

"It would be my pleasure," she managed before crushing her fist against her lips to stifle the sobs racing up her throat.

He nodded. A heartbeat later, he was gone, his voice mingling with Cecelie's laughter as he strode down the hall.

Sophie scooted off the bed. Her legs trembled as she crossed the room. She sat before her dressing table, looked in the mirror, and groaned. It was worse than she had imagined. Her hair looked as if a windstorm had swept through it. Her eyes were mere slits between swollen lids. The skin beneath her lashes was as black as if someone had punched her.

She buried her face in her hands. The ticking of the mantel clock seemed eerily loud amidst the silence of the room.

God had answered her prayers and returned her daughter to her former exuberant self, but would she ever speak?

Sophie breathed deeply. She needed to gain control over her emotions. She forced her thoughts onto the mundane matters at hand. She needed to wash her face and change her dress.

A loud knock on the door saved her from further self-pity.

Jagger entered the room, a pot of steaming water in his hands. His hair was wet, as if he had recently bathed. He wore it combed back from his face, highlighting the strong square cut of his jaw. He was clean-shaven and immaculately dressed in buff, thigh-hugging breaches tucked into knee-high boots.

His crisp white shirt and white cravat emphasized the deep tan of his cheeks. His dove-gray waistcoat hugged the broad expanse of his chest. His deep blue frock coat brought out the blue in his eyes, making them appear as vibrant as the summer sky. His formal attire was more suited to paying visits than traipsing across the countryside with a four-year-old child.

"I thought you might like to freshen yourself before our outing," he said as he filled the washstand basin.

"Where is Cecelie?" Her voice sounded very much like the croaking of a frog.

His smile was so tender and fond, Sophie found herself longing to rest her palm against his cheek and press her lips to his. Oh, he was dangerous to her peace of mind.

He dipped a cloth in the water, slowly rubbed it over her cheeks, then moved it to her forehead. "She is with Cook, packing food for our outing."

She should push him away. She was more than capable of washing her own face, but she lost herself in the soothing warmth of the cloth as he smoothed it over her skin.

She closed her eyes as he blotted her puffy, swollen lids.

A moment later she gasped as he replaced the cloth with his lips, pressing a tender kiss to her eyes, her forehead, her nose. She lifted her chin, silently yearning for him to kiss her lips, hoping he would take the hint.

He did not. He grabbed her brush from the dressing table, moved behind her chair, and stroked it through the tangled mess of her hair. Goodness, but she enjoyed his ministrations.

For a moment, she allowed her mind to wander, to daydream as she had as a young girl still in the schoolroom. She imagined she was a princess and he was her prince, sworn to protect her and madly in love with her.

She met his gaze in the mirror. The skin around his

mouth was drawn tight, but his blue eyes blazed with the same naked longing that burned within her soul.

She lowered her lashes to hide her foolishness.

"I can finish myself," she said, hoping her voice didn't shake with the longing now coursing through her veins.

He placed the brush on the table. He ran his fingers through her hair, rubbing the ends between his thumb and his forefinger. His knuckles grazed her neck and she shivered.

A soft sigh escaped her lips.

She caught his stunned gaze in the mirror. Her breath caught in her throat as his eyes darkened dangerously.

A heartbeat later, he turned and strode out the door.

Sophie quickly knotted her hair at her nape. She should keep her distance. She should stay as far away from this man as was humanly possible.

She ran to her clothespress. For the first time in as long as she could remember, she wanted to wear something attractive, something that flattered her figure and highlighted her hair.

Her fingers tensed as she sorted through her dresses, all of which were old and woefully out-of-date. Most were black. Some were gray. Those she wore to clean the house were brown.

One was a delicate gold. She had never worn it, though it was her favorite dress, one of her mother's castoffs given to her shortly before her death. Once, Sophie had fantasized about wearing that dress at her wedding, back when she was still too young and naïve to realize how cruel the world truly was.

She should have dyed it black long ago, but she could never bring herself to do it. It was too fancy for traipsing out-of-doors, but she had no other options.

A nagging voice in her head argued that she was in mourning for her brother. She should wear black.

"He didn't want me to," she growled as she struggled

into the gown, then rushed out the door, eager to join her family.

At the landing, she paused to catch her breath. Her stomach churned with eagerness and anxiety, as if she were a debutante making her first appearance in society rather than merely strolling out-of-doors with her family.

Her family. Oh, how she liked the sound of that. It filled her with hope. And an inexplicable dread.

She descended the stairs at a slow, dignified pace, one hand firmly clinging to the rail, both because she did not want to trip on her hem and because her legs were shaking so badly she thought she might collapse in an unladylike heap.

Jagger Remington stood at the bottom of the stairs with Cecelie by his side, her hand firmly wrapped in his. His expression was inscrutable as he watched Sophie progress down the stairs. His gaze roamed from her shoulders to her shoes before moving back to her face.

His jaw tightened. Heat flared in his eyes.

Her hand tensed on the post. She froze midstep. Her heart beat a pagan rhythm in her breast. She had made a dreadful mistake. She fought the urge to run back to her chambers and change into one of her older dresses.

She forced herself to continue to move down the stairs, toward him, rather than retreating to the safety of her room.

As she reached the foyer, he took her hand in his. Staring into her eyes, he raised her fingertips to his lips. His hot breath sent shivers up her arm and set the butterflies to trembling in her belly, and that was before he turned her hand and brushed his lips over the sensitive skin of her wrist.

She was in grave danger. She should run while she still had the chance. But she was as incapable of moving as she was incapable of giving voice to her fears.

Chapter Seventeen

"Do not let her fall in," Sophie said as she spread the blanket on the sandy bank near the edge of the pond.

Jagger and Cecelie stood side by side on the boulder, tossing cubes of bread to the swans. He glanced at Sophie over his shoulder. His polite though exasperated smile practically screamed "Do you think I'm entirely stupid?"

Sophie turned her attention to unpacking the basket, unwrapping the chicken and the cheese, anything to keep her gaze and her thoughts off the man who stood so darkly handsome framed against the bright blue sky.

When first he'd arrived at Norwood Park, she had thought him a pirate out to steal her worldly possessions. Too late she realized the treasure she was in danger of losing was her heart.

She stretched out on the blanket, sighing with pleasure as the sun warmed her face. She rubbed her hands over her cheeks. She was unsure if it was the sun or embarrassment that made her skin feel as if it were tingling. Back in her room, she had been mere moments away from throwing caution to the wind and begging Jagger Remington to make love to her.

Thank goodness Cecelie had charged into the room.

Sophie needed time to sort through her tangled thoughts and emotions.

She ran trembling fingertips over her lips, remembering the kiss he had given her, here, by this pond, a kiss as gentle as it was hungry. She could still taste the sweetness of his breath. She could still feel the burning he'd fired within her belly, and deeper still, between her thighs.

A powerful, yet tender moment. Dangerous to her well-being because he had kindled a yearning in her soul for possessions she could never claim, such as happiness and a love of her own.

Now her deepest longings seemed within her reach.

The scent of wildflowers starting to bloom floated on the gentle breeze, mingling with the laughter of father and daughter as they fed the swans. The joyous sound soothed Sophie like a lullaby, carried her to the brink of sleep where she imagined they were a family in truth, rather than a mismatched potpourri thrust upon one another through treachery and deceit.

She blocked that avenue of thought. Jagger Remington had offered her hope, if she had but the courage to reach out and grasp it. That was the question niggling at her mind. Did she have the courage? Or was she a coward in truth, determined to hide for the rest of her life behind walls of stubborn pride?

The ground rumbled with footsteps closing in on the blanket. Sophie opened her eyes and sat up. Jagger trotted toward her with Cecelie riding high on his shoulders. Cecelie was clinging to his ears, laughing and squealing as if she were a normal child who had never suffered the trauma of losing a brother and living in silence for two long years.

Jagger swung the child to the blanket, then stretched out on his side, facing Sophie. He ran his fingers through his hair as if he could salvage some sense of style from the tangles made by Cecelie's hands. Stray locks fell into his eyes, adding to his roguish appeal. He watched her face, his blue eyes so astute, his smile so understanding, she wondered for a moment if he could read her mind.

Trying desperately to focus on anything other than the man lounging across from her, Sophie busied herself by fussing over Cecelie. She settled her daughter into the crook of her arm, clinging to her with all the love in her heart.

Within minutes Cecelie was asleep.

Sophie glanced at Jagger from beneath her lashes.

Never had she felt as awkward and shy as she did at this moment. She did not know what to say or how to behave. Her thoughts seemed foggy and incoherent. The pounding echo in her ears sounded like ocean waves crashing onto the beach.

She settled on the weather as a safe topic. "'Tis an unseasonably warm day, is it not?"

A smile was his only reply.

She forged ahead, determined to conquer her uncharacteristic inability to speak her mind. "It is so peaceful here. Of course, there are other, more cultivated areas of beauty on the estate, but this is my favorite location. I love the wild ruggedness of the landscape."

"Beautiful," he murmured, though he was looking at her, not the scenery. "It is my favorite spot as well."

Heat rushed to her cheeks, and a pleasant tingle spread through her belly, the source of which she refused to contemplate. Was he trying to seduce her?

Did she want him to?

"I fished here once," he said. "As a boy."

He bit his lips, as if ashamed at speaking of his past.

"Did you visit Norwood often?" Sophie asked, suddenly filled with a desperate desire to learn all she could about this man.

"Once or twice." His clipped, icy tone clearly indicated that subject was closed.

The pain in his voice cried out to her. Could his child-hood have been as cold and lonely as hers was?

Perhaps they had more in common than she once thought.

As they stared at one another, the world seemed to fade away until there was just this moment, this blanket, this family. The anguished silence was broken only by the sound of squabbling birds and bees buzzing through the wildflowers.

Jagger reached out, as if to caress her cheek.

Her breath caught in her throat. Anticipation hummed through her veins. As if in a dream, she leaned toward him.

He let his hand fall to his thigh, breaking the spell.

"I left England when I was twelve," he said slowly, as if he were dragging the words from his mouth. "I traveled to India, where I have lived these fifteen years past."

Sophie blinked. What was wrong with her? She had clearly lost the thread of the conversation, simply be-cause he sent her a heated gaze?

She breathed deeply, thankful to break the unbearable tension with idle chatter. "India! How exciting. What is it like?"

"Not as exciting as you might imagine. The English bring their customs and manners wherever they go, and many of the Company settlements, like Calcutta, seem more like English villages, with a society not too dissim-ilar from here. I understand that once it was quite common for men to adopt some of the native ways, but that has long since faded from fashion and is actually quite frowned upon."

"I have read that it is very hot."

"Very hot indeed," he said. But no doubt not nearly as hot as the burning desire she read in his eyes.

Despite her resolve to remain indifferent to this man, an uncontrollable shiver rolled down her spine.

He picked up a plate of food, scooted closer to Sophie

until his shins were touching hers. "The winters are quite pleasant and generally mild."

Until that moment, Sophie hadn't realized her danger. With Cecelie wrapped in her arms, she had no free hands with which to feed herself.

He held out a cube of cheese. "However, the summer months are so hot, it feels as if one is living in a blast furnace."

She lost herself in the deep blue depths of his eyes. Heat spread over her skin as if *she* were staring into a blast furnace and she was in very great danger of being burned.

Slowly, she opened her mouth.

He placed the cheese on her tongue, his thumb lingering against her lower lip, touching her teeth. His gaze dropped to her mouth. Intensity flared in their deep blue depths.

She closed her eyes. Her moan of desire caught in her throat. She wanted him, she realized with stunning clarity. She could no longer deny the truth. Not even to herself.

What was wrong with that? He was her husband. She was his wife. He wanted to build a family with her if only she had the courage to step into the future rather than dwell on the past.

They ate in silence. He fed her as if she were a babe, but her inner reactions were anything but innocent. Every time his finger touched her lips, she fought the urge to dart her tongue out and taste his skin. As the moments passed, she grew exceedingly uncomfortable. An ache built in her breasts, and in her belly, and between her thighs. Sweat dripped down her back.

Were it not for her daughter slumbering peacefully in her arms, Sophie would have squirmed on the blanket.

This, then, was desire.

"The native areas of India are as different from England as you can imagine." His deep husky voice drifted through the sensual spell he had woven around her.

"Very colorful. Very opulent. Their traditions are freer, by far. Mayhap I will take you there and you can see for yourself."

She felt his hot breath against her cheeks.

Her eyes snapped open and she met his mischievous gaze.

His grin was positively wicked. "Mayhap I will turn you into a nautch dancer and you can entice me."

She had no idea what a nautch dancer was but she understood the word *entice*. She felt herself flush to the roots of her hair.

"You should not speak so in front of my daughter," she scolded. "Or me."

"I beg your pardon," he said, though his smile said he was anything but sorry.

She tried to keep her features stern, but she felt an answering smile twitching at the corner of her lips. The beast.

"What made you finally return?"

He shrugged his shoulders.

Sophie read the truth in his eyes.

"My brother tracked you down," she said, unable to hide the bitterness in her voice, her hopes of forming a family with this man dashing away at the vivid reminder of how they came to be married. She had started to believe her foolish dreams. She had started to hope for the future.

Once again, she had played the fool.

He took her hand in his. He did not speak until she returned his gaze. "We cannot change the past. We must look to the future instead. Our future," he said gently.

Too gently, she thought as she felt tears stinging her eyes. She had rarely cried before this day. Now she was turning into a veritable watering pot and she hated it, almost as much as she wished she still hated him.

Jagger caressed her cheeks with the back of his thumbs, brushing away the tears glistening on her satiny skin. If her brother were still alive, Jagger would crush him with his bare hands for causing this woman so much pain.

He understood her conflicting emotions. He had yet to deal with his own anger, his own disgust, at his mother's ultimate betrayal and the secrets of his birth. He had tucked these issues aside to deal with at a later date. It did not really change his plans for his so-called father, nor did it alter his desire for revenge. Besides, he had many more pressing issues to worry about, such as how to win the love of his wife.

He wanted to ease Sophie's distress. He wanted to tell her it mattered not how they'd met or come to be wed. He wanted to tell her that he loved her. She would never believe him, Jagger knew, just as he could not change the circumstances that had brought them together. But he had a plan to win her love. He would settle for nothing less than total success.

"Do forgive me," she said, staring off in the direction of the trees. "I do not know what is wrong with me. I rarely cry, though I imagine you must find that impossible to believe, given my shameful behavior this day."

He believed it all too well. For far too long she was forced to rely on her inner strength to survive. She had built walls of isolation to defend herself, but now those walls were crumbling.

"I believe we must speak frankly," he said.

She pursed her lips.

He feathered his fingertips along her chin until she met his gaze. "If we are to build our future together, we must face the betrayal by your brother. Bring it out in the open."

Her eyelids fluttered closed. When she opened them again, her tears were gone. She thrust her shoulders back and lifted her chin, visibly drawing on her inner strength and pride to meet his challenge.

"Was there someone you loved?" she asked bluntly. "In India?"

"Good God, no."

"There was no one you cared for?"

He smiled tenderly. "No. I was too busy building an empire. I always knew I would return to England at some point. Your brother merely hastened my return."

"And saddled you with a wife and child you did not want."

"Does it matter why we wed? Honestly, at this point, does it matter?"

She looked at him intently, though he could not read her thoughts in her eyes.

"What of you?" he said, finally broaching the subject to which he wanted answers more than anything else. "Is there someone you love? The father of your child perhaps?"

She stared at her daughter, sleeping soundly in her lap.

"He is dead," she said with no trace of emotion in her voice or in her features.

Jagger blew out his breath, unsure if he was relieved or disturbed by her words. It was a beginning, he supposed.

He clenched his hands into fists until his knuckles ached.

Tell me everything, he wanted to shout, but he bit his tongue.

She glanced at him out of the corner of her eye. It was a speculative look that left him holding his breath in anticipation of her next words.

"If we are to build a future together . . . Jagger . . ." She said the word as if it caused her physical pain to use his name. "Then we must have truth between us. Do you not agree?"

Wary of what he might be agreeing to, he slowly nodded.

"How did you know my brother?"

"I believe I mentioned once before that he was a friend of my mother's."

"Where were you born?"

"In England. Not far from here. And what of you?" He swiftly changed the subject. He was not ready to discuss his past, nor was she ready to hear it. "Where were you born?"

She shook her head sadly. "Stephen did you a dreadful disservice in so many ways. Did he tell you *nothing* about me?"

Jagger pursed his lips. What painful secret was she about to impart? He had no doubt it was trivial compared to the secrets that haunted his soul.

She studied her fingernails. "My mother was an opera singer, of Italian descent, who somehow managed to snag herself an earl. It caused quite a scandal, as you can well imagine."

"That explains the golden bronze of your skin," he said, taking her hand in his. "And the glorious burnished mahogany of your hair."

She glared at him as if he had suddenly sprouted horns.

Flattery was obviously not the way to win his lady's heart. But God, she was beautiful. Even when dressed in drab frocks of black or brown, she was more beautiful than any woman he had ever met. But today, when she had first appeared at the top of the stairs, swathed in golden silk, Jagger was certain he'd died and gone to heaven. No mere mortal could look like this.

The sun dipped behind the trees. The fiery reds and golds streaking the sky reflected off the stillness of the water, making it appear as if it were afire.

"Sunset is my favorite time of day," she said, gazing at the horizon, a sudden wistfulness in her eyes. "I have often questioned my faith. I have wondered—if God exists, how can He allow so much suffering and misery and evil in His world? Then I see the sunset and it gives me hope. . . ."

She turned her tortured gaze to Jagger and he could read her thoughts as clearly as if she had spoken them aloud. It gave her hope that, one day, she would see her son again.

His throat started to ache and his eyes hurt.

He wanted to cry, for her pain, for his suffering, for all that was wrong with the world, and for what was finally right.

This moment. His wife.

"It is getting late," she said, effectively calling an end to their interlude. "We should return to the house."

Jagger hooked an arm around her elbow and helped her to her feet. She did not protest when he shifted Cecelie out of her arms and cradled her against his chest.

They turned down the path and headed for the house.

"Shouldn't we retrieve the basket and blanket?"

"One of my men will gather them," he said, surprised at the difficulty he had getting words past the lump in his throat.

She put a hand on his arm. "There is something about which I must speak to you."

It was the first time she had touched him of her own volition. Jagger wished he were naked so he could feel the heat of her palm against his skin.

Her brow was furrowed, with worry or anger he wasn't sure.

"You have altogether too many servants," she said. "Some of them must go. And you cannot hire any more. I am sorry. But there is no help for it."

"I beg your pardon?"

"You saw the accounts. The estate cannot support the number of people now living here. We cannot pay their wages. Honestly, I should have turned Mary away, but she offered to work for room and board and I had not the heart to say no."

He stopped walking, turned to gaze steadily into her eyes. The uncertainty and fear he saw staring back at him was as sharp as a knife thrust into his heart. He wanted revenge upon every male throughout her young life who should have protected her.

"You do not need to scrimp—"

"Economizing is not scrimping," she said sharply, thrusting her chin into the air in a gesture that had become as familiar to Jagger as it was endearing. Were it not for Cecelie cradled against his chest, he would give in to temptation, pull her into his arms, and smother her with his kiss.

He forced himself not to smile. "Sheath your claws, my lady tiger. I meant no insult."

She rolled her lips between her teeth in what Jagger thought was a meager attempt at hiding a smile.

He sought to ease her fears. "Not to mention that your brother has left us a small fortune—"

"Which you said would be tied up in the courts for years."

"So you do listen to me," he teased.

"Every once in a while," she shot back at him. "When you say something of import, and you are wearing your clothes."

Her eyes went wide, as if she couldn't believe the words had come out of her mouth.

Jagger swallowed his laugh. "Do you have any idea why men go to India? I assure you, it is not for the climate."

"For the nautch dancers, of course," she said primly.

He grinned. "Ah. Perhaps those beautiful ladies might entice them to stay once they've arrived, but there is a much more fundamental reason for going in the first place."

"Do not speak to me as if I were an imbecile. I know they work for the East India Company."

"Some do. But those, like me, who truly want to build a fortune, open a private agency house. It is a trading company. Do you understand what I am saying to you?"

She shook her head.

"I am rich, madam. By any definition of the word."

Chapter Eighteen

She turned and stomped down the path in what could only be described as a magnificent huff. Jagger did not know what reaction he had expected from her, but this certainly wasn't it.

Cradling Cecelie's head against his shoulder, he scurried after her. "What is wrong with you?"

When she didn't stop walking, he grabbed her arm.

She glared at his hand. "Release me. At once."

"I tell you we are rich, and you are furious?"

She tapped her foot at a maddening pace as she stared off into the trees.

He lifted his hand away from her. "Please, do not allow me to detain you a moment longer."

How had this happened? One moment, they were talking as if they were friends, laughing and teasing.

Now this complete rift.

Over what?

Over the fact that he wasn't a fortune hunter after all? Over the fact that he had the means to support his wife in the manner to which she should want to become accustomed?

He would never understand women. Now he wished he had paid more attention to the fishing fleet, those English maidens who descended upon Calcutta each year, so desperate for a husband they sailed halfway 'round the world to catch their man.

Then it hit him with painful clarity. She had believed him a fortune hunter. It was the dignity with which she held her head high. It gave her the conviction that she held some small value to him beyond Stephen's terrible betrayal.

His declaration had told her she was of no more value than the pine needles strewn across the path. She was a means to an end in Stephen's grand scheme, and she didn't even know what that scheme entailed.

He hurt so much for her, Jagger wanted to slam his fist into a tree. He planted his feet firmly on the ground. "You will never turn your back on me. Do you understand?"

Furious color rushed into her cheeks. Good. He wanted her angry. He wanted her fighting for her dignity. He had no other means to prove her value at the moment. He could not declare his love for her. She would never believe him.

"We will not be dismissing any of our servants," he said. "Instead, you will let it be known that we are in need of help. Then you will interview and hire servants until all the necessary positions are filled."

Her brows shot up. "You trust me, a mere woman, to accomplish this task? Do you think I can handle it?"

"Do you underestimate yourself?"

Her hands fisted at her sides.

Would she strike him?

She planted her fists on her hips instead. God, she was so beautiful, it hit him like a punch to the gut.

"I do not wish to fight with you," he said.

She studied her foot as she swept it back and forth through the pebbles and leaves on the ground. "Nor I you."

He held out his hand, held his breath as he waited.

She stared at his fingers, then slowly lifted her hand to his. If felt so small within his grasp.

All he wanted to do was protect her.

He searched for a topic that would prove she had value in his eyes. "What do you think we should do about the properties your brother left us?"

She watched him through wide eyes. "You are asking me?"

"Of course. You are my wife and a rather astute land agent, at that. I value your opinion."

He couldn't be entirely certain, but he thought he saw a smile tugging at the corners of her lips.

"Do you think we should give them to your brother, Edmund?"

"Heavens. Why would we want to do that?"

"Because he feels they rightly belong to him and he is willing to fight long and hard to retrieve them."

"But Stephen wanted you to have them. He must have had a reason."

A reason Jagger would never share with his wife. A secret he would take to his grave.

"So you think we should keep them?"

"I think we should have this discussion tomorrow," she said, casting him a sideways glance that stole his breath. "I am enjoying myself too much to discuss such mundane matters as money today."

Good Lord, was she flirting with him?

His heartbeat quickened. He inched closer to her side. He didn't stop moving until his arm touched hers. The scent of rosewater tickled his nose.

He lifted his hand, intent on threading his fingers through her hair and dragging her lips to his.

Cecelie chose that moment to awaken. She wiggled in Jagger's arms until he slid the child to her feet.

She scurried over to Sophie, lifted her hands in the air.

"Do not pick her up," Jagger said, "unless she asks."

Sophie glared at him. "You know she does not speak."

She bent to gather the child in her arms.

"Do not," Jagger said as he pushed himself between mother and daughter. He bent at the waist to bring his eyes to Cecelie's level. "What is it you want, young lady?"

Cecelie pouted her lips and started to whine.

"If you want your mother or me to pick you up, you are going to have to say the words."

Sophie bumped into his shoulder as she stepped around him to rescue her child.

"Stop," Jagger said.

She flashed him a scathing look as she bent to scoop Cecelie into her arms.

Cecelie wiggled away. She ran to Jagger, her hands thrust into the air.

Sophie's features collapsed. "She wants *you* to pick her up."

The hurt in her voice rang through the trees.

Jagger wanted nothing more than to drag his wife and child into his arms. He forced his hands to stay at his sides as he leaned toward Sophie. "Have you ever wondered if the reason she doesn't speak is because she does not have to?"

Sophie's glare could have turned a tropical rainstorm into sleet and hail. "Now you are an expert at raising a child? Tell me, Mr. Remington, how many children do *you* have?"

"One," he said brutally. "And she is standing in front of me." He lowered his voice, tried to gentle his tone. "I know nothing about raising children. But you said yourself, she has not laughed or cried or screamed, let alone spoken, since her brother died. Yet, she used to speak, so we know there is no bodily reason for her silence. And today she has proven that she is indeed capable of speech. Why is it so unreasonable to think that she does not speak because her needs are always met before she even voices them?"

Sophie set her chin belligerently, yet she did not interfere as Jagger turned to Cecelie. "If you want me to pick you up, you are going to have to say the word. Say 'Up.'"

Cecelie's lower lip quivered. Giant tears formed in her eyes. She thrust her hands higher into the air, whimpering as she clawed at his frock coat.

Jagger's chest ached, as if his heart had shattered into a million pieces. He could be wrong, but his instincts told him he was right. She knew how to speak. She simply chose not to.

"Say 'Up.'" He heard the tremor in his voice. How had this child burrowed so deeply and swiftly into his heart?

Cecelie was screaming now, and stomping her feet. Tears as big as diamonds glittered on her cheeks. She made a fist and punched Jagger's knee, then turned and raced away, disappearing around a bend in the path.

"Now see what you have done," Sophie hissed, but Jagger was already sprinting after Cecelie.

For such a young child, she was as swift as a deer.

Jagger was breathing heavily by the time he caught up to her and scooped her into his arms.

He buried his face in her hair, clutched her tightly against his chest. His heart hurt, like a giant fist was squeezing it dry. At that moment, he knew a greater fear than he had ever known in his life. If anything were ever to happen to this child, *his* child, he was certain he would die. He finally understood how much it cost his wife merely to survive.

Sophie tucked the coverlet under Cecelie's chin, then stepped aside so Jagger could say good night.

He perched on the edge of the bed, gathered the child into his arms. Cecelie babbled some incoherent noises at him, then kissed him on the cheek. His love for her was clearly evident in the taut muscles of his arms as he hugged her, in the pain etched into the skin around his eyes, in the tightness of his lips. Sophie's heart ached for his self-inflicted misery.

She placed a hand on his shoulder.

"Might I speak with you," she whispered near his ear.

He kissed Cecelie's forehead, then adjusted the covers around her. They passed silently through the connecting door into Sophie's rooms. She laced her fingers together as she tried to form the words she wanted to say.

He paced before the fire. "You have every right to your anger. I was a pompous ass. I do not know what I was thinking. I know nothing about raising a child. God, had she been hurt, I would never have forgiven myself."

He raked his hand through his hair as he turned to face her. "Have you nothing to say?"

She raised her hands. "You are doing an admirable job at self-flagellation. You do not need my assistance."

"You could tell me in that independent voice of yours to mind my own business and leave your daughter alone."

Sophie smiled, a reaction he was obviously not expecting given the stunned look on his face. "Cecelie was throwing a fit of temper. There is nothing more to it than that. And I, for one, was very glad to see it."

"I cannot believe you are trying to make me feel better about scaring our daughter until she ran away."

"Our daughter," Sophie said on a sigh. "I rather like the sound of that." Her smile broadened until she almost feared she would disappear behind it. "I will admit I was angry at first. I felt you had no right to interfere in matters concerning my daughter. But I was wrong.

"Jagger," she said, surprised at how easily his name rolled off her tongue. "Most mothers would be horrified to see their child behave in such a manner, screeching and crying and hitting! But I was thrilled. Have you any idea why?"

He shook his head.

"Because she is no longer locked in her closet of

silence! While this morning was the first time I've heard her laugh in two years, it was also the first time I've seen her express any emotion at all. Happy. Sad. Angry! I am thrilled!"

She buried her face in her hands. Good Lord, she was on the verge of tears yet again. Where was the strength she'd relied upon to get her through her days?

She heard his footsteps as he walked up behind her. His hands gripped her waist. She turned to face him.

He yanked her against the broad wall of his chest.

She wrapped her arms around his shoulders, nuzzled her cheek into his neck. She could hear his heart beating beneath her ear. She was no longer alone.

"Thank you," she whispered, content to snuggle in his arms until she could find the words to express how she felt.

She listened to his breath moving in and out of his lungs. She felt safe and cherished and valued and loved. It might turn out to be an illusion, but she was willing to take that chance.

Reluctantly, she stepped back. She crossed to the window, putting a safe distance between them.

He watched her silently, almost broodingly.

As they stared into each other's eyes, Sophie no longer had any doubts. "There is something I must tell you—"

A loud knock on the door interrupted her confession.

Damn and blast. Who could that be?

"Yes," she called, hoping she didn't sound as irritable as she felt.

Mary peeked around the door. "Lord Hallowell wishes a word with Mr. Remington. He's brought the magistrate with him," she added in a hushed voice as if relaying a secret.

Sophie's heart started to race, but Jagger did not seem disturbed. He smiled at the maid. "Thank you, Mary. Show them to the library. I will be down in a moment."

"What do you think this means?" Sophie said.

"I have no idea. Mayhap they have some word on Stephen's murder. Let us find out."

He linked her arm though his and led her out the door.

Edmund lounged in the chair behind the massive oak desk that had once belonged to Stephen. He had a cigar clamped between his teeth. The smoke hovering about his face gave him a ghostly aspect. Sir John leaned against the wall behind the desk. His casual stance did nothing to hide the lecherous gaze he bestowed upon Sophie as she walked through the door.

She glanced at Jagger, who was glaring at Sir John as if he were about to rip the man's throat open.

"Sophie, Sophie, Sophie," Edmund said, grunting out of the chair. He dropped his cigar in a glass of what looked to be wine. It hissed sharply before sputtering out.

His gaze wandered over the contours of her dress as he strolled around the desk. "Are you so like your mother you could not pretend to mourn our brother for more than one day?"

Sophie refused to dignify his abuse with a response. She was looking to the future. Not the past.

He no longer had the power to hurt her.

The lingering smell of cigar smoke stung her throat.

She turned to Sir John. "Have you news of the miscreant who murdered my brother?"

Sir John leered at her. "As a matter of fact, I have."

"And?"

Sir John's eyes gleamed with lust as he leaned toward her. He dropped his voice to a conspiratorial whisper that was no doubt loud enough to be heard across the room. "You might have considered my previous . . . proposal . . . more carefully before you wed this man."

"And what proposal might that have been?" Jagger growled as he stepped up to Sir John. The two men glared at one another like two bucks about to fight for control of the herd.

Rubbing his hands together, Edmund cackled. "Ho, ho, Sophie, you've done it up right and tight this time."

"What are you talking about?" she said, stunned by the giddiness in his voice.

"Ask yourself, sister. Who stood to gain the most from our dear brother's death?"

At her confused silence, Edmund chortled. "Your husband, my dear. Your husband."

"That is absurd," Sophie said, looking at Jagger.

No hint of emotion showed on his face.

"Obviously, you have taken leave of your senses," he drawled in a bored tone that shocked Sophie.

Did he not realize the seriousness of these charges?

"He tried to save Stephen's life," she countered. "And he sent to London to hire private investigators to search for the fiends who did this deed."

Edmund blanched, but quickly recovered his composure. "And when Stephen died, your so-called husband won the prize of extensive lands and properties that should have devolved to me!"

"Your argument is upside down, Edmund. Mr. Remington had no idea what terms were in Stephen's will. None of us did."

"Are you certain about that?"

"He was as shocked as you and I when Mr. Feldman read the will."

"Or is he a very clever actor, my dear? How much do you know about this man?"

She stared into Jagger's eyes as she vowed, "Enough to know that he would never have murdered our brother, or anyone else."

Jagger's eyes darkened with an emotion she could not interpret. She held her head high. "This joke of yours has gone too far, Edmund. I must insist that you leave."

"You have no say in this matter," Edmund said.

"There you are wrong. This house is mine, and I have

had enough of this nonsense. Please leave of your own accord, before I have you thrown out."

Edmund laughed. It was a decidedly evil sound. "This house is not yours. Stephen signed it away to this blackguard, along with all his other property. Tell me, Remington, how did you coerce my brother into such a shady arrangement? What drove you to kill him? Getting his property and money wasn't enough? How stupid of me. You had to kill him. You would not have received any of your ill-gotten bounty had he lived."

"Enough." Sophie grabbed the pull rope and gave it a vicious tug. "These same arguments could be turned toward you, Edmund. After all, until the will was read, everyone believed you were the primary beneficiary. Therefore, to all outward appearances, you were the one who stood to gain most by our brother's death. I want you to leave. Now."

Edmund sputtered and fumed. "Afraid of the truth, my dear? We have witnesses that place this man in Stephen's company mere hours before he was ambushed. He alone knew where Stephen was. He alone had motive and opportunity. He alone is guilty of murder." His voice thundered through the room.

"Do your duty, Sir John. Arrest this fiend."

Sir John pulled himself up to his full height. "Jagger Remington, I arrest you in the king's name."

Jagger almost laughed, but one glance at Sophie's stricken features erased his humor at this bizarre turn of events.

The magistrate brushed his sleeves like a cock fluffing his feathers. "My men are outside and await my orders. You may accompany us of your own volition or we can drag you out in irons and chains. The choice is yours."

Sophie grasped Jagger's arm. Her face was the color of a pale moon covered in clouds. "Why don't you say something to defend yourself?"

He covered her hand with his. Her fingers felt small

and cold beneath his palm. "There is no need for you to worry. Why don't you go and check on Cecelie while I clear this up?"

"No, I am not leaving you."

He was afraid of that. She was forthright and loyal to a fault. Naturally, she would not desert him in this, his perceived hour of need. Yet, he wished, just this once, she could be a little less loyal, a little less devoted.

He knew he could clear his name. He had an alibi, for pity's sake. He could no more admit that he had been with another woman at the time of Stephen's attack than he could admit that this "other woman" now worked under this very roof. And she was, at this very moment, entering the room in response to Sophie's frantic tugging on the bell pull.

Jagger was making good progress in winning Sophie's love. He was not about to give her a new reason to hate him.

"Mary," Sophie said. "Fetch Mr. Remington's men."

"That will not be necessary," Jagger said to the maid. "Please return to your duties."

Mary made a quick curtsy, but to Jagger's disgust, she remained in the room, hovering by the door.

He turned to Sophie, dropped his voice to a whisper. "I do not want you to worry. I wish to speak with Sir John in private. Hush now," he said at her protest. "I had intended to meet with him tomorrow anyway, to discuss what, if anything, he has done to apprehend your previous estate manager."

He should be heartened by the worry he read in her eyes. It meant she cared about him, even if she wasn't ready to admit it. But she had suffered so much in her life. He did not want to be the means by which she suffered more.

He gathered her hands in his. "Do not worry, my love. I can prove my innocence."

"How can you behave so nonchalantly when they are accusing you of killing my brother?"

A loud gasp sounded near the door where Mary still stood. Twisting her fingers in her apron, she hobbled toward Sophie.

The maid's face was as pasty as spoiled milk. Droplets of sweat hung on her brow.

"He couldn'a done it, ma'am," she said in an agonized whisper, as if the words were being dragged from her throat.

Edmund glared at the maid, as if he could strangle her with his eyes.

Sir John cleared his throat dismissively.

Jagger wanted to take the maid by the arm and drag her from the room. He was between the proverbial rock and a hard place. Whether she spoke the words aloud or he somehow managed to silence her confession, everyone in the room would know what she was about to say and he would be damned for it by his wife. Though he recognized how tawdry it all appeared, what made him want to rant and rail was the fact that he was innocent.

Sophie took the maid's hand in hers. "If you know anything, anything at all, Mary, you must say so now."

Mary's breathing quickened until she was practically panting. She gulped noisily, then gulped again. "He couldn'a done it," she repeated. "He was at the inn—"

"We already know that," Edmund sneered. "We have witnesses who state he met with the earl. Then he followed him into the woods and attacked him."

Mary shook her head so rapidly her hair fell from her cap and covered her eyes. Her forehead wrinkled. Her mouth twitched. She clutched Sophie's fingers. "'Tis not true."

"How do you know it is not true?" Sophie asked gently.

"'Cause he was with me that night. All night."

Chapter Nineteen

Jagger watched the tableau play itself out in an eerily detached manner, as if the foundation upon which he was building his future hadn't just exploded.

Edmund roared. He grabbed Sir John by the shoulder and dragged him from the room.

"It's not what ye think, ma'am." Throbbing tears shook Mary's voice. "He did not touch me. It's not what ye think."

"Do not distress yourself," Sophie said, stroking the maid's hands as if she were an injured kitten in need of soothing. Her voice sounded bland, almost pleasant, as if she had learned she could not have tea because they had run out of water rather than having discovered her husband was a womanizing lecher who hired his whore to work in his house.

Sophie's face remained expressionless. "Please return to your duties now, Mary."

White-faced and shaken, the maid scurried from the room.

It was surprising how loud the absence of sound could be, Jagger realized as he watched his wife stand in the middle of the room. She did not move. She did not speak.

She did not so much as blink as her gaze met his. Was she even breathing?

Jagger would have preferred a fit of hysterics or female vapors to this prolonged silence. With every beat of his heart, his pulse pounded in his ears. He knew he owed her an apology, but he also knew that any words he spoke would sound like a rationalization of his actions.

She squared her shoulders. She lifted her chin and held up her hand to stop any words he might think to utter. "I do not wish to discuss it. I do not care."

As if that weren't the biggest lie Jagger had ever heard, she continued. "However, if we are to convince everyone that ours is a 'love match,' as *you* suggested, you might want to be more discreet about your indiscretions."

He clenched his jaw to stop the smile that was twitching at the corners of his lips. "You have no reason to be jealous," he said, as pleased at this proof that she cared for him as he was disgusted with himself for shaming her in front of her brother and the incompetent fool masquerading as a magistrate.

Sophie looked down her nose at him as if he were a fly. "With whom you cavort is of no consequence to me. After all, ours is a marriage in name only. I would only wish that you did not bring your mistress into my home, as I would not expose my daughter to such behavior."

"Our daughter," Jagger said gently. "And neither would I. Mary is not my mistress. Not now, not ever. Though I do admit, I had intended to tryst with her that night. You will remember, at that point, we were not yet wed."

"As if that ever stopped any man."

"I am not just 'any man.' Nevertheless, I could not follow through with my plans for the simple reason that I could not get *you* out of my mind."

"Perhaps you consider me naïve, Mr. Remington. But as you might recall, I know something of the nature of men."

Condescension dripped from her voice.

Jagger had no doubt that he deserved her scorn. "I spent

the entire night staring out the window and thinking of you, *Mrs. Remington.*"

"Please, do not insult me with such nonsense."

"It is not 'nonsense,' I assure you. I could not wipe from my memory the taste of your lips against mine. Little did I know you had enslaved me with your intoxicating kiss."

"Ha! As if you had never kissed a woman before."

"I have kissed any number of women, but I knew from the moment your lips touched mine we were destined to spend the rest of our lives together. And *not* in a marriage 'in name only.'"

Hot color rushed into her cheeks. She pursed her lips. "You agreed to those terms."

"Yes. But only until *you* ask me to make love to you."

"Which we both know will never happen." She studied the pattern of the Persian rug beneath her feet.

Jagger wanted to take her into his arms, but he forced himself to stand still. "I have been faithful to you from the moment we met."

"It is of no difference to me."

"This I swear to you on my honor."

She stared at him then, through eyes that had seen too much pain, too much suffering, too much betrayal.

The room seemed to grow inordinately hot. Sweat dripped down Jagger's back as she leveled her steady gaze on him. The walls seemed to press in on him and he seemed to be struggling to breathe, as if all the air in the room had disappeared.

"I believe you," she finally said.

He hadn't even realized he'd been holding his breath until it whooshed out of him. He dragged her into his arms, covered her lips with his, devoured her mouth with his too-hungry kiss. She was everything a man could hope for in a wife. As much as he'd previously condemned Stephen for his treachery, Jagger now thanked him for his foresight.

"Why?" he whispered against her lips. "Why do you believe me?"

She pressed her hands against his chest. She leaned back so she could gaze steadfastly into his eyes. "You are the most honorable man I have ever met," she said simply.

Jagger felt the sting of tears in his eyes. He buried his hand in her hair, pressed her cheek against his chest.

"I can hear your heart beating," she murmured.

It is beating for you, he wanted to say, but he feared she would think him a maudlin fool.

He speared his fingers through her hair, tipped her face to his. The words he truly wanted to say tangled in his throat. He kissed her instead, molding her to the length of his body, smoothing his hands over her back and through her hair. He devoured her lips with his hungry kiss, touching his tongue to her teeth, moaning from deep in his belly as she opened her mouth and welcomed him in.

She clutched his shoulders, dug her nails into his back. Her tongue danced with his and he groaned as passion swept reason away. He wanted to lower her to the floor, to take her there on the carpet, to show her his love in the only way he knew how. But she deserved more than a desperate coupling on the library floor. She whimpered softly against his mouth, an urgent plea for something more.

A hysterical scream rang from somewhere within the house.

He lifted his head. "What the hell?"

He thrust Sophie behind him and ran to the door.

"Stay here," he shouted over his shoulder.

Naturally, she ignored him. He would have to teach her a thing or two about wifely obedience, he decided as he dashed down the hallway, trying to determine the source of the shrieking. When he realized it was coming from the family apartments, his heart hitched painfully in his chest.

He raced up the stairs. Looked left. Then right.

Oh, Christ. The screaming was coming from Cecelie's room.

He burst through the door. Thea stood in the middle of the room, her hands clutching her ears, her eyes scrunched shut, her mouth pried open by the force of her scream.

The nursemaid cowered in the corner.

Jagger raced to Cecelie's bed. It was empty.

His fingernails bit into his palms as every muscle in his body clenched. He turned on the maid. "Where is she?"

He grabbed her arms, shook her viciously. "Where is she?"

The maid blubbered something incoherent.

Thea stopped screaming. Her face collapsed in a puddle of tears. "It was a man. He took her—"

Sophie's skin was as cold as if her blood had turned to ice within her veins. Her thoughts grew murkier with each breath she drew. She could not go through this pain again. If she lost another child, she would not survive.

"Who took her?" Sophie said, as she placed her hands on her companion's shoulders.

Thea raised her trembling hands, pressed her clenched fists into the corners of her mouth. "I don't know. I heard a noise. I knew you were with Edmund, so I came to check on Cecelie. It was dark. It was a man. He was wearing a hat pulled low on his head and a coat with the collar turned up."

"How long ago?" Jagger demanded.

"I don't know." Thea buried her face in her hands. Her shoulders shook as she wept.

Footsteps thundered down the hallway. Mary rushed into the room. Jagger Remington's men gathered at the door.

"Block the exits," Jagger shouted. "Search the house. Every room. Every closet. I want my daughter found!"

Mary wrapped her arms around Thea's shoulders and gently led her from the room. Betsy shrieked, then fell into a faint, landing with a thud on the floor. No one paid her any heed.

Time seemed to crawl to a stop. Every sound in the room intensified, until the ticking of the mantel clock was as deafening as a cannon blast.

Sophie forced herself to breathe deeply, willing the fresh air to clear the fog from her mind. She needed to think clearly, but try as she might, she could not wrap her thoughts around the situation. Who would have taken her daughter?

She turned to Jagger. His face reflected the pain she knew ravaged her own features. She clutched his fingers.

He squeezed her hand in a grip so tight, it hurt. "Have you any idea who would have taken her?"

Sophie shook her head. Her teeth ached from clenching her jaw. An uncontrollable trembling rattled her bones.

"What about the father? Could he have taken her?"

"No. I told you. He is dead."

Or was he? How did Sophie know that for certain? She did not read the papers. She had only his worthless brother's declaration of the bounder's death.

"No," Sophie said, reasoning aloud as she dropped Jagger's hand and paced the room. "I never told him I was with child. I never told anyone his name. He could not have known."

Yet, his brother had been here, in her house, mere days ago.

But he did not know about Cecelie. Or did he?

If he had spent any time in the village—and he must have since there was no place else to sleep in the neighborhood—he would have learned about the twins. It was hardly a secret in these parts. Could she ignore the possibility that he might have abducted Cecelie? That Cecelie might, at his moment, be in his clutches? But what reason would he have to take her? Sophie was the wronged party in their twisted past.

She swung her head in a half circle, as if it hung on a pendulum. She caught Jagger's gaze out of the corner of her eye. "Send men to the village."

"Who are they looking for?"

"Henry Holliston." Sophie was amazed at how bland her voice sounded when she was dying inside.

"Who is he?" Jagger demanded, as she'd known he would.

Sophie did not want to say the words. She did not want to name anyone a relation to her daughter, especially anyone involved in the villainy of Sophie's downfall.

She scratched her fingers over her scalp. "Cecelie's uncle, though I am not certain he even knows of her existence."

Another idea coalesced through the miasma in her brain. She clawed at Jagger's arms. "Could it be Edmund? Could this have to do with Stephen's will? Could he plan to ransom her for the property and money? It makes more sense. Edmund is a monster who has always hated me."

Jagger clenched his jaw and narrowed his eyes. His face twisted into a fearsome mask of rage. "Search this room. Perhaps the bounder left a note of some kind. Whoever the bastard is, if he harms one hair on my daughter's head, he is dead. This I vow on my life."

He pulled Sophie into his arms.

"I will find our daughter," he whispered against her ear. Then he released her and ran from the room.

"I know you will," she said, though he was no longer present and could not hear her words. She was not surprised to realize she trusted him. He loved Cecelie as if she were his daughter in truth. He would die to protect her.

Sophie only hoped it wasn't too late. She caught her sob with her fist. *Dear God, please keep my daughter safe.*

* * *

A search of the house turned up nothing.

Sophie watched in helpless dismay as Jagger dispatched one of his men to fetch Sir John and to round up everyone in the neighborhood who could aid in the search. He set the rest of the men to scouring the grounds while he rode into the village to hunt for Henry Holliston.

Questioning Betsy once she regained consciousness was no help at all. The woman's hysterical ranting was gibberish.

Sophie sent her to the kitchen to have something to eat.

She rubbed her hand over the back of her neck to ease the tension and help her think. She was treading on the brink of hysteria. She needed to keep her wits about her.

After Colin had died, Sophie had thought she could face no greater pain. Now she knew she was wrong. Her daughter was out there somewhere. In the dark. Cold and afraid. Wondering where her mother was and why she would abandon her to a strange man. The never-ending circle of thoughts drove Sophie mad.

She searched the bedroom for some clue. She pulled the mattress off the bed, in case the ransom note had slipped between the headboard and frame. She found nothing.

Mary entered the room, carrying a tea service. "I thought ye might like a cup to soothe yer nerves," she said as she placed the tray on the child-sized table.

Sophie silently stared out the window, studying the stars. In her mind, she was screaming.

"I'm sorry, Mrs. Remington," Mary said quietly. "For the pain ye be goin' through. And for earlier . . ."

Sophie nodded absently. The last thing on her mind was with whom her husband had slept before he married her.

What difference could it possibly make, now that Cecelie was missing?

Sophie wanted to open her mouth and scream, but she was afraid once she started, she would never stop.

Mary fidgeted with her apron. "I admire ye, ma'am."

"For what possible reason?"

"I cannot imagine how much it hurts, losin' a babe," Mary said, her hand absently moving to her stomach.

"You are with child?"

The maid widened her eyes. Her mouth dropped open. "It's not what ye think—"

"Do not distress yourself, Mary. Mr. Remington has explained. And I believe him."

It sounded strange, but it was true. He was a good and honorable man. More honorable than any man she had ever known in her life. Including her brother, Stephen, who once was the standard by whom she had judged all men.

No one she had ever met could compare with Jagger Remington. In the face of a stunning betrayal by Sophie's brother, he had kept his word and married a woman he neither loved nor wanted. Selflessly, he nursed Stephen through the aftermath of his attack, striving to save his life.

Deep with grief in the face of Stephen's death, he turned his anger toward justice. Though others had long since given up the chase, he searched for Stephen's killer still, hiring Bow Street Runners to keep the hunt alive.

But most of all, he loved Cecelie as if she were his daughter in truth, rather than the natural child of another man. Now Sophie wanted to win his love for herself. She wanted him to love her as a husband should love a wife. It was shocking, but it was true. She could no longer deny it. She loved him.

Not that it mattered.

Nothing mattered, now that Cecelie was missing.

Sophie's chest ached. The air felt thick and heavy, as if it was saturated with glue and sticking to her throat.

Though she had no reason to think well of him, Sophie did not believe Henry Holliston was behind Cecelie's disappearance. That could only leave Edmund as the culprit. But why? Because she'd refused to believe his lies about Stephen's death?

That he hated Sophie, he had never tried to hide, but did he hate her so much he would hurt an innocent child?

Suddenly, Thea's words earlier in the day came back to her, as loud as a mallet striking a gong. Thea had seen Betsy and Edmund walking along the carriage drive. Edmund had been in the house mere minutes before Cecelie's abduction.

A wail of agony exploded within Sophie's breast. She raced to the chest of drawers in the corner of the room. It was a small cabinet that held Betsy's clothes and personal items.

Holding her breath, Sophie yanked open the top drawer. It was filled with socks and gloves and other sundry items. The second drawer held shifts and castaway dresses.

Sophie pressed the heels of her hands against her eyes. Had she honestly expected to find some nefarious item that would implicate the maid in Cecelie's disappearance?

As she pulled open the bottom drawer, it took a moment for her brain to register what her eyes were seeing.

Letters. Dozens and dozens of letters.

As Sophie sorted through the missives, shock slithered through her like venom from a poisonous snake, burning her from within her own skin. Most of the letters were written in Sophie's hand. Some were addressed to Stephen. Others were addressed to Mr. Feldman, her brother's solicitor. All were cries for help. All were supposedly posted by Betsy on her trips into the village. All were buried in this drawer.

Now Sophie understood why no one had heeded her plea.

She found a dozen or more letters addressed to her in Stephen's hand, no doubt informing her of his intention to leave England, updating his whereabouts as he traveled, asking after her health and the health of her children.

All the accusations she had flung at Stephen's head came back to taunt her with a vengeance.

Hidden at the back of the drawer, Sophie found a packet of letters addressed to Betsy. They were separated from the rest by a ribbon. The penmanship of the author was very familiar to Sophie. She had seen his writing many times as she grew up. They were from Edmund.

Before she had a chance to read them, Sophie became aware of a distressed voice calling her name. It came from the hall.

A moment later, Thea rushed into the room. Her eyes were so swollen, it was amazing she could navigate across the floor. Her cheeks were as white as the linen shawl draped around her shoulders. She clutched a missive in her hand.

She thrust it at Sophie. "I have no idea what it says. Betsy shoved it in my hand, then ran out the kitchen door."

A strange, dreamlike calm suffused Sophie as she took the letter. Her name was scrawled across the page in Edmund's hand.

She broke the seal.

If you wish to see your daughter alive, meet me at the Lodge. Tell no one. Bring no one. Or she dies.

In a state of perfect composure, Sophie folded the missive, tucked it into her pocket, and headed for the door.

Chapter Twenty

Jagger shoved the barrel of his pistol into the sleeping man's neck. "Where is she?"

The room was dark, save for the sliver of moonlight creeping through the single small window, but Jagger could see the whites of the man's eyes as they opened.

"Who are you?" Henry Holliston said, his voice sounding remarkably bored despite the weapon poised to blow his brains into his pillow.

Jagger pushed the gun deeper into the man's neck, making him flinch. "Where is she?"

"Where is who?"

"My daughter. Cecelie *Treneham* Remington."

"Oh," the man said. "You are Jagger Remington."

The rage pulsing through Jagger was savage. "You have less than one minute to tell me where she is before I blow a hole through your hand. Before you have time to draw breath and scream, I will reload and shoot another part of your body, but in such a manner that won't let you die. Do you understand?"

An audible gulp and a slight nod of the head was his reply. "Am I to understand the child is missing?"

"You know damn well she is missing because you took her."

"I assure you, I did not."

Jagger clenched his finger on the trigger. For fear of shooting the man's head off before he answered, Jagger grabbed the bastard's hand and shoved the barrel deep into the palm.

"I am going to count to three. One."

"I did not take her."

"Two."

"Why would I—"

"Three."

"—when I came here to make amends with her mother." He didn't sound bored now. No, his choked voice held fear and tears and a ring of truth that made Jagger loosen his grip on the trigger. But he did not move the gun away.

"What do you mean?"

"Could we light a candle and discuss this face-to-face? I feel rather at a disadvantage being pinned as I am, in my bed, by a man with a gun."

"Give me one reason to believe you."

"If I took the child, do you honestly think I would be sleeping in this rundown inn waiting for you to kill me? Wouldn't I have fled the scene of my crime?"

Sweat dripped down Jagger's forehead, stinging his eyes. Outside, the melancholy hoot of a barn owl carried on the breeze. Drunken voices drifted up the stairs from the taproom below. The world had not stopped spinning, Jagger realized, though it seemed as if time stood still.

His heart hammered in his ears. He could barely think, given the red rage swirling in his brain. He wanted to kill this man so badly, he could taste it. It was all he could do to release his tense grip on the trigger.

He kept the gun pointed at the man's chest as he backed off the bed. "Light the candle."

A moment later, a dull glow illuminated the same attic room Jagger had occupied the night of Stephen's attack.

The man sitting at the edge of the bed in his dressing gown looked to be about twenty-five, with a sharply angled chin and nose that proudly proclaimed his aristocratic lineage.

"You were at the Park," Jagger said. "The night of the funeral."

"Yes."

"Why?"

"I wished to speak to Miss Treneham—pardon me— Mrs. Remington. I had not heard of her marriage at the time."

"What did you want?"

"To apologize. Though she would not listen. Not that I blame her."

"For?"

He stared at Jagger through haunted eyes. "Does it matter? If the child is missing, should we not be looking for her?"

"I am not convinced that you haven't taken her."

Henry Holliston rose from the bed, grabbed his breeches from the chair. "You can shoot me later. The child is my niece, and I am going to help you find her—whether you want my help or not."

A heavy cast of clouds hung over the sky, blocking the moon. A few slivers of light cut through the dense haze, casting the abandoned hunting box in an eerily desolate gloom.

Sophie was reasonably certain Edmund had not marked her arrival, hidden as she was by the dense growth of trees at the edge of the lawn and the deep shadows. The sound of nocturnal creatures scurrying through the woods seemed perversely loud, while the Lodge loomed before her like a specter in the night.

A sudden gust of wind whipped off the river, swished

through the overgrown grass sloping away from the rundown cottage. Though the breeze was mild, Sophie shivered as she swept the hem of her skirt into her hands and marched across the grass with only the occasional shaft of moonlight to guide her.

Branches and debris from innumerable storms scratched her ankles. Her lungs ached as she sucked in ragged breaths in a futile attempt to calm her shattered nerves.

She forced her thoughts away from Cecelie and the questions that tortured her with each step she took. Was Cecelie frightened? Was she hurt? Was she crying for her mother?

Such thoughts would not save her daughter's life.

Sophie did not try to conceal her approach. She wanted Edmund to know she had arrived. She wanted his focus on her, and not on Cecelie, though she did not have a plan, other than exchanging herself for her daughter's release.

The knife she had strapped to her shin gave her some small measure of comfort, as did Mary's presence behind the tree line, ready to scoop Cecelie up and run with her to safety.

Sophie stopped at the door. She pounded on the sagging wood with her fist. "Edmund. I am here."

She heard a high-pitched whimpering.

Oh, God, it sounded like Cecelie. Was she hurt?

Sophie shook her head to clear the emotions that clouded her reasoning. She pounded on the door again.

The scraping of boots on wood signaled his approach.

Sophie breathed deeply, as if she could slow her pounding heart by sheer force of will. She peered through the cracked wood, but she could see nothing within the darkness.

As if pushed by a supernatural hand, the door creaked open on rusty hinges. A man-sized form hovered in the shadows beyond the door. As she waited for him to speak, Sophie became painfully aware of the scurrying sound from the floor beyond the door that she greatly feared might be rats. She imagined there were bats living along the ridge board of the slate roof, a thought that normally would frighten her, but tonight merely firmed her resolve to rescue her daughter.

Sophie was locked in a conflict she did not understand. She had not even known it existed before Cecelie's abduction.

She waited for him to speak.

"Come in, my dear."

It was Edmund's voice.

Until this moment, Sophie had held out some small hope that it wouldn't be true. She could not understand why her stepbrother would want to hurt her. True, he had seemed to resent her presence in his father's house. He had taunted her cruelly as she had grown up. But did he hate her so much he was willing to destroy his reputation and his family name? For what possible reason? Did family loyalty stand for naught?

"Send Cecelie out," Sophie said, disgusted at the quivering in her voice, a sure sign of weakness he would no doubt relish. She cleared her throat. "Send Cecelie out, and I will come in."

Edmund chuckled. "I'm afraid not, my dear. Without your precious bastard, what reason would you have to do as I say?"

"You have my word. Let Cecelie leave and I will remain."

"The word of a slut does not inspire confidence. If you want to see your brat, you will have to come in."

"How do I know Cecelie is even with you?"

A shadowy movement followed by Cecelie's muffled cry tore a hole in Sophie's heart. "Stop! Do not hurt her."

"You are the key to ending her suffering."

Sophie thrust her chin in the air and marched through the door. He grabbed her right arm, twisted it viciously, then reached around her waist and yanked her left arm until her wrists crisscrossed behind her back. He used a coarse rope to bind them together. He wound it so tight, it sliced through her skin. She bit her lip to keep from crying out. She did not want Cecelie more frightened than she already was.

He grabbed Sophie's shoulder and pulled her through the darkness. She could not see Cecelie, but she could hear her whimpering and her footsteps as he dragged her across the floor.

"Let her go, you bastard," Sophie snarled.

"Tsk, tsk, my dear. Such language from one who would aspire to the aristocratic life."

"What are you talking about?"

"Shut up," he said, pushing his fingernails into the hollow beneath her collarbone. She blinked her eyes to stem her unbidden tears. She would not cry. She would not frighten her daughter more.

He shoved open a door.

A blinding shaft of light hit the darkness.

Sophie blinked to refocus as he shoved her into the room. She landed on her knees. The rotting wood scraped her shins. A sharp pain shot up her leg. No doubt the knife had shifted in the fall and sliced into her skin. She would have preferred a sheathed dagger, but, unable to find one, she'd made due with her sharpest kitchen knife. Her skin felt itchy from the blood oozing out of the wound.

Ignoring the pain, she curled her feet beneath her, wiggled into a kneeling position. She shook her hair out of her eyes, frantically glanced around the room, searching for Cecelie. Edmund was pushing her into a rickety wooden chair. He used the same coarse rope to bind her.

"Let her go," Sophie snarled. "Or I will kill you."

He cast her a glance of unspeakable malice. "Say one more word and I'll knock your brat's teeth down her throat."

Cecelie's tormented tears wrenched Sophie's heart.

She watched Edmund pace before a meager fire burn-

ing in a grate that hadn't been used in years. Smoke
streamed into the room, rather than up the chimney.

Would they burn to death before Jagger arrived?

She prayed he would get her message before it was
too late.

She had to find a way to cut through her bindings, but
she couldn't get at the knife with her hands twisted
behind her back. She was not agile enough to slide her
hands under her bottom and reach her shins.

"We won't be here long. We're waiting for our ride."
He glanced at his watch. "Then again, we might have
enough time."

"Please let Cecelie go. She's an innocent child."

He dropped to his knees beside her. "Sophie, you will
never know how long I've dreamed of this."

He shoved his hands into her hair. Lowering his head,
he smashed his mouth into hers. He thrust his tongue between her teeth. Bile rose in her throat as he probed
deeper and deeper into her mouth. His hands covered her
breast, squeezing hard, hurting her. She bucked and
kicked, but he pushed her hard against the floor until she
was flat on her back. Her hands were crushed between
her bottom and the floor.

Her shoulders twisted in their sockets. Spasms of pain
shot down her neck. He sprawled full-length atop her. He
was as heavy as a board piled high with rocks.

He locked her feet in place with his knees. His breath
wheezed in and out of his chest. He was going to rape
her, right here, in front of her daughter's eyes, and there
was nothing Sophie could do to stop him.

She twisted her head until she managed to break free of
his mouth. "Not with Cecelie in the room," she gasped.

"If I let her go, you will not fight me?"

Sophie nodded. She could survive anything as long
as she knew her daughter was safe.

A shriek came from behind them. Betsy flew across

the room and smashed him in the back with her fist. "Liar. You said it was me you wanted."

Edmund roared to his feet, his hand landing with a loud crack against Betsy's jaw. "Stupid fool. Never touch me again, or I'll kill you."

Betsy clutched her mouth. Blood seeped between her fingers, dripped onto the floor.

"Is the boat here?"

Betsy shook her head.

"What's taking them so long?" He pointed a finger at Betsy. "Take the child outside and wait for me."

Betsy fumbled with the ropes binding Cecelie to the chair.

"There, there, sweet one," she whispered, her words whistling through her broken teeth. "I won't let no harm come to you. You are my daughter now."

Cecelie had long since stopped crying. Her face was pale. Her eyes were blank. Sophie greatly feared her daughter had retreated into her shell of silence.

Sophie wished she could retreat as well. She felt as if she had fallen into a witch's spell where evil was everywhere and nothing made sense.

Edmund turned to face her. His eyes glowed with lust.

Sophie cringed. "Why are you doing this? I am your sister."

"You're no more my sister than that slut of a maid is."

"Mayhap not by blood, but by marriage."

"Your mother was an Italian whore and so are you. But you're going to be *my* whore," he said as he pushed her legs apart with his booted feet. "I've worked long and hard for this moment and I'll not be denied."

He unbuttoned his breeches and sank to his knees. He wrapped his hands around her ankles, then slid them up her shins. His eyebrows shot up. He pushed her skirt past her knees. "What is this?" he said, pulling the knife from its binding, slicing her leg in the process.

She bit her lip to keep from crying out. She would not give him the satisfaction of knowing he'd hurt her.

Nor would she ever let him know how scared she was.

"You are too clever by half, my dear," he said, flinging the knife over his back. He grabbed the neck of her dress, rent it down to her waist. "But not clever enough to stop me."

Chapter Twenty-one

"Thank the good Lord," Mary said as Jagger jogged to the edge of the trees with Henry Holliston fast on his heels.

He had left his horse a quarter mile back so as not to alert Edmund to his presence. He'd picked his way through the trees, moving so swiftly he was panting for breath. "Where is your mistress?"

Mary's features were grave. "Inside the house, sir."

"Damn and blast." Holliston spat the words. "She should have waited for you to return."

Jagger couldn't agree more, though he wasn't surprised. She was headstrong and much too brave for her five-foot frame. Jagger admired her and cursed her within the same breath. Now he had twice the worries than he'd had a moment before.

Though he couldn't stop the sweat plastering his shirt to his back, Jagger had finally tamed his rampaging emotions.

There would be time enough for anxiety and fear after he rescued his family. Right now, he needed to focus his rage into action and his thoughts into battle plans.

"You watch the front," Jagger told Holliston. "I'll circle around the back."

Holliston nodded.

They crept along the tree line until they were parallel with the house. Jagger held up a hand, waiting until a dark cloud moved over the moon before slicing it through the air, gesturing Holliston to move by the flick of his hand.

Both men ran to the house, then inched along the wall in opposite directions.

A sound carried on the breeze whipping around the corner of the house. It came from the back.

Jagger froze. A heartbeat later, a hand gripped his shoulder. Jagger knew without looking it was Holliston's hand, in a gesture meant to assure Jagger that he wasn't alone.

Jagger buried the resentment he felt toward this man. He had no idea if Edmund was working alone. Until Jagger's servants arrived, Henry Holliston was the only help he had.

He peeked around the corner of the house. The meager moonlight ripping through the clouds scattered shadows across the grass like specters in a horrific dance.

A swath of light escaped through the cracked boards covering one of the windows. A door creaked open. A figure emerged from the house. Jagger thought it must be a woman because it was far too small to be a man.

She carried a bundle over her shoulder like a sack of potatoes. As they moved away from the house toward the river, a cloud broke and moonlight caught on the woman's hair. Jagger recognized the nursemaid. The bundle in her arms was Cecelie.

The roaring in his ears was deafening. Never before had he harmed a woman, but now an overwhelming desire to kill the nursemaid filled him from head to toe. The only thing that stopped him was the knowledge that her screams would alert Edmund to his presence.

The maid was muttering to herself as she walked toward the water. Sprinting forward, Jagger reached her before she could react to the sound of his boots on the ground. He covered her mouth with one hand, slid the other hand around her waist.

Holliston reached them a moment later. He ripped off his cravat, shoved it into the maid's mouth to keep her from crying out. He pried Cecelie out of the maid's arms.

Cecelie's eyes were wide, but she seemed unaware of her surroundings, as if fear had shut down her mind. Perhaps it was a blessing, Jagger thought, for the nightmare wasn't over yet.

Cradling Cecelie against his chest, Holliston rushed away.

Jagger used his neck cloth to bind the woman's arms. He shoved her to the ground, ripped a strip off her petticoat and used it to bind her feet. That should hold her until the magistrate arrived.

As he crept toward the door, he heard a man howl.

Jagger grabbed his pistol from his belt.

With his pounding heart trying to leap into his throat, he sprinted through the door into a dirty room cluttered with broken furniture and filled with smoke. With a warrior's efficiency, his gaze swept the room. Sophie stood along the far wall. She clutched a knife in her hand. She swayed on her feet as she pointed it at Edmund, who stood a few feet away from her holding a gun aimed at her chest.

"Hallowell," Jagger shouted, to draw his attention away from Sophie. Edmund turned, but he kept his gun trained on Sophie.

Jagger was normally an excellent shot, but his hand was shaking so badly, he greatly feared he might miss. He glanced at Sophie. Her face was the color of day-old ashes. The bodice of her dress was ripped, exposing her breasts.

An icy rage sliced through Jagger.

He counted silently.

One. He lifted his left hand to support his wrist.

Two. His finger tightened on the trigger.

Three. He fired, catching Edmund in the shoulder.

The next few seconds passed so quickly, time seemed to blur. The impact spun Edmund a half turn to the right.

He still had his gun in his hand, which was now aimed at Jagger. A cry gurgled from Sophie's throat as she streaked across the room, knife poised to strike.

Jagger bolted toward Edmund as Edmund's gun went off. The ball grazed his side. It hurt like the devil but Jagger kept moving. He was only vaguely aware of Sophie screaming his name.

He staggered forward. He reached Edmund before Sophie. He slugged him in the jaw. The bastard crashed to the floor. His head bounced on the hard wood. Up. Down. Up. Down. Like a puppet controlled by an unseen hand. The repeated blow knocked him unconscious.

Sophie dropped the knife. It clattered to the floor as she rushed to Jagger's side.

She wiped the hair from his brow, murmured his name.

"I must have died," he said. "For this is surely heaven."

"Stupid man," she said, kissing his brow.

"Did he . . ." Jagger couldn't bring himself to say the words.

She shook her head. "No. But he tried."

"How did you free yourself?"

Her lips against his brow curved into a smile. "Let us say, I have a mean way with my knee."

Jagger laughed, then grabbed his side. "You are a re-markable woman, my dear wife."

"And you are a remarkable man, my dear, dear husband."

Sir John burst through the door, followed by Jagger's men, armed with pistols, muskets, and swords.

Jagger pulled Sophie against his chest. He shrugged out of his jacket, then wrapped it around her shoulders.

"That man abducted my wife and daughter," Jagger said, nodding at Edmund's still-unconscious form on the floor. "And I suspect, if you question him when he comes around, you will find he killed Lord Hallowell as well, or he hired thugs to do the deed."

Sir John nodded.

Jagger wrapped his arm around Sophie's waist and together they hobbled toward the door. Outside, the constable had secured Betsy. Mary and Henry Holliston stood back from the crowd. Cecelie sat on the ground between them.

As Sophie and Jagger walked past a torch, Cecelie jumped to her feet.

"Up," she cried, running as fast as her little legs would carry her. "Up. Up. Uppie!"

She flung her hands into the air. She leapt into Jagger's arms. She reached one chubby hand toward Sophie to gather her into the hug. Two years of silence broke. As her cries of "Mama" and "Uppie" echoed through the night, Jagger could not tell if the tears wetting his cheeks were his or his wife's.

Jagger paced the drawing room.

His side ached, but he refused to sit down. The doctor had declared it a superficial wound. After a thorough cleansing and wrapping with bandages, he pronounced Jagger as good as new.

"Sit down, Remington. The doctor will speak with you as soon as he finishes his examination."

Jagger glared at Henry Holliston as if he could burn the man with his eyes. "Give me one good reason why I shouldn't kill you."

Now that the danger had passed and Sophie and Cecelie were safe within their rooms, Jagger's pent-up emotions battered him with a vengeance. Holliston was as good a target for Jagger's rage as anyone, given that his despicable brother had plunged the whole nightmare into motion.

Holliston had the audacity to smile, albeit weakly. "Were it not for me, you would not have met your wife."

That stopped Jagger midstep. "How do you figure that?"

"She would have made a respectable marriage years ago. As such, she would not have been waiting here for you."

Jagger grabbed the pup by his collar and hauled him out of his chair. "Mayhap you should not remind me of your nefarious deeds. I may kill you yet as a matter of honor."

Henry Holliston nodded gravely. "As would I in your position."

Jagger shoved him back in his chair.

Holliston rubbed his thumb and forefinger over his eyes. When he finally looked at Jagger, his gaze held the haunted hollowness of the irrevocably damned. "You cannot imagine how I berate myself for my part in what happened to her. I was young and irresponsible at the time, much influenced by my brother, but that is no excuse. A man of honor would never have acted such. I am ashamed."

Jagger imagined that confession had cost the young man plenty of pride, though it did nothing to ease the murder lust flowing through Jagger's veins.

He stalked to the liquor cabinet, poured two snifters of brandy, then thrust one at Holliston. "Tell me the details, and I may spare your life yet."

Holliston's chuckle was anything but merry. "Charles, my late brother—may his soul rot in hell for eternity—was as wicked as they come. After this night's events, you may not be surprised to hear he claimed a close friendship with Edmund Treneham."

Naturally. It made perfect sense. A suspicion as ugly as it was perverse materialized in Jagger's mind. He tossed back his brandy as he waited for Holliston to continue.

"Charles came to me one night, giddy with a grand

scheme and a pocketful of blunt. He had wooed this wall-flower. Said she was 'ripe and ready' for the plucking."

Jagger growled, an animal sound from low in his throat.

Holliston flinched. "Those were his words, not mine. The only problem was she wouldn't sleep with him without marriage. He told her they would elope to Gretna. Of course, what she thought was Gretna turned out to be a small village this side of the border."

"What vicar would marry them there? It would be illegal."

"Naturally. That's where I came in."

Jagger narrowed his gaze as it hit him. "You pretended to be a man of the cloth and you 'married' them."

"I was as drunk as a monk. I hardly remember the 'ceremony,' though I remember Miss Treneham clearly enough. She was but seventeen and stunningly beautiful."

Holliston stared into his brandy, his voice heavily laden with despair as he continued. "Were I not so far gone with drink, I like to think I would have dragged her out of there and taken her home to her family. As it was, I performed the mock ceremony."

She had thought she was legally wed. It explained so much.

Jagger clenched his fist to keep from smashing it into Henry Holliston's face. "He got her pregnant. Why did you not step forward and tell Lord Hallowell what had happened?"

Holliston held up his hands. "And have him shoot me? I told you, I was young and foolish. I also didn't learn about the babes until well after they were born. Besides, I have a feeling she would not have welcomed my confession."

The misery reflected in Holliston's features did nothing to thaw the icy anger ripping through Jagger.

He grabbed the brandy decanter and refilled Holliston's glass. "Were you telling the truth when you said you wished to make amends?"

"Naturally."

"I have an idea."

Jagger crept into her bedchamber. He did not want to disturb her if she were asleep.

She was not. She sat on a cushioned window seat, her back resting against the wall, her eyes lingering on the night sky.

She had her knees drawn up and tucked beneath her dressing gown. She wore a shawl casually draped across her shoulders, the ends loosely grasped in one hand. Her hair spilled wildly about her face, as if she had yet to tame it from the night.

Jagger crossed the room tentatively. She seemed so peaceful. He did not want reality intruding upon this moment, no matter how fleeting the current tranquillity.

"Thea tells me Sir John was here," she said, not turning her gaze from the stars. "And that Henry Holliston has left."

Jagger smiled. His ever-practical and overly brave wife would not allow herself to hide behind any illusions. No doubt a habit learned from years spent depending only upon herself for her safety. He sat opposite her on the bench.

"That is true," he said.

She looked at him then, and Jagger saw the depth of her grief in the dark clarity of her eyes. "What did Sir John have to say?"

Her neck was red and puffy and bore the finger imprints from her brother's hand. Jagger wanted to kill the man.

He was too late, though. "Your brother is dead."

She closed her eyes, dropped her head back against the wall. "By his own hand?"

"Yes."

She nodded, as if it were a fitting end for his villainy.

Jagger would have preferred to string the man up by his toes and flay him alive.

"How did he get the gun?"

"After Edmund made his confession, Sir John sought to give him the honorable way to atone for his crimes. As if he deserved a quick and easy death."

The bitterness in his voice brought her gaze back to his.

"I am well-pleased," she said. "I would not want to spend the rest of my life wondering how he was planning to hurt me or Cecelie next."

Her eyes held a deeper grief than Edmund deserved.

She pushed her lips together as one does when sorting through painful thoughts. "Why did he do this? Did he say?"

Jagger wanted to stroke her cheek. He wanted to kiss the bruises from her throat. He wanted to draw her pain into himself. He settled for taking her hand in his.

He stared at her palm, so fragile, yet so strong. But was she strong enough to hear the truth? It was no less than she deserved, given the suffering Edmund had caused her.

"It appears that your stepbrother had an obsession with your mother from the moment she first wed your step-father."

Sophie smiled painfully. "That would make him, what, ten and six, a mere boy. Did she, how can I say it—"

"You do not have to say it. The answer is yes. She knew how he felt and she used it against him. She used him and manipulated him until the day she died. At which point, he turned his obsession to you. I gather because of the resemblance you bear your mother."

She did not reply, but her fingers tightened around his hand. The red line around her wrist made him ache with fright and burn with rage that someone would dare to harm her, that he had almost lost her.

"How did Betsy become involved?" Her voice trembled ever so slightly as she tried to make sense of the latest betrayal in the long list of betrayals by those she had trusted.

"He seduced her."

Sophie laughed darkly. "Of course. How else does a man get a woman to lean his wicked way? Are we all so desperate for someone to love us that we have no sense of self-respect?"

"Do not seek to compare your mistakes with hers. You sought to harm no one, where she knew what she was doing. By all accounts, she was frivolous enough to believe he would marry her. Though she swears she did not know he intended to snatch Cecelie or force himself on you, a fact which has caused her to repent her evil ways. Now she lists his misdeeds as worthily as any wronged Shakespearian queen. She will have time aplenty to repent her sins once she's transported to Newgate Prison."

"Let us not discuss this further tonight. I am tired," she said, leaning toward him. Angling herself sideways on the seat, she lifted his arm, wrapped it around her shoulders, then snuggled against his chest.

Jagger held his breath, half-afraid that any motion, even the simple rhythm of his breathing, would cause her to move away from him. He wished he'd taken the time to remove his coat and waistcoat. He greatly feared the buttons and creases would make her uncomfortable. She felt small and fragile in his arms. He longed to ease her suffering.

She smoothed her hand over his belly until it came to rest above his bandaged wound. Her simple touch seemed to burn through his clothing, setting fire to his skin.

"I am sorry for this," she said, her voice ragged with raw emotion. "Were you not forced to wed with me, you would not have been in such danger."

"I was not 'forced to wed with you.'"

She made a sound of disbelief.

He tipped his fingers beneath her chin until she raised

her eyes to meet his gaze. "I know you won't believe this, but I wanted to marry you. You are loyal and brave and kind, not to mention a devoted mother. You are spirited and lovely, as well. I would have been a fool to let you get away."

He wanted to kiss her, but he refrained for fear his emotional needs would consume her.

An agonizing moment of silence passed. A moment in which her heart beat hard against her chest. A moment when a terrible trembling traveled beneath her skin, down her arms, down her back, to her toes.

Her face felt brittle, as if it would break into a thousand slivers should she try to smile. There was only one tale left to tell. Then she could close the door on her past and step into the light of her future.

His hand tightened around her shoulder. "Whatever it is, you do not have to say it."

"Yes, I do. If we are to build a future together, I would have no secrets between us. You deserve better than that. As do I."

She pressed her cheek against his chest. The steady thrum of air moving in and out of his lungs was a comforting sound. "I already told you that my mother was a nobody in the eyes of society. An actress of Italian descent."

She felt his chin nod against the top of her head. She drew a deep breath. "Naturally, she was not seen as an equal by her husband's peers, though not for lack of trying. For years she chased society's approval, only to be ridiculed by the matrons who guard the entrance to that coveted portal. But among the men, her fame increased a hundredfold as she made her way across the bedrooms of the *ton*."

His arm tightened around her shoulder in a silent signal of support. She ran her tongue over her lips to ease their dryness. The ache in her throat surprised her.

She had not expected this to be so difficult. "As you can well imagine, the scandal was extreme, though I did not learn any of this until I was much older, as I was only eight when they married."

She closed her eyes, trying to blot out the visions in her mind. "I was sixteen when she died. The details of her death were all hush-hush, so I assume it was more scandalous than any of her exploits until then. Unfit for my tender ears. A year later, my stepfather decided it was time to rid himself of any reminders of his irresponsible marriage to my mother. He summoned me to London, clothed me in the finest fashions of the day, launched me upon an unaccepting society and planned to marry me off to the first poor fool who looked my way."

The steady rhythm of Jagger's breathing accelerated beneath her ear. His heart rate quickened, but he spoke not a word.

Sophie ran a shaking hand over her aching throat. "Why he felt the need to give me a Season, I have no idea. He could have easily fobbed me off on some poor unsuspecting country squire rather than some fancy fribble in Town. Perhaps he felt guilty about the years he had pretended I didn't exist. Or perhaps he wanted to humiliate me, as my mother had humiliated him during their marriage. Whatever the reason, he didn't seem to think it would take long to get rid of me. I am told I resemble my mother and inherited her beauty, though I do not see it."

She held up her hand. "I do not say that to gain a compliment from you. It is merely a fact. Unfortunately for my stepfather, society shunned me as they shunned my mother."

"They are fools," Jagger said vehemently. "They would not recognize true nobility were it to bite them on the arse."

Sophie almost laughed. "Nor did he take into consideration my shyness. I had not spent much time in the company of others, and I found London overwhelming. Then there were the whispers and innuendos about my mother. I didn't understand most of it, but I caught the general meaning."

Of course, Edmund had been more than eager to explain. Sophie wondered if the stunning depths of his cruelty would always haunt her.

She rubbed her fingers in the silken folds of Jagger's shirt. "I hugged the wall at more than my share of balls and routes. Until I met a man. It was as if he had walked out of my dreams. Tall. Handsome. And attracted to me. We talked for hours. We met again and again. He said he loved me."

She choked, but she took a deep breath and hurried her words before she lost her nerve. "He said he wanted to be with me always. I thought he meant he wanted to marry me. In truth, he wanted to bed me. But I would not. Not without marriage. He suggested we elope. A runaway marriage with the man I loved seemed dashing and romantic at the time."

"The bounder deserved to be shot," Jagger growled. "It's a shame he is already dead. I would so enjoy doing the deed."

She did smile, then. He was her knight in shining armor, riding to her rescue, but he did not know the princess he was rescuing was tawdry and cheap.

Her smile faded. "We set off for Gretna. Or what I thought was Gretna—I still do not know the name of the village where we passed that final night."

She sat up to look in his eyes. "I was young and naïve. How could I have known it was a trick? How could I have suspected anyone could be so treacherous?"

Jagger smoothed his hand over her cheek. He tucked her hair behind her ear. His smile was tender and held not a trace of the condemnation she'd expected. "He was a despicable cad who took advantage of a young girl. It was not your fault."

Her throat ached and her eyes burned. Good Lord,

was she going to cry again? Would her nightmare never cease?

"His brother was a vicar, or so I thought at the time. He performed the ceremony before witnesses, a pair of his friends. After the wedding dinner, the man I thought was my husband drank himself senseless."

She fisted her hands in Jagger's shirt as angry tears dripped down her cheeks. She had suffered through the pain and brutality of her so-called wedding night.

"You need not say more," Jagger whispered brokenly. "I have already gathered the man was a monster. Were he alive, I would kill him for you."

Sophie smiled, a wobbly stretching of skin that tugged the bruise tightening her neck. "As he dressed the next morning, it was readily apparent that he was preparing to leave me."

He had stood by the bed, glaring down at her. "I can still hear his words. *Did you honestly think I would marry you? The daughter of an Italian whore?*'"

She laughed. It was a harsh, melancholy sound that seemed almost hysterical to her ears. "I believe he expected me to protest, but I was relieved! You are right. The man was a monster and I was grateful for my narrow escape. When I learned I was with child, I refused to name the father, just as I refused to divulge any of the details surrounding my fall from grace, including my so-called wedding."

Her stubborn pride had refused to allow her to admit to such stupidity. "I knew my stepbrother would either kill the man or force him to marry me in truth. I would rather live with the scandal of an unwed pregnancy than suffer a lifetime of abuse at the hands of that man. I could never entrust the future of my unborn child to that fiend. You do not seem surprised."

Jagger smiled tenderly. "Given your independent and fiercely honorable nature, I had already surmised your motives in not marrying the father of your children. You are an amazing woman, Mrs. Remington. And I am honored that you are my wife."

She shook her head. "I am not so amazing. And not strong at all. When Colin died, I plunged into a darkness the likes of which I never imagined. For two years, I struggled back from the depths of despair, barely making it through my days, relegating the care of my daughter to servants, the running of my estate to a thief."

Tears flowed freely down her cheeks, scalding her skin. Her heart beat a staccato rhythm within her chest. "Then you showed up with your preposterous claim to my hand, just as I was regaining control over my life and my land. Please, do not stop me. I want you to understand how I feel. We married for all the wrong reasons, out of duty and honor and to appease the wishes of a dying man. But do you know what I think? I think Stephen was wise beyond his years, that he chose better for me than I chose for myself."

His eyes went wide. "What are you saying?"

She smiled a wobbly smile. "I have come to know you, Jagger Remington. You are decent and kind, honorable and caring, and you do not hold the circumstances of Cecelie's birth against her. In fact, I very much suspect that you love her as if she were flesh of your flesh. You asked me if we could cry friends. If we could be partners in this life we now have entwined together. But I want more than that."

"What do you mean?"

"You are my husband. I am your wife."

"And?"

"I want a marriage in truth."

There. She had said it.

You do not want children, her inner voice screamed, but she knew she would kiss him just as she knew where her boldness would lead. The marriage act was a beastly thing, filled with pain and humiliation. Yet, she could not deny this powerful attraction that was inching her closer to this man.

To her husband. It was not just a physical attraction, though she certainly could not deny his incredible good looks. She was drawn to his inner strength, his sense of honor and duty, his commitment to justice.

She felt safe in his arms.

He slid his palm along her neck. The warmth of his touch rippled down her back. He made no move to help or hinder her.

"You do not want children," he said, his voice low and husky and rough with desire, an alluring aphrodisiac.

"I do not," she averred, but she wanted this moment in his arms. "You said there were ways . . . to prevent conception."

She couldn't believe the words had come out of her mouth, but he did not appear shocked.

He merely nodded. "I also promised you I would not claim my marital rights unless *you* asked me to."

He was using her words to give her a chance to escape.

"Are you asking me to?"

She had only two options. She could withdraw, retreat into the safety of loneliness, or she could commit to this man, commit to this marriage in truth. He would not force her.

Their future was hers and hers alone to decide.

She drew a deep breath, and slowly, oh so slowly, inched her lips toward his. Though he remained motionless, his mouth opened on a sigh. His warm breath beckoned her closer.

Sliding her hands into his hair, she drew his head down until his lips were a whisper away.

Chapter Twenty-two

"I want you to," she said, then pressed her lips to his.

The moment their mouths touched, heat spiraled down her arms and legs. With a growl, he swept her into his arms and carried her to the bed. She was surrounded by his strength, by the firmness of his chest, by his seeking fingers speared through her hair. He came down atop her, pushing her into the mattress. She should be terrified, yet never had she felt so protected, so cherished, so needed as his mouth clung to hers, almost desperately.

He traced the seam of her lips with his tongue, urged her to open her mouth, to invite him inside. As she welcomed him in, a terrible throbbing ache built between her legs, a need to be filled with this man. She had never felt such sensations. She should be horrified, but she was lost in his kiss, in the heat of his touch, and the depth of her desire. She breathed in his hot, masculine scent as his lips moved over her jaw.

She shivered as his breath tickled her ear. A giggle escaped her as he nibbled her neck. She felt his smile against the hollow beneath her throat.

"Do you like that?"

She could not have replied had her life depended on it. She was too lost in the sensations he was building within her. She turned her head, pressed her mouth to his neck, ran her fingers through his hair, then down his back. She felt the muscles of his shoulders tighten and stretch beneath his form-fitting coat. She could not deny it. She wanted this man.

There was no sin. He was her husband. She was his wife.

It was her duty to lie with him.

And to give him children, her traitorous mind taunted her.

She pushed that thought into the darkest corner of her thoughts as she surrendered to the sensations he was arousing within her. This was it. This was passion. She had thought she'd understood what it was, but she was so wrong, so naïve.

He leaned on his elbows, framed her face with his hands. His deep blue eyes were as dark and as turbulent as a storm-tossed sea. "Are you certain this is what you want? If you have any doubts, say so now, while I still have control of myself."

She hated the understanding and concern she saw in his eyes. He deserved so much better than her. She bit her lip to stifle a cry, turned her head to the side to hide her distress.

He would not let her escape. With the tips of his fingers, he tilted her face to meet his gaze.

"Do not be concerned," he whispered raggedly. "I understand. I am willing to wait."

She closed her eyes. "It is not that."

"Tell me what it is you want."

She did not know how to say it. She did not want him to be so understanding, so sympathetic, so . . . so perfect. He deserved much more in a wife than he was getting with her.

"It should be the first time," she whispered, barely able to give voice to her shame.

"Look at me," he said.

When she finally met his gaze, his eyes appeared bright and moist and filled with such raw emotion, Sophie felt as if she had just gazed into the center of the sun.

"It *is* the first time," he said fiercely. "It is *our* first time."

And Sophie tumbled headlong into love.

With a moan of surrender, she kissed him with all the desperate emotion in her heart. She could not admit her feelings. He had married her out of duty and obligation, but she silently vowed she would win his love. Then her mind ceased to function as his hands cupped her breasts. His mouth followed his hands and he ran his lips along the swells of her breast where her skin met her dressing gown. Good Lord, what a rush of sensation shuddered through her. She was nearly mindless by the time he slid her dressing gown from her shoulders, then moved his fingers to the collar of her night rail. Slowly, he eased it over her skin, revealing her shoulders, trapping her arms by her sides. She was helpless to touch him as he ran his mouth from her neck to her elbows and back to her lips. He pulled the fabric lower, releasing her arms, revealing her breasts, before promptly covering her aching flesh with his palms. He rubbed her sensitive mounds with his thumbs, lowered his mouth to her breast, drew her aching nipple between his teeth.

She felt as if she were about to perish beneath the sweet torture of his mouth on her flesh, his hands squeezing and kneading and igniting a yearning to run her hands over *his* naked flesh. Good Lord, she was wanton. She shoved her hands beneath the lapels of his frock coat. Never removing his lips from her flesh, he sat back on his knees, dragging her with him so they knelt face-to-face. He leaned back and smiled at her then, as she pushed his coat over his shoulders and down his arms.

She tried to return his smile, but her lips trembled. She felt an overwhelming urge to look away from his scorching gaze, to let him handle the removal of his own clothing as well as hers. A small voice in her mind protested such cowardice and would not let her hide. This moment was of her making. She would not step back and put all the responsibility on him, nor all the blame for having been swept away with desire.

She fumbled with the buttons of his waistcoat, unraveled his cravat, which he slowly pulled from her hands and slid under the pillow, much to her confusion. Conscious thought fled as she drew his shirt over his head. She choked on a sob as she ran her hands over his bandaged wound. She replaced her hands with her lips and he shuddered. Clutching her shoulders, he dragged her mouth to his, smothering her with his kiss.

She ran her hands over his chest, amazed at how much she wanted to touch his flesh, to feel the hardness of his muscles beneath her fingertips, to run her fingers through the dark patch of hair on his chest. His skin was golden brown, as if he spent many hours naked in the sun. The thought fascinated her. But when he dropped his hands to his breeches, she could not help herself—she closed her eyes.

Without warning he flipped her onto her back and she laughed, she actually laughed! Then she moaned as he slid his hands along her sides, dragging her night rail over her hips, down her thighs, until finally she was naked to his eyes.

Never had she felt so totally exposed nor so vulnerable. She fought the urge to cover herself with her hands. The cool air made her shiver, or perhaps it was the heat of his gaze as he knelt above her, caressing her skin with his eyes. She trembled with unbearable need as he returned his gaze to her face, and then slowly lowered himself over her body.

She thought he would kiss her then, but he buried his face in her belly, mouthed hot, wet kisses over her stomach, the swells of her breasts. His hands ran over her thighs, then slid between her legs and she moaned. He touched her in ways she had never expected. She could never have dreamed that such things passed between a man and a woman.

Surely he was wicked, moving his fingers within her deepest folds, drawing moans and sighs from her lips, setting fire to her belly and her womb. He stroked her and touched her and kissed her and suckled her breasts until she was quivering from head to toe and covered in sweat. He murmured tantalizing words against her skin, asking her if she liked how he touched her, if she liked where he kissed her, if she wanted more.

Yes, she wanted to scream, but she could not bring herself to reply, not because she was afraid of appearing wanton before his eyes, but because she was afraid she might cry.

For the first time in her life, she felt beautiful. She felt worshiped. She felt loved.

The sensations within her were rapidly building. She was reaching for something. She didn't know what, but she was afraid that if she so much as moved, the moment would be lost and she knew it would hurt her.

"Jagger," she moaned in spite of herself, and he shuddered in her arms.

He groaned against her lips. "Sophie. Say it again. Please, say it again."

His whispered words filled her with an overwhelming surge of power. Did he like the sound of his name on her lips as much as she liked saying it?

"Jagger," she said as he slid between her thighs.

She tried not to worry, but she couldn't seem to control the fear that caused her to tense her legs.

"Do not be afraid," he murmured against her lips as he smoothed the hair from her brow. He slid himself between her legs, and in another moment he was inside her. Instead of unbearable pain, Sophie felt only an intensification of the pleasure his fingers had stroked to life within her.

As he moved above her and within her, Sophie reached a pinnacle of exquisite pleasure. She cried out his name.

She wrapped her arms around his shoulders, buried her lips against his neck. This is what it meant to love a man.

Without shame. Without pain. With total surrender.

I love you, she wanted to shout, but she bit her lips to keep the words locked inside. He hadn't asked for her love, didn't want her love, but he did want to build a future with her and that was enough. They were married. They were a family.

Then why did she feel so bereft when, at the peak moment of his pleasure, he grabbed his cravat from under the pillow, withdrew from her body, and spilled his seed into the cloth?

Chapter Twenty-three

She was having the most delicious dream. Sheltered in her husband's arms with her back tucked tightly against his chest, surrounded by heat and security, she floated through a sensuous sea of longing and fulfillment. A hint of regret tugged at the back of her mind, but it drifted away as quickly as it appeared.

"Wake up," he whispered in her ear.

Languidly, she moved her head to one side. She breathed slowly, sleepily. "No," she whispered.

She could not remember the last time she had slept so deeply and for so long. She was reluctant to relinquish this moment of serenity. His hot breath sent sultry shivers up her spine. He nibbled her earlobe.

An unexpected giggle bubbled from her lips.

"I like the sound of that," he murmured.

She smiled and stretched in his arms, rubbing her back against his chest, sliding her bottom over his erection.

A moan of desire throbbed in her throat. She was trembling, deep inside, aching to feel his hot mouth along the tender skin of her neck, longing to feel him slip inside her womanly depths.

"I would like to oblige you," he said, his husky voice vibrating along her shoulder. "But we must get dressed."

Sophie opened her eyes. The room was still dark. They had another hour, mayhap two, before Cecelie would awaken and come bounding through the door a morning routine that Sophie realized would have to change now that her husband shared her bed. But she would not worry about that now.

The door was locked. No one would disturb them.

"Not yet," she murmured. Boldly entangling her legs with his, she shifted slightly until his hot flesh was poised at the entrance to her womanhood. Another small movement and she slid him deep inside her until he thrust against her womb.

Their simultaneous moans echoed through the room. The ache intensified as she slowly swayed her hips in a rhythm that built to a shuddering peak. She shivered. She gasped. She had no idea that married love could generate this longing to share this physical connection. His hands covered her breasts, lifting them, squeezing them, making her moan.

"You slaughter me," he growled ferociously as he leaned into her and over her, his hands clutching her arms as he thrust his hips, pushing himself deeper and harder into her core until she cried out from the tension, until she collapsed from the pleasure. A moment later, he pulled himself from her body and, once again, spilled his seed into his neck cloth.

The twinge of regret that had haunted her dreams returned with a vengeance.

Jagger searched her features, looking for any sign of disgust for the ferocity with which he had just taken her.

Her face gave no hint to her thoughts.

He couldn't believe he was growing hard again, that he wanted her, again, though mere moments had passed since their coupling. He would never have enough of her, he suddenly realized. His hands shook at his helplessness, at the power she now possessed to destroy him.

He fought the urge to declare his love, until his throat

ached and his jaw throbbed. Her dark eyes studied him intently, but she said not a word.

I love you, he wanted to shout, but fear kept the words locked behind his teeth. Before this moment, he had never suspected that he was a coward.

"Will you join me for breakfast?" he asked, opting for safety within the mundane.

She nodded her head, her eyes grave, her mouth flat. She pulled the covers up to her chin. Her cheeks were flushed from their lovemaking. A sheen of sweat glistened on her shoulders. The alluring scent of her arousal clung to the sheets.

If he stayed there another moment, he would be leaping upon her like a randy dog covering a bitch in heat. She deserved better than that. She deserved better than him. But he would never let her go.

A hint of gray light filtered through the crease in the draperies. He rose on trembling legs, crossed to the windows, pulled the panels wide. A swirl of vivid reds, pinks, and gold fired the horizon as dawn burned away the night.

He would have to return to his own rooms to wash up, shave, and change into clean clothes. For now, last night's garments would have to do. Her eyes never left him as he moved. The intensity of her gaze made him self-conscious, an altogether unpleasant sensation that trapped the air in his lungs and tightened to an ache in his chest. He was excruciatingly aware of every move he made, of his naked butt and his hairy chest. Of his broad shoulders and his erection, unmistakable evidence of his overwhelming desire for her.

Turning his back to the bed, he tugged on his shirt, then realized it was inside out. He didn't think she could tell from this distance. Rather than admit his embarrassing mistake, he yanked on his breeches. His hands shook as he fumbled with the buttons. Good Lord, what was wrong with him? He grabbed his boots as he strode to the bed. He slid one hand through her hair, covered her mouth in a kiss so powerful it reverberated through him like thunder shaking the wind.

She leaned up on her knees, pressed her palms against his chest, moved her tongue against his lips. A soft moan escaped from her throat, a purring sound that fueled his desire.

It took all his strength of will to release her. She sat back on her heels, the covers tangled around her knees, her breasts bared to his gaze. He dared not speak for fear of what words might come out of his mouth.

He turned and stalked barefoot out of the room.

Sophie grabbed her dressing gown from the edge of the bed as she struggled to her feet. She crossed the room on trembling legs. She had hurt his feelings with her silence, she realized.

He had treated her with unfailing kindness, had made love to her with a gentleness that had bordered on reverence, and she had trampled his feelings as if he had none.

How could she put words to her thoughts when confusion clouded her senses? When she had no specific idea of what was bothering her. She simply felt uneasy, agitated by some notion she could not even name.

Good Lord, what was wrong with her? She would not countenance such gloominess when the day ahead of her—nay, the future ahead of her—was hopeful and bright.

Eager to attack the chores of the day, she washed up and dressed in a simple gray dress. When she passed into Cecelie's room, Jagger was there already, sitting cross-legged on a massive pillow before the child-sized table. Cecelie sat upon another massive pillow, with a third one apparently waiting for her. The table held three plates overflowing with poached eggs with burnt butter, spiced bread, and gooseberry jam. The cheerful domestic scene brought a tender smile to her lips, even as it touched upon emotions she was unprepared to face.

Jagger grinned as he came to his feet. Good Lord, he truly was a handsome man. He wore a frock coat of blue superfine that accentuated his vibrant blue eyes. He took her hand in his. His intimate smile brought a burning sensation to her cheeks.

"I thought it prudent to start a *new* morning ritual," he said. "Given our activities of last night." His voice dropped to a whisper, low and seductive. "Activities I hope to repeat tonight and every night for the rest of our lives."

A delicious shiver tickled her spine as his words seeped through the sensual fog surrounding her. He pressed his lips to her fingertips. The heat in her cheeks spread to her neck.

Good Lord, she must look as if she had a fever.

"How intuitive," she said, not recognizing her own voice hidden in the low sultry tone. She stared into his eyes, lost in the magical spell he was weaving around her.

Cecelie grabbed his hand, ending the moment and dragging her back to the present. "Uppie. Mama," she said, taking Sophie's hand in hers and leading them both to the table.

She pointed at one of the cushions. "Mama. Sit."

Sophie had thought herself long past tears, but the sweet sound of her daughter's voice nearly unraveled her. She turned her head to study the floor, then shifted her gaze to the ceiling in the hopes of hiding her emotions from her ebullient child. She was afraid Cecelie might misinterpret her tears as grief instead of joy.

"How elegant," she said as Jagger helped her onto her cushion. She lost her balance, tipping precariously toward the floor. He set his hand in the center of her back, firmly locking her in an upright position and saving her dignity.

Sophie's laughter mingled with Cecelie's giggles.

Jagger coughed into his fist, an ineffective method

of hiding his grin. "Why don't you show Mama how it is done?"

Cecelie plopped on her cushion, wiggled her bottom until she was positioned exactly in the middle, then crossed her legs in front of her, her skirt snagging around her ankles.

"I feel so exotic," Sophie said, gripping the table with one hand as she imitated her daughter's movements. The other hand she used to tug her dress to hide her knees.

Once she was certain she wouldn't topple to the floor, she let go of the table. She did not bother to hide her fascination as she watched Jagger fold himself onto his cushion with all the elegance and grace of an Indian prince. All he was missing was a turban and jewels and a hookah pipe.

He spread his napkin on his lap. "What are your plans for this day, madam?"

"First, I must inspect the house to determine which rooms need cleaning. I have fallen dreadfully behind, given the circumstances of these last few weeks."

Determined to put the past behind her, Sophie ruthlessly banished the bad memories trying to invade her consciousness.

At Jagger's dark look, she smiled. "Then I will draft an advertisement seeking domestic service. Does that please you?"

"Greatly," Jagger drawled, his tone clearly teasing, though approval and something darker, something earthier, burned in his eyes. "You will not let me see you with a feather duster in your hand, madam. Nor a mop nor a broom, nor any other instrument, for that matter."

She could not stop the wry smile that curved her lips as she slowly nodded her head in agreement.

He scooped up a forkful of eggs. "Now, why don't I believe you?"

Sophie laughed. "I cannot imagine."

She could not remember a moment in her life when

she had felt this happy, other than the day her children were born. Though she would never forget her little boy or the pain of his death, she finally felt hopeful for the future.

"Uppie said ride. Jack," Cecelie said around a mouthful of eggs. Her curls bounced up and down as she nodded her head. Her eyes sparkled with excitement.

Sophie stared at Cecelie, amazed at how quickly her silent, withdrawn daughter was transforming into the jubilant child Sophie had known before Colin's death. Even the trauma of the night before seemed to have left no ill effects. If for no other reason, she would love Jagger Remington for giving her this. But there were so many reasons to love him, she thought as she caught him gazing at her out of the corner of her eye.

"I have promised our daughter an adventure," he said. "I hope you do not mind."

"Of course not."

"Would you care to join us?"

"No. I have too much to do. I need to organize the staff. I do not know your servants or what positions they have held in the past. It is long since time I conducted an inventory of the storerooms and linens. And so on."

He smiled at her. "I have estate business to see to as well."

She raised a brow in silent query.

"After Cecelie and I finish our ride, I plan to visit the tenants. I want to prioritize any needed repairs. I wish to evaluate the home farm and determine the number of workers we need. And so on," he said, repeating her words, his smile evident in his voice. "But perhaps you would do me the honor of spending the afternoon with me? I have a surprise for you."

Honestly, she shouldn't smile so much. She was making a cake of herself. But she couldn't seem to stop. His words pleased her greatly, as did the intimacy of his voice and this new family tradition.

He tossed his napkin on the table. "What say you, princess? Are you ready to ride?"

Cecelie leapt to her feet, hands high in the air. "Up."

Jagger swung the child into his arms. Supporting the back of her head with his hand, he cradled her against his shoulder and closed his eyes.

The poignancy of the moment brought fresh tears to Sophie's eyes. Never could she have imagined she would cry more out of happiness than she had in despair.

After a hasty good-bye, father and daughter strode from the room. A moment later, Mary appeared, followed by the village seamstress and a dozen or more girls carrying armfuls of the most beautiful fabric and dresses Sophie had ever seen.

Chapter Twenty-four

"Do not open your eyes."

Sophie laughed. She clung to his neck as he carried her to her "surprise." "I can hear dried leaves crunching beneath your boots, and that rustling sounds like squirrels dashing through the trees."

"So you think you know our destination, do you?"

"Yes, I do. You should put me down. You must be tired by now."

"Tired? You insult my manhood, madam. I assure you, I am capable of carrying you for miles."

The sound of crunching leaves stopped. She could feel the warmth of the sun on her face. The brilliance of the light glowed orange through her eyelids. They were nearing the pond.

"Remember, do not open your eyes," he said, as he set her on her feet. He stood behind her, his fingers brushing the nape of her neck as he deftly untied the lacings.

The frock was a new creation, ordered over a week ago by Mr. Remington, or so the seamstress had told Sophie that morning. It had needed only minor alterations, as the seamstress had taken apart one of Sophie's older dresses, also delivered by Mr. Remington, in order to fashion the pattern.

It was made of the softest green silk Sophie had ever had the pleasure of caressing with her hands. An overskirt of sheer green netting shot with gold gathered at the waist, just under her breasts. The rounded neckline was shockingly low.

With a gentle pressure, he turned her to face him. He slowly inched the fabric over her shoulders.

Her breathing quickened. Her neck grew warm. His fingers, grazing her collarbone, sent a delicious shiver skittering over her skin. She could hardly believe he planned to make love to her here. Out-of-doors. It was improper. It was decadent.

It was exciting beyond anything she had ever imagined.

Her stomach felt fluttery. Her knees grew soft, almost incapable of supporting her weight. She dropped her head back, exposing her neck, silently imploring him to kiss her there.

Her dress slipped down her sides and pooled at her feet. She held her breath as he skimmed his knuckles over the curves of her breasts above the neckline of her shift.

She wore no stays, a habit that would change as soon as she hired a lady's maid. Or perhaps he could act as her valet.

The idea enticed her. She could well imagine him sliding his fingers along her back as he drew the laces. Her skin was afire. She wanted to feel his hands on her flesh.

She was wearing only her shift, made of thin, nearly transparent cotton that she imagined left nothing to his imagination. She felt exposed and utterly aroused.

Her breasts ached for his touch. If only she weren't so modest and shy, she would grab his hand, place his palm at the juncture of her thighs, urge him to stroke his fingers over her sensitive flesh. She opened her mouth to say—what?

Make love to me? I want you?

She had no idea what words to use to express her desire.

He touched his fingertips to her lips. "Shh."

Good Lord, was she so desperate that this simple touch could make her weak? Yes, she was, but she was not ashamed.

He moved away from her then. She peeked at him from beneath her eyelids. He had lifted his foot and was removing his boot. She choked back a giggle, a nervous habit she had never outgrown. She heard a thud as first one boot hit the ground, then the other. He stripped off his socks, his frock coat, his waistcoat, and then his shirt, though he left on his breeches. His golden skin glistened in the sun.

A moment later, he knelt before her and removed her shoes.

As his warm hands wrapped around her ankle, she decided that having Jagger Remington undress her was the most erotic experience of her life. Well, not as erotic as the way he had touched her last night in her bed, but she knew that was coming.

She shuddered in anticipation, then laughed as he swept her into his arms. Her laughter turned into a shriek as she heard him splashing into the pond. Her screech startled a family of swans, sending them paddling for the opposite shore.

The cold water lapped at her heels as he waded deeper and deeper. "What do you think you are doing?"

His smile was as wicked as the devil's own. "I am teaching you to swim."

"I have absolutely no desire to learn how to swim. Put me down."

"As you wish," he said, sliding her slowly along the length of his body, into the water, until her feet sank in the slimy mud. "But you *will* learn to swim. I insist."

Finding herself waist-deep in the pond shocked all romantic feelings out of her. The water was frigid, despite the warmth of the air. She shivered. "I will catch a cold, you brute."

"You are made of stronger stuff than that, as I know from experience. No, you will learn to swim, if for no other reason than it might one day save your life."

"It's not much of a surprise." She heard the whine in her voice, but she was too frightened to care. When she had fallen into the pond—when he had pushed her, her treacherous mind chimed in—she had truly thought she was about to die. It was the first time she had feared her own mortality.

She was not eager to repeat the experience.

He laughed, pointing to the shore. "Delicious food and drink await you, my love. But first—you learn to swim."

He had spread a blanket, arranged a basket with food. Pots stuffed to overflowing with flowers sat at each corner of the fabric, anchoring it from blowing away in the wind. From this distance, Sophie could not tell what type of flowers they were, but the picture was beautiful.

She blinked rapidly, in tune with her thundering heart. She tried not to read too much into his actions, though it was nearly impossible to keep her hopes from soaring.

She smiled. "Teach me. I'm yours."

During the next hour, Sophie realized that learning to swim wasn't such a bad idea, especially with Jagger Remington as the teacher. He wrapped his powerful arms around her waist, kept her back snuggled tightly against his chest. His warm breath tickled the nape of her neck. His hands brushed the swells of her breasts as he taught her to move her arms back and forth as if they were wings. His fingers grazed her calves as he showed her how to pump her legs in circular motions, sending delicious shivers down her spine that had nothing to do with the temperature of the water.

He called it "treading water." She called it "a last gasp before dying" as she dipped below the surface. But then he quickly wrapped his arm around her waist and dragged her against his chest. She gazed at him with wide eyes and a quivering heartbeat and a rapidity of breath that nearly sent her into a swoon. Gooseflesh shivered across her skin.

Her palms rested on his chest. His skin was hot beneath her fingertips. His muscles flexed. His shoulders hardened. And pressed against her lower body was the undeniable proof that he wanted her as badly as she wanted him.

It was time to take matters into her own hands.

She slid her palms up his chest, wrapped her arms around his neck, buried her fingers in his hair, and drew his lips down to hers. She felt his sharp intake of breath against her mouth before awareness slipped away and she lost herself in the heat of his kiss. He slanted his mouth over hers, but she took control of the kiss, tentatively touching her tongue to his lips, then slipping it deeper within his mouth, stroking the sensitive skin, tasting his breath.

"Delicious," she murmured, pulling him deeper into her embrace.

A deep moan slipped from his throat. She felt powerful, aware of his need, aware of her desire. Never could she have imagined how arousing it was to touch a man's naked flesh.

She explored the hard ridges of his back, the muscles flexing and stretching beneath her palms. When she reached the waistband of his breeches, she paused, but only for a moment before she smoothed her hands over his bottom.

Her bold touch drew a frenzied response. He thrust one hand into her hair, devoured her mouth like a man half-starved. He pushed his other hand into the small of her back, pulling her closer and closer until he held her so tightly against his chest, she felt as if they were one person, with no end of her and no beginning of him.

"I want you," he growled against her lips. "I want you right here. Right now—"

"I want you, too," she breathed, before he once more possessed her lips in a mind-numbing kiss. She lost conscious thought as his hands roamed her body, palming her breasts, cupping her bottom.

His mouth dropped to her throat, and she moaned. She slid her hands to the front of his breeches, and slowly, boldly, popped the buttons. His chest heaved. A low groan rumbled in his throat as she peeled back the flap and took his erect flesh into her hands. She felt wicked and wild and wondrously thrilled to learn that she had the power to make him moan. To learn the physical union between a man and a woman was a pleasurable act, when shared in love. She half expected him to drag her from the water and take her on the grassy bank. She never expected him to raise her shift, lift her in the water, wrap her legs around his waist, and slide himself within her.

What strange, yet altogether arousing sensations shuddered through her as she rotated her hips until the delicious friction built to a shattering peak. She clung to his shoulders, her lips melting against his. With a sudden groan, he released her, withdrawing himself at the last moment. Sophie knew she should be happy. He was an honorable man above all things.

He would never break his word. He would never contribute to her heartache by giving her another reason to grieve.

He would never give her a child.

As they reclined side by side on the blanket, the scent of roses drifting on the breeze, Jagger felt a contentment he'd never known in his life. *Are you happy?* he wanted to ask her, but the words tangled on his tongue.

He had no notions of romance or chivalry. He was a stumbling clod out to win the heart of the woman he loved—and he hadn't the foggiest idea how to proceed.

She rolled onto her stomach. Resting her cheek against the back of her hands, she cast him a sideways glance.

"It seems a bit unfair," she said. "You know so much about me. And I know so little of you."

He propped himself on his elbow so he could better see her, better gauge her reactions and her mood. He stroked her hair, tucking a stray strand behind her ear. "What would you like to know?"

She shivered, bringing a smile to his lips. She was so sensitive to his touch. It filled him with manly pleasure and no small sense of pride. She had experienced little happiness in her life. It pleased him greatly that she found such joy in his arms. It was only a matter of time until that joy turned to love. No doubt he was turning into a mindless fool, but it was a path he now willingly traveled.

"Where were you born? Who are your parents? What was your childhood like? Why did you go to India? What made you stay in such a faraway place? How did you know Stephen . . . ?"

Her voice trailed off after the last question, and her gaze shifted away. No doubt she regretted interjecting her brother's name into the conversation, considering how they had come together in the first place.

He stroked her cheek as he contemplated his answers. How much could he tell her without scaring her away? They were beginning to forge a future together. He had no intention of disrupting that process for the sake of honesty. There was plenty of time for the truth to come out. He wanted to secure her love. Only then could he bare his soul.

And hope she would understand.

"Let us discuss Stephen, shall we?" he said. "Let us get his chicanery out in the open, once and for all."

He waited until she met his gaze. "Stephen asked me to marry you. I agreed because I thought you were willing."

"But why? Please answer me."

"He assured me that you were fair of face and form, that I would not find you displeasing. I am shallow. I admit to being intrigued by his description of you. But I must also admit, he misled me on that score. You are far more beautiful than any words invented by mortal man can describe."

A flush spread over her cheeks. She smiled shyly. "You flatter me too graciously."

The emotion shining in her dark eyes entranced him. "I think not. But I have a lifetime to convince you of that truth."

"In all seriousness, why did you agree to wed me?"

He breathed deeply. He would have to share some of the truth. She deserved that much. "I thought I told you already, but perhaps I didn't sufficiently answer your worries. I owed your brother a debt of honor for helping me as a young man. Quite frankly, he saved my mother's life."

Sophie's shocked gasp did not surprise him.

"How do you mean?"

Jagger swallowed. Never before had he discussed the events of that fateful moment that had sent him running into the night, broken and bleeding and begging for help.

"My father," he began, but an odd lump lodged in his throat and he had to pause for breath. "My father was a brutal man. He lived by the rule: 'Spare the rod and spoil the child.' As many a man does, I have since learned. Though it does not make it right."

The sympathy shining in her eyes showed her clear understanding of the words he omitted about the shadows and menace that had haunted his every waking moment throughout his childhood. "My mother did nothing to stop him. As an adult, I understand a woman has no power against a monster like that, but as a child, I hated her for letting him hurt me."

The sounds and smells of the pond drifted away, and Jagger found himself lost in the memories of that awful night. "One evening, when I was twelve and he was particularly brutal, she stepped between us."

A burning sensation stung his eyes. He blinked hard, damned if he would allow himself to cry. "It was the first time I fought back. Then I carried my mother to the only person I knew who I thought might help us."

"My brother," she said, her voice hoarse, as if she were fighting back tears.

He nodded. "Despite the law, Stephen sheltered my mother from my father's wrath. He brokered a separation, by which my mother was allowed to live on her own in the country and my father would make no demands upon her."

At the time, Jagger had wondered why his father had agreed so readily to the arrangement. At first, Jagger had convinced himself that the man was afraid Jagger would return and pummel him to death. It was the logic of a green youth with no experience of the real world and how it worked.

In reality, Stephen had possessed those damning letters and he had used them as a weapon to secure the separation. What hurt Jagger the most was the realization that his mother had provided Stephen with those letters.

She must have discovered them early in her marriage and used them to blackmail her husband into accepting Jagger as his son, thereby securing Jagger a title and position in society. Then she had hidden from Jagger the truth of his parentage, a truth that could have set him free from the chain that had dragged him down for so long—the terrifying fear that he would grow up to be as brutal as the man who had raised him.

Sophie rolled onto her side to face him. She reached out her hand, traced her fingertips over the jagged flesh beneath his eye. "He did this to you."

It wasn't a question, but a statement of fact. Balancing on the precipice of his past, Jagger was overwhelmed by his love for this woman. And that was before she leaned forward and kissed his withered cheek.

"I am sorry for your pain," she whispered.

His chest hurt, as if his heart were being squeezed in a vise. He had never known until that moment that one's heart could actually ache, not with pain, but with a love so great, it could no longer be contained.

He cupped her cheek. "Have you any idea how much I admire you?"

Her eyes widened. "Admire me? Whatever for?"

"I can only imagine—" His voice cracked with barely suppressed emotion. "If my mother had possessed one ounce of your courage, how different my life would have turned out."

"I do not understand."

"You did not name the father of your child because the man was a brutal monster who raped you."

"It was not rape," she said, her voice low and trembling with shame. "The beast was guilty of many a thing, but not that. I went with him willingly."

Jagger tried to keep the rage he felt for the bastard out of his voice, but he failed miserably. "The man deserves no such kindness from you. And it was rape. He took what he wanted with no regard for your innocence. He was brutal and he caused you pain. No doubt he would have abused you and your children had you allowed your brother to force him to wed you. Society may judge your actions harshly, but I know you acted to protect yourself and your babes."

A tear slipped down her cheek, which he wiped away with his thumb. "My wife. My beautiful, brave, compassionate wife. Mother of my child." He laughed. "I can hardly believe that I once thought I never wanted children. But you have given me the most miraculous gift. A precious daughter."

He shook his head, amazed at his own misguided thinking. "It is getting late. We should head back to the house."

"I don't think my shift is dry yet," she whispered as she rolled him onto his back.

"I have let it be known in the village that we are taking on staff," Sophie said, smiling shyly at Jagger as they walked hand in hand through the French doors leading to the gallery.

He slowed his step, as if reluctant to let this afternoon draw to an end. "I am glad to hear it, as I never want to see you cleaning the house again. Not even with your infamous feather duster."

He was teasing her about the day they met. Then, Sophie could not have imagined how pleasant it was to laugh and tease with a man she loved. So much had changed.

She used her free hand to pat her hair into place, to smooth the wrinkles from her overskirt. "Did Cecelie enjoy her ride?"

"Tremendously. Though she was not pleased when Mary came to collect her. Two hours was not long enough, it seems."

Sophie laughed. It felt so good.

When she noticed how much it pleased him, she laughed again. What had she done to deserve such happiness?

She was laughing still when they passed through the gallery into the drawing room. At their arrival, a man stood up. He was an older man, fastidiously dressed in the fashion of the day in striped trousers and a white waistcoat under a bottle-green cutaway dress coat. His well-tailored clothes were expensive, as was the leather satchel on the floor at his feet.

Sophie frowned. She did not recognize the man.

She glanced at Jagger.

He smiled at her. His eyes seemed mildly curious, but not alarmed. He tucked her hand into the crook of his arm. "Might I help you, sir?"

The gentleman cleared his throat.

"Here we are," Thea said, coming through the door with a tea tray in her hand. She saw Sophie and Jagger, and she smiled. "Thank goodness, you are back. I see you have met Mr. Matthews."

She set the tray on a satinwood table. "Mr. Matthews is an emissary from the Duke of Mannering."

Something in Thea's calculating smile raised an alarm in Sophie's mind and that was before Thea shifted her gaze to Jagger. Sophie glanced at her husband. His cheeks were pale, an unhealthy starkness made more noticeable given the unruly flurry of thick dark hair framing his face.

He caught Sophie's gaze. His eyes appeared haunted. This man would bring trouble to the fragile start of their future together. Sophie felt this truth in the marrow of her bones.

She did not want to know who he was, or why he was here, but she had never been a coward. She thrust her chin in the air and stepped forward.

"I am Mrs. Remington. Might I please inquire as to the purpose of your visit?"

The man did not reply. He kept his gaze on Jagger.

The tension between the two men pulled and stretched.

Jagger finally turned to Sophie and took her hand in his. "Why don't you check on our daughter, madam? I will deal with whatever issue has arisen."

Sophie recognized his words for what they were: an attempt to get rid of her so he could speak in private with this man. Perhaps it was a good idea, but she was tired of secrets and lies and betrayals popping up to hurt her.

She wanted the truth. "Your business, sir?"

The man kept his unreadable gaze on Jagger. "It is with the greatest sadness that I must inform you of the death of your father, the Duke of Mannering."

Chapter Twenty-five

His father was a duke.

Sophie twisted her hands in the folds of her dress as she paced her bedchamber. Far beyond rational thought, she was floating in an abyss filled with pure emotion. An intense feeling of betrayal ripped through her. He had made her fall in love with him. Now he had yanked the rug of illusion from beneath her feet. Yet again, she was played for a fool.

The door snapped open and Jagger entered the room.

"Get out," Sophie spat, embarrassed at her inability to suppress her anger. What difference could it make at this point? He had seen her naked. He knew all there was to know about her. But she had known nothing about him. It was a fantasy world in which she had allowed herself to believe.

"We need to speak."

He sounded calm and rational, which only escalated the fury flowing within her veins. Her thoughts were incoherent, as if her brain had melted into a soggy mess.

"Get out of my room," she bit out through her teeth. "Get out of my house." Her voice rose an octave higher. "Get out of my life," she shouted, turning her back on him.

She scanned the room, looking for something to throw at his head. She could not be held accountable for her actions.

He strode across the room, wrapped his hands around her arms, and forced her to meet his gaze. His mouth was hard and flat, the muscles in his neck taut. Icy control, and a deeper menace, glittered in his narrowed eyes.

"You will listen to me," she said, schooling as much dignity as she could into her voice. "I don't want you here."

"So that is it? One tiny setback and you are ready to cut and run? I thought you made of sterner stuff than that."

"One tiny setback?" she sputtered. "Your father is a duke."

His fingers tightened on her arms. "Was a duke. He is dead."

"As is our so-called marriage. I want a divorce."

He smiled at her then, but there was no warmth to the curve of his lips. "No court will grant us a divorce. We have no grounds."

She thrust her chin in the air. "You can claim adultery. Given my reputation, no one will doubt your veracity."

His features softened. Some emotion crept into his eyes. It looked like pity, which set the small hairs at the back of her neck on end and whipped her chin up.

"Sophie," he whispered in his achingly appealing voice.

She shook off his grip and raced across the room.

Standing by the windows, she folded her arms over her chest. Even though she felt as if she were dying, she knew she continued to draw breath. She could feel the air moving in and out of her lungs, and it hurt. "All this time, you were masquerading as a common man, when in reality, you were a—what? An earl? A marquess? Not that it matters, for now you are a duke." She clutched her fist to her chest. "Is Jagger Remington even your true name?

Perhaps you need not seek a divorce, after all. Perhaps we are not legally wed."

The tendons in his neck bulged as he clenched his jaw.

"Oh, it is a legal marriage, I do assure you, madam," he said through clenched teeth. "My given name is James Jagger Spencer Remington, though no one has called me James since I was very young, and then, only Stephen. Make no mistake. All the documents are legally signed and witnessed, as was the marriage itself. You are my wife, and my duchess, and so you shall remain."

He would never understand. She could never explain.

"Am I to expose my daughter to society's scorn merely to please you?" She pressed the back of her hands to her lips until she was able to speak without choking on her words. "I think not. I want a divorce. You will weather the scandal easily enough. You are a duke, after all."

He stared into her eyes as if he could see into the deepest recesses of her mind. He held her gaze for what seemed like an hour, though mere minutes passed.

Finally, he gave a curt nod, then stalked from the room.

It was what she wanted. She should be happy, but Sophie greatly feared she would never be happy again.

She stood beside her bedroom window. The morning sun seemed unbearably bright. She would have much preferred rain today. He was leaving.

The rumble of his deep voice floated on the breeze from the courtyard below. Why she remained by her window, she couldn't say. Perhaps she wanted to torture herself. She had reached too high. She had dared too much.

Now she had to pay the price.

His horse restlessly shifted its feet, its hooves striking the packed-earth drive. The voices of the servants who had gathered to bid him farewell waned beneath the sound of her breaking heart. She buried her face in the draperies. A sharp ache twisted the pit of her stomach. She wanted nothing more than to run after him and beg him to stay. But it was impossible. He was a powerful peer of the realm. He needed a wife who could mingle with royalty, not a woman with scandal branded into her name.

Oh, she had no doubt that society would pretend to accept her, if for no other reason than to toady up to her high-born husband, but he deserved better than that. He deserved better than her. Still, the sad truth did nothing to ease her pain.

She loved him. She always would.

If she were honest with herself, she had loved him from the moment she'd met him, only she had been too afraid to admit it. Afraid to take the chance that he would not betray her, as everyone else she had ever loved had betrayed her in the past.

And he had. By keeping his birthright a secret, he had allowed her to dream, to hope, that he might grow to love her, truly love her, regardless of her past and her shame.

She should have known better.

The ache in her stomach turned to unbearable pain. Despite her better judgment, despite her determination to stay in her room, her feet started to move, seemingly of their own accord. Slowly, at first. Then faster and faster until she raced from the room, through the hall, down the stairs.

She flung open the front door just in time to see him kick his horse into a canter and disappear around the bend in the road. His name caught in her throat and threatened to choke her. What had she done?

Cecelie stood on the top step, her face buried in her hands, her anguish clearly visible in the sobs racking her back.

To see her daughter suffer so wrenched Sophie's heart. Thea offered what little comfort she was capable of giving, stroking Cecelie's hair, murmuring soft, soothing words.

With a calmness that belied her own breaking heart, Sophie knelt and gathered her daughter into her arms. Cecelie's tears soaked through Sophie's gown, searing her skin like a whiplash.

Thea plunked her hands on her hips. "I never thought I would call you a fool. But you are. A fool."

Sophie closed her eyes, silently pleading for Thea to go away. But Thea seemed determined to speak her piece, each word sharper than the prick of a knife.

"That man loves you," Thea said. "And you sent him away. I wish a man would love me that way."

Thea was right. She was a fool. But there was nothing she could do about it now. She had made her decision. She was the one who had to live with the consequences.

But why did Cecelie have to suffer so?

"My love," Sophie crooned. "It will be all right."

Cecelie was crying so hard she could scarcely draw breath. "I w-want Uppie. I want U-Uppie."

"I know you do, darling." So do I, Sophie thought, though she would never say the words. She held her daughter at arm's length, forced herself to smile. "Now, you must stop crying so. You will make yourself ill. Can you do that for me?"

Cecelie hiccupped. "I d-don't know."

"Here," Thea said, taking the child by the hand. "Why don't you and I have a steaming cup of chocolate and a tart or two? What say you?"

Cecelie stuck the pinkie finger of her free hand in her mouth and started to suck. Breathing raggedly through her nose, she followed Thea into the house.

Thea paused at the door. "Do not worry, Sophie. I will not leave her alone. Why don't you try to get some rest?"

Sophie nodded, but she knew she wouldn't sleep. She went to the garden instead. Hoping some routine work would keep her mind occupied, she fetched her pruning shears from the shed and attacked one of the rose bushes.

Thoughts of Jagger plagued her relentlessly, despite her best efforts to keep her mind blank. Like a hurricane, he'd swept into her life and turned her world upside down. He'd shattered her defenses. He'd earned her trust, then her love.

Then he betrayed her.

She should have ignored the stirrings of her heart. She should have heeded the lessons she'd learned from the past. She should never have let herself fall in love with the blasted man.

Viciously, she worked the shears. The mutilated branches piled up around her feet, but she kept cutting, as if in a trance, until the plant was decimated.

She threw her shears to the ground. Obviously, this wasn't working. Restless energy besieged her. She roamed the Park, her thoughts as wild as the gathering wind. To her utmost despair, everywhere she went reminded her of Jagger.

Standing by the pond where they shared their first kiss, she closed her eyes, traced her fingertips over her mouth. She remembered the heat of his lips against hers and she moaned.

Here, they had dined alfresco and Sophie had felt the first stirrings of love in her barren heart as she'd watched him play with her daughter, drawing Cecelie out of her silent cocoon, her raspy laughter sweet music to her mother's ears.

Later, he'd taught Sophie to swim. Later still, they had made love beneath a sun-brightened sky.

The memories here were too painful.

Determined to conquer her wayward emotions, Sophie strode back to the house. As she passed the stables, the crisp scent of hay and horse beckoned her in. As if pulled by a force beyond her control, she walked into the first stall.

Jack, the Welsh pony Colin had loved so much, nuzzled her hand. Colin. Her beautiful son. Dead these many months.

Sophie had kept her grief for him locked deep inside because she was too afraid to let it out. Afraid she would go insane, or worse, afraid that her memories of Colin would fade until he was no more than a brief annotation in her life. Referred to once, and then forgotten.

She laid her head against the pony's neck. It was warm and soft and smelled of dust. Jagger had helped her face her grief. She had not put Colin's death behind her, but she had learned there was no sin in seeking her own happiness.

Her chest felt hollow, as if some unseen hand had reached in and ripped out her heart. Once, she had thought she could live with this loneliness, but that was before Jagger Remington had walked into her life. He had loved her. He had cherished her, and she had chased him away.

Now her life would never be the same.

She had claimed she remained on the estate to protect Cecelie from society's scorn. But the lie tasted bitter on her tongue as she suddenly realized she was protecting herself. What a coward she was. She'd had the chance for love and laughter in her life, but she'd let it slip away because she was too afraid to confront her fears.

The pony rubbed his head against her shoulder, as if he could sense her despair and wanted to ease her anguish.

"'Tis a sad day indeed, when a woman must seek comfort from a horse," Sophie said, as if the horse could understand her.

He pawed the ground.

She rubbed her hand down the animal's neck and remembered the day she had confided in Jagger her greatest mistake, the truth behind Cecelie and Colin's conception. She had expected him to turn away from her in disgust.

Instead, he'd gathered her in his arms and made her realize she wasn't to blame.

Determined to shake off her self-pity by cleaning the rugs, Sophie headed for the house. It would make him furious if he knew, but he wasn't here to stop her. She covered her face with her hands as she choked on a sob. What had she done?

Outside the stables, she bumped into Henry Holliston— Viscount Holliston now that his brother was dead.

Her jaw dropped open. "What are you doing here?"

The wind ruffled his light brown hair. His eyes were narrowed in concern. "Searching for you."

Sophie gave silent thanks that Cecelie was in the house with Thea, safely tucked away from this bounder. She drew a shaky breath. "What do you want?"

"I want to be an uncle to your daughter and a brother to you," he said, his jaw tense and his head erect, as if he had no shame. "I want to make amends."

"You have no claims on her."

He reached for Sophie's hand, but she quickly backed away. He let his arm drop to his side.

She marched toward the house.

"I might not be able to change the past," he said as he strode along beside her. "But please allow me to make what amends I might."

"That is impossible."

"Not as impossible as you might think."

"What is it you believe you might do to rectify the damage you've inflicted? Will you restore my reputation? Provide my daughter with legitimacy?"

"That is exactly what I propose to do."

She turned to stare at him then. "You have taken leave of your senses."

"No, I have not. I plan to petition the courts to recognize your marriage to my brother and the legitimacy of your children."

Sophie couldn't help herself. She laughed. "That

might be a possibility had a true marriage taken place, but you and I know that it did not."

"The laws of Scotland are different than those of England. All one need do to contract a valid marriage is to pledge one's troth before witnesses. As I witnessed that pledging, along with several others all ready to swear to the same, I foresee no difficulty in proving my point."

"Except we weren't in Scotland. We were in England."

"Says who? Not I, nor any of my friends. We say we were in Scotland, and we are prepared to testify to that effect. As I am the current Viscount Holliston, I cannot imagine anyone will question my veracity."

"How on earth did you ever arrive at this ridiculous scheme?"

"I admit I did not devise it myself. Your husband, in his greater wisdom and knowledge of the law, pointed me in the right direction. I have no doubt we shall succeed in our endeavor."

Completely at a loss for words, Sophie stared at him. She wondered if she appeared as stunned as she felt.

Her knight in shining armor was racing to her rescue yet again? It seemed somehow obscene after she had treated him so shabbily and banished him from her kingdom.

Somehow she managed to suppress the hysterical laughter building at the back of her throat.

Viscount Holliston held her gaze. "Your daughter is rightfully styled the Honorable Cecelie Holliston. In deference to your recent marriage, I will agree to attach Remington to her name, and I will provide a dowry for any marriage she might make. Though your son did not survive, he was rightfully Viscount Holliston during his short life, as his father, my brother, died before him."

She blinked, then turned her gaze to study the clouds.

"Your husband and his solicitors are drafting the bill. Your rights will be protected, as will those of your daughter. Your husband, and you as her mother, will be named Cecelie's guardians. I will not interfere in her upbringing. This I swear, on my honor. Though I can well imagine you believe I have none. And with good reason."

She studied his face, saw the sincerity shining in his eyes. "I do not know what to say."

"There is no need to say anything." He cleared his throat. "There is one other thing I must tell you. I have a message from your husband."

She wished he would stop saying that. "Your husband" this and "your husband" that. As if everything were right in the world and "her husband" wasn't at this moment on his way to London to obtain a divorce.

She sucked her lower lip between her teeth. Part of her didn't want to know what the message was. The part of her that was weak and afraid.

He pulled two letters from his frock coat pocket. "He wants you to read that one first."

Her hand shook as she took the missives. She was confused. The letter he'd indicated was addressed to Jagger. It was in Stephen's hand. The seal was intact, indicating that Jagger had never read it. Why would he give it to her?

She was vaguely aware that Henry Holliston had turned and strode toward the house, no doubt to give her privacy. She stared at the missive. She was afraid to open it. Afraid of what secrets and lies it would reveal.

Finally, she broke the seal. Her hands were shaking so badly, she had trouble focusing on the words.

My Son.
If only you knew how I've longed to tell you the truth. I am your father. But your mother bid me guard this secret well. . . .

Sophie closed her eyes. Pain swelled in her breast. She ached for Jagger, for the little boy he once was who had never known a father's love. She ached for his mother, who was forced into a brutal marriage by a legal system that left a woman with few choices and no rights. Though

Sophie had chosen a different path for her life, she understood only too well why Jagger's mother had shielded the secret of his birth. She had sacrificed her life to protect her son from society's contempt. It was the greatest sacrifice a mother could make.

But most of all, Sophie ached for her brother, who was forced to stand by as another man, a cruel monster, claimed his son. Now Stephen's actions made perfect sense. He could not provide for his son during his lifetime, so he found a way to do so after his death. All the pain she had felt at her brother's scheming disappeared in a heartbeat, replaced by a soaring admiration she'd thought lost forever.

She shuffled the letters, so that Jagger's missive to her was on top. Holding her breath, she ripped open the seal.

My Dearest Wife,
  For that is who you are. My wife. And I refuse to let you go. My business in Town will take no more than a day or two. Then I shall return to you. No longer a duke. Just an ordinary man in love with his extraordinary wife.
        Until I see you again, I remain,
        Forever Yours

The wetness on her cheeks took Sophie by surprise. She read the letter again and again, hearing his voice in her head as she memorized his beautiful words.

He loved her. He wanted her, so much so he was even willing to sacrifice his heritage because she had told him she could never be married to a duke. He was proving by action, not by words, that he wanted her. And it had nothing to do with treachery and betrayal or duty-bound honor. It had nothing to do with Stephen's wicked scheme. He wanted *her*. He loved *her*.

Happiness was within her grasp, if only she had the courage to reach out and grasp it. Could she throw caution to the wind and claim what *she* wanted, what *she* needed?

Clutching the letters to her chest, she ran to the house, up the stairs, through the door held open by Viscount Holliston.

He smiled as she raced past him, but she paid him no heed.

"Cecelie," she cried.

A few moments passed before her daughter appeared, followed by Thea. Dear, wonderful Thea, who sent Henry Holliston a shy smile as she followed Cecelie down the stairs in what could only be described as an undignified, unladylike trot.

Sophie started to laugh. "Cecelie, my love. We're going to London."

Chapter Twenty-six

Jagger stalked through the ballroom of Mannering House in search of his uncle. All of society's finest seemed to have gathered there, the women dressed in black velvet and bombazine, the men sporting black bands around their arms in a show of respect for the late duke. Jagger would have laughed if he didn't feel more like committing murder.

A thousand shimmering candles dripped hot wax from the candelabra above. The crush of bodies generated a stifling heat and pungent aroma. The guests were beginning to stare at the stranger in their midst. The men cast sly, covert glances Jagger's way as they sized him up. The women openly admired him, their eyes inviting him hither, as if he were a sultan and they were his harem, eager and anxious to do as he pleased.

The scene made him sick.

He was not in the mood. Conversation was not on his list of things he wanted to do tonight. He wanted nothing more than to finish his business and return to his wife.

He found his uncle cowering behind the potted ferns near the terrace doors. A healthier, more robust version of the late duke, his uncle had thin gray hair, dark gray eyes, and a bulging waistline. He offered Jagger a timid smile.

"What is the meaning of this?" Jagger demanded, barely keeping his anger in check.

Anthony's fat cheeks flushed. "Now, Jagger."

"I requested a private audience with you."

"I wanted to introduce you to a few of my friends. After all, you are the duke now—"

"Keep your voice down," Jagger snarled. He nodded toward a small chamber off to the side of the French doors. "Let us speak privately."

Anthony nodded. "As you wish."

Velvet-covered chairs circled a polished mahogany table, upon which sat several wooden boxes filled with cigars, as well as a number of glass bowls to hold the stubs and ashes. The air in the room was thick with smoke and oppressively hot from numerous candelabra and wall sconces, all burning brightly.

A variety of choice liquors in crystal decanters caught Jagger's eye as he prowled the perimeter of the room.

His uncle was watching him steadily.

Jagger cleared his throat. "I wanted to inform you in person. I am relinquishing my title."

"What?"

Anthony's shout brought the conversation of those standing outside the room to a grinding halt. No doubt they were eager to learn the next juicy *on-dit* to tell their friends. They were society sharks feasting on the emotional blood of their prey.

Jagger had no intention of feeding them today.

He slammed the door, then stalked to the table. He poured two bumpers of brandy, slid one along the polished wood to Anthony, before dropping onto a chair.

Trying to tame his rampaging emotions, he pinched the bridge of his nose. At first, he'd thought he would use his title and influence to avenge the cruelty society had heaped upon Sophie during her Season. When she refused to be married to a duke, he'd abandoned the idea.

Now he needed to devise another plan, but he wasn't worried. He had the rest of his life.

God, he missed her so much. It seemed forever since last he'd seen her, rather than mere days. What was she doing right now? Did she miss him half as much as he missed her?

Would he have to fight to get her back?

Or would she accept defeat gracefully?

Accept defeat? What the hell was he thinking? She had never admitted defeat in her life. She was a fighter, with the courage and fortitude of a dozen men. And she would fight to protect her daughter, no matter the cost.

But this time, Jagger knew it wasn't Cecelie she was trying to protect. In her misguided notions of honor, she thought she was protecting him by letting him go. He had never loved her more than when she had thrown him out of her life.

He understood her reasons. Because of her scandalous past, she thought herself unworthy to be his wife, now that she knew of his title and precedence. She thought he deserved better than her, as if there were anyone in this world who could compare with his beautiful wife. His life.

It was she who deserved better than him, but he didn't care. She was his and he would never let her go.

Anthony's shoulders slumped. "Please, forgive my outburst. But you took me by surprise. Might I ask you to explain?"

Jagger sipped his brandy. It was velvety smooth with a hint of honey and oak. "When I first returned to England, I wanted the title. If for no other reason than to make my father pay."

"I know how he wronged you," Anthony said quietly.

Jagger slammed his glass on the table, sloshing liquid onto the polished wood. "Wronged me. 'Tis not nearly a strong enough word. I suppose you also know that I am not his son by blood?"

Anthony nodded.

"Ah. It seems I was the only one who did not know."

"How could she tell you?"

"How could she not? It would have been a relief. The man was a monster." Jagger held his uncle's gaze and asked the question that had bothered him most since learning the truth about his parentage. "Why have you kept this secret? The title is yours by rights. Yet you are willing to let a bastard inherit?"

Anthony sighed. "Even if I wanted to contest it, which I do not, I would have no grounds. You were born within a legal marriage. My brother never disclaimed you. It would cause a scandal for no good earthly reason. In truth, I have never wanted the title. Unlike most younger sons, I never envied what my brother had. I was content with my life. I still am."

Both men were silent.

Jagger stared into his drink.

"She did it for you," Anthony said.

Jagger quirked a brow. "How so?"

"How much do you know of your birth?"

Jagger pursed his lips. "Not much. And now that she is dead, as is my blood father, I will never know the truth. The duke must be laughing in his grave. It seems he won after all."

Anthony tapped his fingers on the table. "Jagger. My brother didn't tell me who your father was. Your mother did."

Jagger leaned forward in his chair. "What?"

"I knew my brother was cruel. Verbally abusive. But I had no idea that he used his fists, until that terrible night . . ."

Jagger swallowed hard.

Anthony continued. "Stephen summoned me to Norwood Park. He was frantic. You were missing. I saw your mother's face and I knew the hell she had lived through. The hell you'd lived through, too."

The muscles in Jagger's back tightened painfully.

Anthony shrugged. "You were a wonderful little boy and I was proud to be your uncle. I still am. Mayhap I need to atone for my sin of ignorance. Of looking the other way."

"There was nothing you could have done to prevent it," Jagger said through teeth clenched so tightly, his jaw ached.

"Please, do not release me from my culpability." Anthony grabbed a cigar, but he did not reach for a taper to light it. He simply held it in his hand, as if he needed some sort of talisman. "She was very young when I met her. Very beautiful. She did not want to wed your father."

"Do not call him that. He was not my father."

Anthony coughed. "Sorry. Old habits die hard. But, whether you like it or not, he was your father in society's eyes. Never mind that. She wanted to marry Lord Hallowell. Her uncle, who was her guardian at the time, insisted she wed the duke. He wanted the highest title for her and to rid himself of the expense of supporting her and her younger brother. Later, she confessed to me that she wanted one night with the man she loved. She went to Lord Hallowell the night before the wedding. Of course, he never dreamed she would go through with the ceremony. But she did. And there was nothing he could do about it. He was too much of a gentleman to tarnish her name."

"He must have suspected I was his son."

"Why would he? He didn't know the state of their marriage. And you do not resemble him in any way. You take after your mother."

"The duke must have been furious."

"Quite the contrary. Since he had a ready-made heir, he was free to, how do I say it, pursue his own interests?"

Jagger clenched his hands into fists. "I understand your meaning. Did he know Lord Hallowell was my father?"

"He must have. Why else would he have asked him to be your godfather? They were never close. At the time, he said he wanted to please his wife as she and Lord Hallowell were friends all their lives. Although she never spoke of this, I now believe it was another of his cruelties. Something he could taunt her with through the years."

Jagger nodded. "That sounds like something he would do."

"Believe me, Jagger. Had I known of his brutality, I would have intervened."

Jagger shrugged off his words like an unwanted coat. "What could you have done? Once wed, a man is free to do as he pleases, under the law. Even beat his wife senseless, so it seems."

It was one of the many reasons Jagger admired Sophie so much. Rather than wed a man who would use her and her child cruelly, she chose to remain unwed. In a world where women had no rights at all, to protect herself and her child, she had braved society's scorn. It was impossible for Jagger to express the depth of his love and respect for his wife.

Words were meaningless. She was his life.

And he wanted to go home.

He pushed to his feet. "Anthony, the title is yours, and I wish you good luck with it."

"Sit down," Anthony said, his voice ringing with unexpected authority.

Jagger sat.

"I will not let you do this," Anthony said.

Jagger tried to explain. "I used to dream of this moment. My sweet revenge against my 'father.'" He spat out the hated name. "But now it is meaningless."

"I do not understand. You would tarnish your mother's reputation? Declare yourself a bastard before the world? No one will believe you. Your parents were legally wed at the time of your birth. That makes you his son in the eyes of the law."

"I possess letters that would prove such a claim, though that was never my intention."

Jagger would never sully his mother's name. She had sacrificed too much to protect him.

He rubbed his thumb and forefinger over his eyes. "Rumor already abounds that James Remington is dead. I merely thought to present you with proof that he drowned at sea after his ship went down in a storm. Then I will merrily live out the remainder of my life as Jagger Remington, devoted husband of Sophie Treneham. It is not an elaborate scheme, but it will work. Society sees only what it wants to see."

"There are holes in your plan."

"How so?"

"There are people who already know of your return from the dead."

"Who? Your solicitor? He is in your employ, therefore bound by strict confidentiality. Besides, I have already pointed out to him the wisdom of his silence in regard to his career. There is no one else, other than my wife's companion, who has given me a vow of silence. No, it can be contained. A rumor may surface here or there, but those will be easily squelched by you."

"What if I fight you on this?"

"My wife—"

"Will be best served as your duchess."

Jagger shook his head. "No. You were right. You have no notion of what is at stake."

He held up his hands to dam his uncle's protests. "It's as simple as this. She will not be married to a duke. To any nobleman, for that matter. Given their abominable treatment of her, who could blame her?"

Not to mention the manner in which they came to be wed.

Jagger loved her, but she would always believe that

he'd married her for honor's sake, which simply wasn't true. The feisty termagant who'd stood toe to toe with him banging a feather duster at his chest had stolen his heart, and he had no intention of letting her give it back.

The memory brought a smile to his lips. "If she had her way, she would never have married at all. Anthony, I love her. I would sacrifice anything to be with her. So you see, I haven't any choice. The title has to go."

Anthony nodded slowly.

Jagger stood to leave.

As he opened the door, he became aware of the unnatural silence in the ballroom. Everyone was looking in the opposite direction, pointing and nodding their heads at the door.

Suddenly, the silence broke and everyone began talking at once. Jagger caught snippets of conversations.

A man's voice said, "I never thought we'd see the likes of her again."

Then a woman's. "Can you believe her nerve?"

"The disgrace of it all," someone snickered.

"And Holliston is with her."

The comments grew nastier as the crowd parted to make way for the woman walking across the room. She held her head high. Her gold gown shimmered like a bright star in a barren sky. Candlelight caught the auburn highlights in her mahogany hair.

Jagger was torn between two conflicting emotions. One was a murderous rage. He wanted to issue a challenge to every man in the room for the present insults aimed at his wife. But he forced himself to breathe deeply and schooled his features to reflect a calm he did not feel.

Beyond the rage was a deep and powerful rush of love that nearly drove him to his knees. He longed to race across the room and drag Sophie to safety, away from the wolves and the harpies, but he didn't want to shame her by making a scene.

She deserved this grand entrance. Besides, he was certain his legs would buckle if he so much as tried to move. He knew how much it cost her to come here like this. And the fact that she came here for him brought tears to his eyes.

She wore her mahogany hair loose. It flowed over her shoulders, curled about her face. Her eyes seemed huge. Her confident smile belied the tension Jagger knew she must be feeling inside. She kept her gaze trained on Jagger as she approached, flanked on one side by Henry, Viscount Holliston. On her other side walked Cecelie dressed in white linen and lace. The child's eyes, the same deep brown as her mother's, scanned the unfamiliar crowd, the pinkie finger of her free hand fastened securely in her mouth—until she spotted Jagger.

She dropped her mother's hand and raced across the room as fast as her tiny legs would carry her.

"Uppie," she squealed, launching herself into his arms.

Everyone around them gasped.

Jagger gathered the child against his chest, kissed her cheek, stroked her hair. "My sweet, sweet Cecelie. How I have missed you. Have you missed me?"

"Uh-huh. And Mama did, too," she said, then promptly stuck her finger back in her mouth.

Jagger smiled, his heart so full of love for this child, he thought he might weep. He stared at his wife as she came to a stop before him. Her lips curved into an intimate smile, a silent signal of her love.

There was so much he wanted to say, but he couldn't find the words. Her chin tilted proudly in the air, and he smiled.

Everyone around them gawked, though no one spoke.

Never loosening his grip on his precious child, Jagger sketched an elegant bow. "Madam. This is quite a surprise. Albeit a pleasant one. Might I ask, what brings you to Town?"

Sophie shrugged, a mischievous gleam in her eyes. "I could not stay away."

He quirked a brow.

She smiled tenderly. "You were about to make a grievous mistake."

"How so, when the woman I love will have me no other way?"

"The woman you love realized she was a fool and she came here to tell you so." She dipped a deep curtsy. "Your Grace."

A loud buzzing filled the room as those standing closest to the scene strove to be first to spread the delectable tale.

Anthony laughed. He clapped Jagger on the shoulder, then nodded at Sophie. "Well done, my dear. Very well done, indeed. May I have your attention." He shouted to be heard above the din. He waited until the room fell silent. "I would like to present to you, my nephew, recently returned from India, and his wife. The Duke and Duchess of Mannering."

The buzzing grew thunderous. The crowd closed in around them, but Jagger ignored them all.

He stared at his wife. "I don't understand. What made you change your mind? About me, I mean."

Tears glistened in her eyes. She stroked her fingertips along his jaw. "After you left, I realized the undeniable truth. I love you. Be you of common birth or be you a duke, nothing will ever change that. I love you."

Jagger laughed. Propriety be damned, he dragged her into his arms, crushing Cecelie between them, and covered Sophie's mouth with his. He possessed her lips in a deep, devouring kiss that could only hint at the depth of his love. She smiled as she kissed him, and he knew. She felt the same way, too.

Epilogue

The sheets were soaked, their bodies covered with sweat. The scent of their lovemaking clung to their skin like the sweetest perfume. Sophie smiled as she cuddled in Jagger's arms. Mere hours had passed since their return to Norwood Park, but so much had changed. She wanted to tell him how she felt, but all the words she could think of seemed shallow, too weak to convey the happiness in her heart.

The fire, snapping in the grate, cast a tawny glow across his skin, making his eyes seem more black than blue. She pressed her lips against the scar on his cheek.

He smiled. "I still can't believe you came to London."

"How could I not?" She stroked her fingertips over the jagged flesh beneath his eye. "Do not misunderstand. I could have lived without you, as I had for many years. Before you even left, I knew I didn't want to. But I was too afraid to say the words. Your love gave me the courage, the self-respect I needed, to reach out and fight for what I wanted. And what I wanted was a life with you. As your wife. Words cannot do justice to the love I feel for you."

She pressed her fingertips against his lips to keep him from speaking. All the tenderness and love she felt for this man welled in her heart, burned in her throat. "I know I cannot express myself well. I can only repeat the words a wise man I know once said. I am, and always will be, forever yours."

A wicked gleam lit in his deep blue eyes. He smiled his pirate's smile as he leaned over her, the rigid length of his sex pressed against her thigh. "I have waited so long to hear you say those words. There is only one thing more I want."

He paused, his brow furrowed in a look of uncertainty, as if he never meant to say the words.

She set her palm against his cheek. "What is it you want?"

He shook his head.

"Please tell me."

He closed his eyes.

A look of indescribable agony flitted across his features.

"To give you a child," he finally said, his voice shaking, as if he had dragged the words from the very center of his soul. "Our child. A brother or sister for Cecelie. If it would please you."

She heard the doubt in his voice, saw the tension in his eyes, as if somehow she would deny him that which *she* wanted most. How could he think such a thing? How could he not, when she had told him in no uncertain terms that she would never bear another babe?

She wrapped her leg around his hip.

"I do not want *a* child of yours, Jagger," she said with a smile as she guided him inside of her. "I want ten."